SPOOK NIGHT

David Robbins

BESTSELLING AUTHOR OF *PRANK NIGHT*

Fearing he's losing touch with his wife and teenage children, John Grant moves to a little town named Spook Hollow. Once away from the pressure of city life, he's sure he can save his marriage. But he doesn't know about the local ghost stories—or the legendary specter that has left more than one of the townspeople real dead. As Halloween night approaches, spirits rise and panic spreads. And if John can't find a way to stop the phantom terror, his dream home will be filled with deadly nightmares that will destroy his family.

Other *Leisure Books* by David Robbins:
HELL-O-WEEN
SPECTRE
THE WRATH
THE WERELING
BLOOD CULT

David Robbins

LEISURE BOOKS   **NEW YORK CITY**

To Judy, Joshua, and Shane.
To Roy and Dela White, good friends.

A LEISURE BOOK®

October 1995

Published by

Dorchester Publishing Co., Inc.
276 Fifth Avenue
New York, NY 10001

Printed in the United States of America.

Chapter One

Kip Grant opened his blue eyes. Rolling over, he glared at the jangling alarm clock on the nightstand and wished for his dad's shotgun so he could blow the little monster to kingdom come. What lousy timing. It had ruined a perfectly wonderful dream. Kip swore that he could still smell the minty fragrance of Amy Westbrook's lustrous brown hair and feel the soft touch of her lips on his.

Sitting up with his back to the headboard, Kip picked up the clock and said to himself, "I'd like to meet the lame dork who invented these things." Then he pressed the alarm button and tossed the clock to the foot of the bed.

Sunlight streaming in the west window bathed the small room in a rosy glow. Kip stretched, idly roving his gaze over the posters on the walls and the models on his oak desk and mahogany dresser. Maybe, he mused, it was time he put them all up in the attic.

Until about three months earlier, Kip had been heavily into science fiction. He still had several horrible aliens poised as if to attack him and some exotic spacecraft that seemed to be strafing the furniture. But of late, he had developed a new passion in life. His new passion sometimes made Kip's head swim as if he were dizzy, and caused his pulse to race a mile a minute, among other things. In a word, Kip Grant had discovered girls.

Suddenly rock music blared in the room next to his. Kip bounded out of bed and dashed to his closet. Since his mother always threw a fit if he walked around in his underwear, he pulled on a pair of jeans before opening his door and racing to the bathroom.

Just as Kip passed the next room, 16-year-old Shery Grant stepped into the hall and squealed, "No fair! It's my turn to go first, you little twerp!"

"Sorry, slowpoke," Kip said. "I have to leave early."

Shery started after him, but he beat her to the bathroom and slammed the door shut in her face. Royally ticked off, she smacked a palm against the lintel and warned, "If you don't let me in there right this second, I'll go down and tell Mom."

When Shery heard water running, she drew back a foot to kick the door, but thought better of doing so. Sighing in frustration, the petite blonde pulled her heavy green robe tighter around her and marched back to her bedroom.

"One of these days," she muttered as she closed the door. Sometimes it seemed as if her bratty younger brother had been making her life miserable since the day he was born.

Shery couldn't wait for her 18th birthday so she could strike out on her own: She'd get an apartment and a car, and she'd never again have to share her bathroom with a snotty smart-ass. It would be a dream come true!

"Ugh!" Shery said when she saw her reflection in the full-length mirror. Her long hair looked as if it had been caught in a wind tunnel, and there were bags under her eyes because she had stayed up so late cramming for a history test. Three hours of sleep just weren't enough.

Yawning, Shery stepped to the window, which faced due west, affording her a clear view of stark South Mountain less than half a mile away. According to her father, South Mountain, the highest peak in the area, was part of the Blue Ridge Mountain chain, which ran from Pennsylvania clear down to Georgia. In fact, he had told her, the local range was known as the South Mountain Range. She couldn't have cared less. Geography, in her opinion, ranked down there with algebra and economics as three of the most boring subjects on the planet.

All that mattered to Shery was that her folks had forced her to give up the life she had loved back in Philadelphia and dragged her way out into the sticks to live in a hick town called, of all things, Spook Hollow. She hated living there, just as she hated the old farmhouse in which they lived—and now that she thought about it, just as she hated the sight of that ugly old mountain. Give her skyscrapers over mountains any day.

Shery glanced down at the backyard and the ancient springhouse, which sat near the edge of the woods. Shrouded in shadows cast by encircling maple trees, the structure never failed to give her a creepy feeling. She couldn't say why; it just did.

Tossing her head, Shery took a seat at her vanity. She rummaged in a small drawer for her file and fiddled with her nails while waiting for her brother to vacate the bathroom. This morning was the third time in the past two weeks Kip had needed to get ready before her. Before, he had always been content to lie in bed until dragged out by one of their parents.

Noises rose from downstairs, the same noises Shery heard every morning: There was the clank of the coffeepot, the dull thud of the refrigerator door closing, and the squeak of the back screen door. Sometimes it seemed as if the farmhouse walls were made of paper instead of wood and plaster. Everyone heard every little thing: yet another reason to hate the place.

*   *   *

Spook Night

Unknown to Shery, hate was also on the mind of the woman in the kitchen. Laurie Grant had never hated a stove so much in her life. Impatiently tapping her foot, she repeatedly twisted the control knob to the right front burner. As always, the pilot light would not ignite the gas, and the smell of the fumes made her queasy. She flicked the knob one more time. At last, blue flames spread around the burner cap. Setting the coffeepot on the ring, she turned to the counter and reached for the carton of eggs she had just taken from the fridge.

A peculiar whine drew Laurie's attention to a large brown dog standing just outside the screen door. "What's the matter with you, Buck?" she asked. "I just let you out. You don't get back in until you do your stuff."

When the mongrel whined again and pawed at the screen, Laurie snapped, "You heard me." She had breakfasts to fix, and was in no mood to put up with his shenanigans. "You're a country dog now. You can't go around being scared of your own shadow."

In her 32 years, Laurie had never known any dog so cowardly as Buck. As a puppy, he had spent half his time cowering under a table or chair, only coming out to play with the children or eat. She had considered it a phase and expected him to grow out of it after a while. But in the five years her family had had him, he had not grown braver. When visitors stopped by, he'd go into a panic. At night, he refused to step out of the house unless someone went along.

Laurie looked at him and sadly shook her head. He had been such a handsome pup, with a square muzzle and wide shoulders and a rich brown coat. No one could have foreseen how he would turn out. As the old saw went, appearances were deceiving.

A deep cough from down the hall reminded Laurie that the same words applied to people. Her husband was up. She had once given her heart to him, but for the life of her, she could not quite remember why. Like the pup who had become a wimp, her Prince Charming had become a loathsome toad.

When Buck whined again and looked back into the yard as if there were something out there, Laurie opened her mouth to scold him. The sight of the dense forest that covered a third of their property gave her pause. She had to remember that they were living in the South Mountain Range, hemmed in on all sides by lush state forest. Bears lived there, and so, according to some of the locals, did a cougar or two. Maybe the dog really had a reason to be upset.

Going out, Laurie took a few strides along a flagstone walk, which led to an old woodshed. Other than a few sparrows fluttering in a laurel bush and a squirrel scampering around in their cherry tree, she saw no wildlife. Then she noticed that Buck was staring to the west, not to the north—right at the old springhouse.

Laurie frowned. This made the fourth time in

as many days Buck had acted oddly while looking at the springhouse. Just the evening before, she had been peeling potatoes when she had been startled to hear the dog snarl and snap as if he were fighting for his life. On racing outdoors, she had found him bristling at the springhouse, his lips drawn back to expose his sharp teeth. Yet then, like now, nothing was there.

"I'm tired of this, you idiot," Laurie grumbled. Seizing him by the collar, she pulled him toward the source of his fear. "I'm going to show you that you have no cause to be afraid."

Buck yelped and tried to jerk loose. The closer they came to the squat stone building, the harder he fought. Digging in his claws, he twisted and thrashed.

"No, you don't," Laurie said. She gripped the chain collar with both hands and threw all her weight into hauling him the entire 40 yards. Ignoring his pathetic whines, she stopped in front of the massive, rusted iron door.

According to the real-estate agent who had sold her family the property, the springhouse had been built back in 1813, at the same time as the farmhouse. It had served as the sole source of water until decades later, when a new owner had seen fit to sink a well much closer to the house.

Laurie was glad she hadn't been born back then. It would have been hell to lug buckets up to the house day after day, month in and month out.

"What is the matter with you?" Laurie said, seeing Buck act as if he were paralyzed with fright. His eyes were wide, his nostrils flared. She let go of him with one hand to gesture at the springhouse. "Do you see anything here? No, of course you don't. You're just being a sissy."

Unconvinced, Buck whimpered and squirmed, and Laurie said, "What will it take to get you to stop?"

Impulsively, she balled her fist and struck the door squarely in the middle. It boomed hollowly, like a giant gong. "See? Nothing happened. So quit behaving like a grade-A wienie."

Suddenly, the door boomed to another blow— one delivered on the inside. Gasping, Laurie jumped backward. She inadvertently released Buck, who bolted for the farmhouse as if all the demons of Hell were on his tail.

"What the—" Laurie exclaimed, pressing a hand to her throat. She stood in tense bewilderment, waiting for the sound to be repeated. After waiting a minute, she stepped close to the huge portal. "Hello? Who is in there?"

No one answered. On all sides of the springhouse, the maples rustled in the brisk breeze.

"Answer me," Laurie said.

Gripping the metal handle, she pulled with all her might, but the door would not so much as budge. But that wasn't surprising since no one had been able to open it for years. Laurie's husband had tried when the realtor first showed them the property, and the realtor had mentioned that, as far as she knew, the only key had been lost ages ago.

Thinking that the culprit must be one of her son's impish friends, Laurie stepped back and said, "Whoever you are, I want you to show yourself right this minute."

After no one responded, Laurie placed her ear flush with the cool metal. But the springhouse was as silent as a tomb.

Peeved, Laurie raised a hand to pound on the door once more, then realized that she might be making a big mistake. What if it weren't one of Kip's buddies inside? What if it were a complete stranger—someone who might harm her? She was defenseless in her robe and bunny slippers.

Pivoting on a heel, Laurie hurried to the house, casting glances over her shoulder. She was almost relieved to see her husband in the kitchen—until the memory of their recent argument reminded her how far apart they had drifted. Entering the kitchen, she said curtly, "There's someone in the springhouse."

John Grant looked up from the newspaper he had just unfolded. He was a tall man; in his college days, he had been firm and well-muscled over every square inch of his 220-pound frame. An avid track-and-field man, he had always prided himself on his physical fitness.

Then had come graduation and the real world. John had gone into computers, and 18 years of sitting on his backside ten hours a day had taken their toll. Whenever he saw the doughnut around his midsection and the soft flab where once there had been solid muscle, he wanted to pound his head against the wall.

His handsome face bore more than its share of wrinkles. In his dark eyes lurked a hint of sadness as he regarded his wife in mild confusion. Never one to bounce out of bed in the morning raring to go, he was still drowsy. "What did you just say?"

"Are your ears plugged up?" Laurie asked. "I said there is someone in the old springhouse."

John looked at her, really looked. He could still see, under the surface, the college beauty who had caught his eye many years earlier. But her beauty was clouded by the constant scowl she wore and the ever-present spite in her eyes and her tone. Their marriage was on the brink of disaster and they both knew it. To his dismay, though, she did not seem to care.

"Are you going to sit there or go see who it is?" Laurie asked. "I mean, you are the man of this house, aren't you?"

The way she laced her words with scorn almost made John Grant flinch. Putting the paper down, he walked past her without saying a word. The chilly air invigorated him.

Where had they gone wrong? Once, they had been deeply in love. Once, there had been laughter in their hearts, joy in their souls. But somewhere along the line, things had turned sour.

Abruptly, the great iron door loomed in front

of him. John had been so deep in thought that he couldn't remember crossing the yard. He pulled on the huge handle without result. Bunching his shoulder, he tried a second time, but the door was securely locked. Nothing short of a hand grenade would open it.

Feeling sheepish, John hollered, "This is John Grant. I own this property. If there is someone in here, you'd better speak up."

"That's telling them," Laurie said from behind him.

John was so shocked that he whirled and nearly tripped over his own feet. His wife stood there, a butcher knife clutched in her left hand. "I didn't hear you." To cover his embarrassment, he nodded at the knife and said, "What the devil is that for?"

Laurie shrugged. "Just in case." She couldn't say why she had grabbed it and followed him. It had just seemed like the right thing to do.

"That door is locked," John said, "just like always. What makes you think someone is in there?"

"I was out here with Buck, and I heard somebody pound on the other side."

Perplexed, John tried to open the door again, but failed. Because his wife was watching, he threw his whole body into the attempt, even going so far as to brace his right foot against the jamb and heave until his face turned red and the veins on his neck bulged. He might as well have been trying to open a sealed mausoleum. He headed for the corner, examining the wall as he went. "Well, if anyone is inside, he must have found another way to get in."

Laurie tagged along, even though she was certain they were wasting their time. There was only the one way in and out of the springhouse. "I don't know what you're looking for," she said.

"Maybe there's a hole or something we've missed," John told her lamely, "or maybe part of one wall has collapsed. You know how old these buildings are." He didn't believe his words for a minute, but he would rather be doing something than acting as if he were a helpless boob. Laurie had too low an opinion of him as it was.

All sides of the springhouse were covered with luxuriant ivy. John had poked around shortly after they moved to the farm and hadn't found a trace of a second entrance. That did not stop him, however, from probing high and low now. He recoiled when a large black spider scuttled across his hand, and had to endure his wife's mocking laughter.

Even as Laurie chortled, she regretted doing so. She hadn't meant to. The laugh had simply slipped out, as had many comments she had made recently. A cause-and-effect pattern was at work. The more bitter she grew toward her husband, the more caustic she became. Almost against her own will, she was turning into a shrew. Yet being aware of it did little to help her stop it from happening.

John continued to run his hand over the ivy,

but he was more alert for spiders and other creatures. His neighbor down the road, Bobby Harper, had warned him to watch out for rattlesnakes and copperheads. They were fairly common in the area and every so often, a careless local would be bitten. For all John knew, the reptiles were partial to ivy.

Laurie considered their search a waste of her time. She glanced at the three-story house, thinking of the eggs and bacon she needed to cook before their kids headed for school. "I can't stay out here all morning. Shery and Kip will be late if I don't get in gear."

"You head on back," John said, glad to be free of his wife and her carping. "I'll keep looking."

"Just be careful."

John mustered a wan smile. "I didn't know you cared anymore."

Despite herself, Laurie responded, "I just don't want to have to rush you to the doctor's."

"Haven't you heard?" John said. "Old Doc Syms is one of those rare physicians who still makes house calls."

In the act of swiveling around, Laurie looked to the south, where Spook Hollow shimmered in the morning haze. "It figures he would be," she said. "Everything else about this town is behind the times."

John did not move until the screen door closed behind his wife. Then he walked around the corner, closed his eyes, and bowed his head. Sadness caused his broad shoulders to droop.

He did not know how much more he could take. For two years, they had been at each other's throats like a pair of bloodthirsty piranha, and the bickering was growing worse every day. What did he have to do to turn their relationship around?

A wavering moan cut John's reflection short. Shocked, he glanced around to pinpoint the source, and heard the moan again close to his feet. The ivy quivered, as if a mouse or a copperhead had passed through it. His mouth going dry, his temples pounding, John squatted and gingerly inched a hand to the spot. Warily, he parted the leaves, then laughed at his own fear.

At the base of the wall was a hole about the size of John's fist. Through it cool air blew, producing the groans and shaking the creepers. Bending, John detected a dank, earthy scent. He heard nothing out of the ordinary.

The next moment, a twig snapped loudly in the woods behind him. John rose and spun. Bobby Harper, the neighbor who had told him about the snakes, had also advised him to be on the lookout for black bears. The brazen beasts liked to raid garbage cans and make nuisances of themselves. Harper had assured John that the animals were harmless enough. But John recalled hearing about a tourist at a national park who had been ripped to shreds by one. If he ever saw a black bear heading toward him, John would go the other way just as fast as his legs could carry him.

When over a minute passed and no large animal appeared, John walked to the west side of the springhouse. As he rounded the corner he drew up short. Goose bumps broke out all over him. He had entered a peculiar pocket of air so frigid that it made him feel as if he were in a freezer. Mystified, he moved his arms up and down, testing to determine how large the pocket might be. It rose higher than his head and extended to the ground.

A single step took John out of the cold air. He stuck a hand back into the pocket to feel the chill tingle his fingers. Not knowing what to make of the anomaly, he shrugged and went on to the front of the building.

There were no new openings. Since no one could get into the springhouse, his wife had obviously been mistaken. John gnawed on his lower lip, debating how to tell her. He couldn't come right out and say that she had imagined the whole thing. She would be on him like a pit bull on raw meat.

John Grant made for the house, which he regarded fondly. The farm was his last hope to repair his shattered marriage. It had been his idea to move to Spook Hollow. Laurie and the kids had fought him every step of the way, and of the three, only Kip had adapted so far. Somehow, John had to make his wife and daughter see the light. With a little luck he could, provided no new problems reared up unexpectedly.

The hopeful husband hastened off. He could

David Robbins

no longer hear the moaning sound. Nor could he hear a faint scraping noise on the inner surface of the iron door. If he had, he would have jumped to the only logical conclusion: Something was in there—and it wanted out.

Chapter Two

Kip Grant ran out the front doorway of the farmhouse. Blinking in the bright sunshine, he crossed the wide porch and raced down the neatly trimmed yard toward the winding drive. "I can't be late," he told himself. "I just can't."

Since the house sat on a high hill, the yard sloped steeply at the bottom. Combined with the fact the grass was slick with dew, it was no wonder then that Kip's feet shot out from under him as he neared the gravel. Yelping in surprise, he landed on his backside and slid the final 15 feet. Somehow he was able to hold onto his schoolbooks. When his backside grated onto the gravel, he winced in pain.

What a klutz! Kip reflected as he stood up. Twisting, he found the back of his light jacket and jeans were practically soaked. Even worse, grass marks stained the jeans. He hesitated, debating whether to run back up to the house and change. If he did, he would not get to the bridge in time. And that was more important than a few measly grass stains.

On Kip ran. The drive wound through some maples and oaks until it came to a narrow, rutted asphalt road. At that point Blackgap Road, as it was called, looped in two directions. Directly ahead, it went due south for over a hundred yards, to a short bridge over a small creek. To Kip's right, the road extended westward about three quarters of a mile, passing other homes. It came to a dead end deep in the forest.

Kip had heard his dad and Bob Harper talking once. Apparently, the county had planned to extend the road another 20 miles when they first built it, to another town. But they had run low on funds and never bothered to raise the money to finish the project.

Cradling his books in his left arm, Kip glanced westward. Down the road a slender figure approached. He had made it in time. Smiling, playing it cool, he strolled south as if he had not seen her.

The asphalt ended 20 yards from the covered bridge, but was linked to the bridge by a stretch of cobblestone road. It was the same on the other side. As a sign proudly proclaimed, Monongahela Bridge and the cobblestones had been there since colonial times. They were an historical landmark. Kip knew that the chamber of commerce had put out a pamphlet about the site, and from time to time tourists would make the mile-long ride from town just for the thrill of rattling over the old bridge and back again.

Today, Kip came to the bridge and leaned against the west rail. He watched the gurgling water flow underneath, then thought to look south to where the other stretch of cobblestones ended. Tommy Lee Harper was already at the bus stop and had not noticed him yet. Which was just as well.

It wasn't long before Amy Westbrook came around the bend. She had on a white blouse and beige pants and her long brown hair was in a ponytail. Kip suddenly wanted to run off before she got there. He was making a fool of himself, he was sure. But his legs, the traitors, wouldn't budge. He stood rooted to the spot and plastered what he hoped was a charming smile on his face. "Morning, Amy."

The ninth-grader stopped dead, then exclaimed in her musical voice, "Kip! I didn't see you in the shadows."

"Sorry," he mumbled, stepping into the open. "I didn't mean to scare you."

Flashing a friendly smile that showed her braces, Amy walked up to him. "So how do you like Spook Hollow now that you've lived here three months?"

Kip stared into her green eyes and his mouth went as dry as a desert. He answered slowly, picking each word with care and lowering his voice to sound more manly, more mature. "It's quite a change from Philly. But Spook Hollow has more going for it than I ever counted on." He was referring to her, of course, and congratulated himself on being so darned clever.

"Do you have a cold?" Amy asked. "You sound all stuffed up."

"Just a frog in my throat." Kip coughed and headed across the bridge. It was cool there, under the timbers. They strolled along shoulder to shoulder, almost touching. Kip recalled his dream, and peeked out the corner of his eye at her rosy lips. To die for, he thought.

"Are you ready for our math quiz?"

"Our what?" Kip said absently. He was so thrilled to be talking to her that his brain did not seem to be working right.

"The quiz Mr. Harkness is giving us, silly. He told us yesterday."

"Oh. That quiz," Kip said. "No *problemo*." The truth was, though, that he had forgotten all about it. He had spent most of the evening thinking about Amy, coming up with all kinds of ways to let her know how he felt about her. Now, try as he might, he couldn't remember a single one.

"Mr. Harkness is awful nice, don't you think? I mean, he could have sprung the quiz on us, but he gave us advance warning. For a teacher, he's not half bad."

"If you say so," Kip replied, bothered by a tinge of jealousy. Brian Harkness was a married guy, but that did not stop half the girls in the junior high from having a crush on him. So what if he was only 24? So what if he resembled some hotshot soap opera star?

They walked to the end of the bridge in silence. Then it was Amy who coughed. "Are you planning to go to the Halloween dance?" she asked.

"I hadn't given it much thought," Kip admitted. "I'm not much of a dancer."

"Neither am I," Amy said, "but it's a lot of fun to get all dressed up. And everyone has a great time. I did last year." She paused and looked at him. "Even though I went by myself."

Was that a hint? Kip wondered. She kept on staring at him as if she expected him to say something, perhaps to ask her to be his date. The insight dazed him. Here was the very moment he had waited for, and all he could do was smile dumbly while his mind whirled around and around like a car engine stuck in neutral. "I . . ." he began, struggling to make his mouth form the words.

"Yes?" Amy said expectantly.

Just then a loud whoop rent the air. Tommy Lee Harper bounded up and clapped Kip on the back. "Howdy, neighbors! Are you all set for another day in the coal mines?"

The moment was gone. Amy turned away. Kip frowned and said nothing. He couldn't bring himself to pop the question with someone else there.

Tommy Lee beamed at both of them. He was

a stocky kid, the only one at Spook Hollow Junior High who wore his hair in a crew cut. There were two reasons for that. One, his mother cut his hair. Two, his father made no secret of his belief that any male with hair below the ears had to be a sissy or a liberal, and no son of his was ever going to be either.

Kip did not quite see what long hair had to do with anything, but he was not about to disagree with Bob Harper to Harper's face. The man was as big as a redwood and had a voice that sounded a lot like sandpaper rubbing on rough wood.

Tommy Lee was Kip's new best friend. Why they had hit it off, he couldn't say. They were complete opposites. Where he was quiet and thoughtful, Tommy Lee was outgoing and talked nonstop. Where he liked books and science, Tommy Lee was into sports and cars.

The Harpers had lived in Spook Hollow for only a year. Before that, they had lived in Virginia, where they had "more kin than fleas on an old coon dog," as Tommy Lee had once phrased it.

Now Tommy Lee draped an arm over Kip and Amy's shoulders and steered them toward the bus stop, saying, "Don't you just love this time of year? The trees are changing color and the critters are fattening up for the winter. And Halloween is almost here. I wonder if the Spook will show itself."

"The what?" Kip asked.

Spook Night

It was Amy who answered. "The Spook. That's what everyone calls the Headless Horror of Spook Hollow. I know a few people who have seen it."

If anyone other than the girl he adored had made that statement, Kip would have laughed in the person's face and said to quit yanking his chain. But to her all he could say was, "I never heard this before."

"You're new, dumb-wad," Tommy Lee said, chuckling. "You have a lot to learn about scary old Spook Hollow. All sorts of strange things have happened over the years."

"How would you know?" Kip challenged. "You've only been here a year. That hardly makes you an expert."

Tommy Lee was unruffled. "I like weird stuff. Ghosts, monsters, gory deaths, you name it. So I've done a lot of asking around. My pa too. He takes all the talk mighty serious. When he was a boy about my age, he saw a bogeyman way back in the Appalachians."

"You're putting us on," Kip said.

"Am not. You just ask my pa. He was out camping with a bunch of scouts and they spotted this big hairy creature. Over seven feet tall it was, and it stunk to high heaven. Left tracks over a foot and a half long. What else could it have been but a bogeyman?"

Kip glanced at Amy to see how she was taking this nonsense. To his surprise, she had clasped her books close to her chest and wore what he could only describe as a fearful expression.

"As for the Spook," Tommy Lee went on, "just ask around like I did, and before long you'll be a believer. Too many people have seen the thing. That doesn't count all those it's killed."

There was only so much Kip could stand. "Killed? Now I know you're feeding me a line of bull. If there was some kind of ghost going around murdering people, it would be in the news. I would have heard of it, even in Philadelphia."

Tommy Lee shook his head. "Nope, nope, nope. The killings don't take place all that often. And it's not as if the folks hereabouts go around bragging on the Spook. Would you, if there was a Headless Horror in your town?"

The whole tale was too preposterous for words. But Kip had to confess he was curious to learn more. He would have too, if the bus had not picked that very moment to pull up to the stop with its brakes squealing. Amy climbed on, then Tommy Lee.

Mr. Kimble, the retired postal clerk who supplemented his Social Security by working as a driver for the school district, smiled wryly at Kip and said, "Don't tell me. She's late again."

Kip had completely forgotten about Shery. He half turned and spied her at the far end of the covered bridge, running just fast enough to show she was hurrying but not fast enough to mess up her hair. "Here she comes," he said.

"Tell me, son," Mr. Kimble said confidentially.

"School has been in session for over a month now, and she hasn't made it here once before me. Is that sister of yours ever on time for *anything*?"

"Not that I know of," Kip said. "My mother says she was even ten days late being born."

The driver found that highly amusing, and he was still chuckling when Shery Grant got there, paused to catch her breath, and came up the steps as if she were ascending the marble stairs of a regal palace. "Sorry I'm a wee bit late," she said. It was the same thing she said each and every morning.

The only ones on the bus were her brother, Tommy Lee, and Amy Westbrook. Shery took a seat across from Amy and offered a polite smile. While they knew one another, they were hardly close friends. Shery, after all, was in *high school*. She couldn't be bothered to associate with those who were so much younger. Compared to her, they were mere children.

As the driver backed the bus onto the gravel strip bordering the asphalt so he could turn around and head back into Spook Hollow, Shery opened her purse and took out her compact. A check in the mirror showed that her hair was in place and her lipstick had not been smudged.

Shery needed to look her best. Today was the day she planned to snag a date for the Halloween dance, and she had the perfect catch in mind. Bryce Harcourt was his name, and he just happened to be the varsity quarterback and class president. It didn't hurt that he was the son of the wealthiest man in Spook Hollow and drove a flashy red Corvette.

In due course the bus turned off Blackgap Road into a neighborhood northeast of town. The vehicle made several stops, then skirted downtown Spook Hollow to pick up more kids in neighborhoods to the south. By five minutes to eight it wheeled down Madison Street. On one side sat the high school, on the other the junior high.

Shery had laughed the first time she set eyes on them. As she had joked many times, the two schools combined weren't big enough to fit in the lunchroom of her old high school back in Philadelphia. Her brother had called them dinky, and for once she had agreed with the twerp.

Today Shery was the first one off the bus. Kip called her name and waved, so she gave a little toss of her chin to acknowledge he was alive, then hurried along the sidewalk to the school entrance. Few students were loitering. The bell was about to ring, giving her no time to look for Bryce.

She had to settle for making her play later. On purpose, she was wearing a sweater so tight that her father had once threatened to toss it in the trash, and a skirt so short that the air tickled her fanny when she walked. It was her sexiest outfit, the type few girls at Spook Hollow High had the nerve to wear. Which, she hoped, would give her the edge she needed.

Lunchtime came. Shery had finished loading her tray, and was almost to the end of the line when she saw her quarry at a table with Jerry Dern and Debra Coker. Her lips pinched together. Coker, who was the head cheerleader and the daughter of the town banker, was her only serious rival for Harcourt's affections.

By rights Shery should have despised the girl. But they were so much alike that the two of them had become quite close. They had the same taste in boys, the same taste in clothes, and the same dislike of small towns and small-town life. Coker couldn't wait until her 18th birthday so she could spread her wings and fly to the nearest big city, and Shery didn't blame her. When she graduated, she was heading back to the real world herself, back to Philadelphia.

After paying for her food, Shery sashayed over to their table. She had spent hours practicing her slinky walk in her mirror. Once, her brother had caught her and quipped that if she slung her hips any farther, she'd throw her back out of whack. He'd thought it hilarious. She had been quite flattered by the back-handed compliment.

Setting her tray down on the other side of Harcourt, Shery cleared her throat to get his attention. "Yo. What's happening?" she purred in her best Philly brogue.

Bryce shifted, raked her from head to toe with the sort of look that would make her rabidly feminist aunt see red, then winked. "Whoa there, Shery baby. Major raw, if I do say so myself."

Delighted by the praise, Shery curtsied so the dress would hike higher up her thighs, and said sweetly, "Thank you, kind sir. It's so nice to know that all my hard work wasn't in vain." She slid onto her chair and folded her arms in front of her, causing her breasts to swell. "Am I missing anything?"

"Naw," Bryce said. "We were just wondering what to do this weekend. Jerry wants to go to Gettysburg, but Deb wants to make a run to the big mall up in Harrisburg. What do you think?"

"Gettysburg?" Shery said, much as she might say "acne" or "homework." The national park was about ten miles east of Spook Hollow. Thanks to the many thousands who flocked there yearly, the town boasted four thriving motels. "What's there but a bunch of old cannons and graves?"

Jerry Dern looked at her. "It's a nice ride. And there's a place that sells great ice cream."

Shery smiled. Dern was a linebacker, and the only person she had ever met whose IQ was lower than his height. All he ever thought about was food, food, and more food. She'd heard all about how each year at the Spook Hollow Woodchuck Festival he claimed top honors in the pie-eating contest. The last time, he had polished off 12 apple pies in three minutes to win the crown. "I agree with Deb," she said.

Dern held his ground. "You would. It's hardly a secret that the two of you were born mall crawlers."

A sharp retort was on the tip of Shery's tongue, but she didn't voice it. Jerry was Bryce's main man. If she insulted the lunkhead, Bryce might get upset. And she couldn't have that. "I'll let you big, strong men hash it out," she said. Leaning close to Bryce, she added coyly, "This weekend isn't that important. *Next* weekend is. Have any plans?"

Debra Coker, about to take a swallow of orange juice, swung around. "Oh, no you don't! He took me last year and he's going to take me this year as well."

"Why don't we let him decide?" Shery said.

Bryce Harcourt had a piece of meat loaf speared on his fork. He set it down, glanced from one of them to the other, and laughed. "Do I look crazy? If I ask one of you, the other will slit my throat. No thanks."

"I don't get it," Jerry said. "What's this all about?"

"The Halloween dance, ding-a-ling," Bryce explained.

Shery was not about to take no for an answer. The dance was the first big social event of the year. It would be a real coup for the new girl in town, namely her, to show up on the arm of the studliest hunk in Spook Hollow.

Leaning against Bryce, Shery whispered into his ear, caressing it with her warm breath. It was a trick she had learned in the seventh grade. A few puffs on the average guy's earlobe and he would bend over backwards to please her. "You're going to have to make a choice, handsome." She paused to breathe heavily a few times. "From what I hear, you already know what Deb has to offer. But it's nothing compared to the good time I can show you."

Bryce Harcourt was staring at her cleavage. His throat bobbed a few times. Straightening, he reached into a pants pocket. "There's only one way to settle this and be fair to both of you," he announced. "I'll flip a coin."

Debra Coker flushed red. "You can't! I've been taking it for granted that you would go with me. I even told some of my other friends."

"Never take a man for granted," Shery scolded playfully. "Haven't you learned that by now?"

A shiny quarter was clasped between Bryce's fingers. He flipped it high into the air, then caught it in his left palm. Before anyone could see which side was up, he covered the coin with his other hand. "Okay. Who wants to go first?"

"Not me," Debra declared. "I don't call this fair," She pouted at Shery. "And you! I thought you were my friend!"

Shery arched her eyebrows. "I don't see what you're in a huff about. It can't be that you're afraid of a little competition. I gave you more credit than that."

"You did?"

Adopting a hurt look, Shery played her trump

card. "How long have we been hanging out together now? Five or six weeks? And in all that time have I ever tried to take advantage of you? No. I value our friendship too much. So if it upsets you that Bryce can't make up his mind, I'll drop out of the running and he can take you."

Coker was touched. "You'd do that for me?"

"What are buds for?" Shery asked, and knew she had won when the brunette lowered her head in shame.

"I call heads," Debra said softly.

The quarterback raised his right hand just enough for him to see the coin. "Damn. Too bad, gorgeous," he said. "It's tails." Without showing the quarter to any of them, he shoved it into his pocket and beamed smugly. "I guess I have no choice. I'll have to take Shery."

Time was growing short, so they concentrated on their food. Shery was so giddy from her triumph that she polished off her salad without tasting a single bite. All she could think of was having Bryce Harcourt all to herself for one whole night, a night she was determined he would never forget. By the time she was done with him, he would be wrapped around her little pinky for as long as she wanted him to be.

No prick of conscience bothered Shery over having hoodwinked her friend. If there was one lesson she had learned over the past few years of sheer hell at home, it was that regrets were for losers.

To Shery's way of thinking, life was meant to

be lived to the fullest. A person had to take what she wanted, when she wanted. Being happy was all that counted. Not love or loyalty or any of that other crap. Simply being happy. Anyone who lived otherwise was just asking for misery.

Shery's mother was a case in point.

For years Laurie had given her all to make the marriäge work. She'd given up a nursing career to raise Shery and Kip until they were both in school. Then she had taken grueling night courses to get back into her chosen field. She'd gotten another job, and spent long hours every day at the hospital, dragging herself home every night to do the thousand and one things that had to be done around the house. All that hard work, all that devotion, and what had it gotten her? Misery. Now the marriage was coming apart at the seams. Hardly a night went by that Shery and Kip weren't treated to another shouting match between their parents. It was so bad that Shery had made herself a bet they would be divorced by the end of the year.

The same thing would never happen to her, Shery vowed. She would never let herself grow attached to one man, never let a family weigh her down with responsibilities. Fun, fun, fun was the only thing that mattered. She was going to live her life to the max, and she didn't give a damn who she stepped on along the way.

Yet even as Shery entertained the thought, she saw Debra Coker sulking and felt a twinge of guilt. She promptly dismissed it. Rising to take her tray back, she laughed inwardly at herself.

Some days she was too weak for her own good.

Chapter Three

It was shortly after one in the afternoon when John Grant heard a vehicle winding up the drive. He was in his office, a front corner room on the bottom floor with a window overlooking the town. Curious, he rose and looked out. His curiosity mounted when a yellow van bearing the painted image of a huge key and the words "GEORGE'S LOCK SERVICE" crunched to a stop on the gravel between his station wagon and his wife's sedan.

John Grant put two and two together, and stiffened. Quickly, he went to his computer and hit the save button so that the document he had worked on most of the morning would be stored on his hard drive. Then he hurried down the hall to answer the rap on the front door, but his wife got there before him.

Laurie Grant had spent the morning organizing. They had moved from Philadelphia on such short notice that when they arrived at the farmhouse she had simply stored items wherever it was most convenient. Since then, day after day, she'd rearranged, putting things where she wanted them to go.

Laurie had just gotten done transferring the silverware from a small drawer beside the stove to a larger one under the cupboard which held her plates and bowls when the van pulled up.

She looked a mess in her dirty jeans and frumpy flannel shirt, but she didn't care. She never had been one of those women who were finicky about their appearance. Even when younger, and boy after boy had told her how stunning she was, she had never let the praise go to her head. For one thing, she knew that boys told that to all pretty girls. For another, she had always believed that real beauty was under the skin, not on the surface.

Swiping a hand at a bang which persisted in drooping over her eyes, she went down the hall. The rest of her blond hair was swept back in a tight bun so it would not bother her while she worked.

As Laurie reached for the knob, she saw her husband approach. "Don't let this interrupt your work," she said icily, and opened the door to forestall a reply.

On the porch stood a thin man with a cropped beard as white as snow. He had on bib overalls, and pinned to the right shoulder strap was a name tag which identified him as "GEORGE ELDRIDGE." "Hello," he said politely. "You must be Mrs. Grant?"

"I am," Laurie confirmed. She pulled the door wider so Eldridge could see John. "This is my husband. We want to thank you for coming out on such short notice."

The locksmith chuckled softly. "Spook Hollow ain't like that big city I hear you folks are from. It ain't like I've got more business than I can handle, ma'am."

It surprised Laurie a little to hear that people were talking about them behind their backs. For a moment fear flared, fear that everyone in town knew about their marital problems and that they were a prime source of gossip. "Who told you about us?" she asked. "What did they say?"

Eldridge shrugged, then smiled in a kindly fashion. "Oh, the usual stuff. Folks do love to gossip." He gazed over her shoulder into the interior of the house. "Especially about this place."

Laurie wanted to inquire what he meant by that. But John Grant picked that moment to confirm his hunch by saying, "It was my wife who called you. Are you here about the springhouse?"

"Yes indeedy," Eldridge said, and jiggled the big case he carried. "I want to thank you for the challenge too."

"The challenge?" John repeated, puzzled.

The locksmith nodded, his eyes twinkling.

"Yes, sir. You see, I've been in this business so long that there's hardly a lock in town I haven't repaired or replaced at one time or another. I know 'em all like I do the back of my hand." He scratched his beard. "I don't mean to brag on myself, but I've gotten so good at my job that it don't take me but a few minutes at the most to take care of most locks. There ain't that many challenges, like there were when I was just starting out."

"Oh. I see."

Eldridge nodded at the house. "Yes, sir. This place of yours is one of the oldest in the area. Some of these locks are older than I am. And from what your missus was telling me about the springhouse, I could be in for a real treat."

John had seldom seen anyone so eager to get to work. Grinning, he said, "I'll take you down there."

"We both will," Laurie declared. She was going to be present when the door was opened whether her husband liked it or not. She saw the locksmith pucker his lips and regard the two of the closely, and for a few fleeting moments she had the feeling that he could see right through them, that he knew they were having a spat for no real reason at all. To justify herself, she said, "I heard someone pound on the inside of the springhouse door. My husband insists it must have been the wind. We're hoping you can settle the issue."

"I'll do my best, ma'am," Eldridge promised.

Spook Night

Brilliant sunlight bathed the hill and the valley below. In a nearby tree a mockingbird sang. In another, a robin chirped. Colorful butterflies flitted about the flower bed.

Eldridge inhaled loudly. "It's so beautiful here most of the time, ain't it? I've lived in Spook Hollow pretty near thirty years, so I'm used to it. But this must be quite a change for you folks, coming from the big city and all."

"It is," Laurie admitted, recalling how hectic her life had been in Philadelphia and how the everyday routine had slowed down since the move.

John merely nodded. The change was one of the things he had hoped would helped mend their stricken marriage.

"They say a drastic switch like that can put people on edge," the locksmith continued as innocently as could be. "Make 'em a mite irritable. Why, I remember when Martha and me first came to Spook Hollow from Pittsburgh. We snipped at one another like a cat and dog for pretty near a whole month before it sunk in that we were making fools of ourselves. I sure hope that you two don't go through the same nonsense, because it's as plain as the nose on my face that you make a fine couple."

Laurie and John glanced at one another. For an all-too-short span, tenderness replaced the resentment which both harbored. For all of five seconds they looked into each other's eyes as they had long ago when they were young and head-over-heels in love. Then the locksmith announced "Here we are!" and the moment passed. They halted before the door, each reminded of the other's lack of faith. Their resentment returned.

"My, oh, my," Eldridge said in amazement while running a hand over the pitted surface of the immense portal. "What on earth would anyone want with a door this size?"

"I have no idea," John said.

Eldridge bent to inspect the lock, and giggled like a kid given his heart's desire for Christmas. "Will you look at this beauty! In all my years I ain't never seen the like! Why, there hasn't been a key made to fit a door like this one for over a hundred years or better."

"Does that mean you might not be able to open it?" Laurie asked, worried the mystery would remain unsolved.

"There's no telling, ma'am," Eldridge answered as he set his case down. "I told you I'll do my best, and I will." He opened the case, revealing a tremendous number of keys and picks and files. "With this here kit I should be able to handle any lock known to man, but there's an exception to every rule." From out of a pants pocket he took a pencil flashlight. Aiming the beam into the keyhole, he pressed an eye to the lock. "Mercy. These tumblers look like big teeth."

"Is that good or bad?" John asked.

"I'll be up front with you, Mr. Grant," the locksmith said. "This is a lever tumbler lock, first used way back in the 1700's. The trick to opening one of these babies is to raise a lever in the mechanism to just the right height. The proper key would do it in an instant. But without it, using my tools, it's going to take a long time."

"How long?" Laurie asked. She wondered if the man was trying to gouge them, and decided he was simply too honest a person.

Eldridge swiveled around. "I have no way of knowing, ma'am. I've never worked on a lock like this before. I could surprise myself and open it in an hour. Then again, it could take days. And I don't think you want to spend that kind of money, do you?"

"No," Laurie admitted.

The locksmith pondered a bit. "Tell you what I'll do. I've got the rest of the afternoon free. And I would like to give this lock my best shot. So if I haven't opened it by five or so, I'll call it quits and only charge you for an hour's work. How would that be?"

"Remarkably decent of you," John Grant said.

The man snickered. "Don't make me out to be a saint, mister. You'll find that most people in Spook Hollow are just as decent. It comes from having their priorities straight. Here, we don't worship the almighty dollar like most of those guppies in the big cities."

John nipped a laugh in the bud. "They're called yuppies, Mr. Eldridge, not guppies."

"Whatever. But if you ask me, anyone who

goes around chasing his or her own hind end just to get ahead is a lot like a fish out of water, going nowhere fast." Eldridge paused to study a row of picks. "The Good Lord didn't put us here to work ourselves to a frazzle. Take that as gospel and you'll live to a ripe old age, just like me."

John and Laurie hung around to watch for a little while. The locksmith poked and prodded with his picks and files, but made no headway. At length Laurie said, "Well, I've got a kitchen to set right. If you need anything, give a yell."

"Thank you kindly, ma'am," Eldridge responded. "But if I snack between meals, my Martha is apt to take a baseball hat to my noggin."

Laurie smiled at him and walked off. John stared after her, wistfully wishing that she had smiled at him as well. He tried to remember the last time she had, and couldn't. Was their marriage that far gone? If so, it didn't stand a prayer. He turned to see how the locksmith was doing, and instead found himself being scrutinized.

"It's none of my business, of course," Eldridge said amiably, "but I never have been one to stand by when I see folks hurting. And I couldn't help notice that the two of you ain't on the best of terms. Having a bad day, are you?"

John frowned. He disliked discussing his personal life with a complete stranger. But he had kept so much pent inside for so long that his mouth seemed to move of its own accord. "A bad life is more like it. I thought moving here would solve all my problems, but it isn't turning out that way."

"Places don't solves problems, Mr. Grant, people do," Eldridge said. "And if you're saying what I think you're saying, it's been my experience that all a man needs to do is show a woman that he loves her, *really* loves her, and it will set most everything right again."

John was going to say more when it abruptly hit him how ridiculous he was being. The man was a locksmith, for crying out loud, not a minister or a psychiatrist. And here he was, about to spill his guts. "I'll keep that in mind," he said lamely as he turned to go. "Now if you'll excuse me, I have work to do."

"What kind of work would that be?"

"I'm a freelance computer systems consultant," John said. Since he did not know if Eldridge was at all familiar with computers, he elaborated. "I advise clients on things like how to buy the right computer to fit their needs and how to get their hardware up and running."

Eldridge appeared impressed. "You do all that out of your house?"

"With a modem and a fax, a man can do just about anything out of his home these days," John explained. Then he climbed the hill, and along the way noticed Buck lying under a maple tree.

The locksmith also spotted the big mongrel. He whistled to the dog and beckoned, but the animal showed no interest in being friendly.

David Robbins

"Suit yourself," Eldridge said, devoting his attention to the task at hand. He whistled as he inserted a slender steel file and tried to jimmy the tumblers. One moved, the rest didn't.

"This is going to be a bear," Eldridge said. From a small compartment in the bottom of the case he removed a can of lubricant and gave it a few hard shakes. It appeared to be half full. Attaching a thin red strawlike extension to the nozzle, he slid the tip into the keyhole and pressed his thumb down on the red knob at the top. A loud hiss ensued. Tiny drops of smelly lubricant splattered out of the hole, onto his wrist. He sprayed until the can was empty, then set it down and hunkered to wait. The lubricant would take a few minutes to seep into every nook and cranny in the mechanism.

Eldridge suddenly sensed that he was being watched. Twisting, he beheld the large brown dog a dozen feet away. Evidently lured by the hissing, it held its head cocked to one side and its ears pricked. "Come closer if you want, big fella," he coaxed. "I won't hurt you. I've been a dog lover since way back when."

Buck whined in confusion. His every instinct indicated the man was friendly, but his inherent caution would not let him get any closer. In his canine way he wondered what the old one was up to, and glanced apprehensively at the huge door.

"You're a smart one, aren't you?" Eldridge said pleasantly, knowing that animals often responded to a calm, soothing voice. "I can tell by that look in your eyes." He stared at the building. "There's something about this old springhouse that you don't like, isn't there? What is it?"

Buck whined again, then pawed the ground.

"I appreciate the concern, friend," Eldridge quipped, "but there's nothing in there that can hurt us. I've been in old springhouses before. The worst that I've ever seen was a cranky rattlesnake, and he went crawling off lickety-split. Rattlers ain't as mean as most folks think. Truth is, they'd rather run than fight."

Lulled by the man's tone and attitude, Buck edged nearer. But when the man reached out to pet him, he sprang backward and crouched, poised to flee.

Eldridge laughed. "Skittish rascal, ain't you? A friend of mine had a mutt like you once. That pooch was scared of its own shadow. He had the harebrained notion to take it duck hunting once so it could retrieve the ducks he shot. But the first time his shotgun went off, that yellow-belly turned tail and hid under the pickup. Wouldn't come out for anything."

The locksmith could tell that he was wasting his time. The mongrel was not going to let him touch it. Leaning on an elbow, he pulled a pack of gum out and treated himself to a stick. It was the only vice his Martha allowed, and even then the gum had to be sugar-free or he was in for a tongue-lashing.

Refined white sugar, Martha claimed, was the

bane of Western civilization. According to her, it was sheer poison, worse than hard liquor and cigarettes combined. It slowly destroyed the bodily organs and . . .

What was that? Eldridge asked himself as a faint scratching broke out on the other side of the door. He listened as it grew steadily louder. Rising, he pressed an ear to the keyhole and thought he heard a low gnarl, just such a sound as he had heard raccoons and opossums make on occasion. "Why, a varmint got in there somehow and can't find its way out again," he told the dog. "That must be what your missus heard. It bumped into the door and she figured it was somebody knocking."

The scratching ceased. Eldridge squatted and attacked the lock with renewed vigor. Unless he got the door open, whatever was inside might starve to death. He picked and pried and poked. He jimmied and pushed and pulled. But no matter which tool he used, he made no headway.

The sun arced toward the western horizon. Eldridge was so caught up in his work that he didn't realize hours had gone by until he glanced at his watch and saw that it was well past four o'clock. "It's hopeless," he declared, sitting back. "I could fiddle with this antique until doomsday and never get it open."

Buck, dozing on his stomach, raised his head and yawned.

"That's about how I feel," Eldridge agreed. He started to replace his tools, but stopped when he heard the scratching for a second time. Louder than before, it went on and on, as if the animal were desperate to gain its freedom.

"I'll try once more, little fella," Eldridge said wearily. But what was left to try with? he mused. He had already resorted to every pick and file and key which might do the job and none had. As a last resort he grabbed the one tool he hadn't touched yet, an ordinary screwdriver.

"Talk about tilting at windmills," he muttered as he stuck the head into the hole. It wedged under a tumbler, and he applied as much leverage as he dared without breaking the screwdriver. The tumbler grated against another, but would not rise high enough to activate the lever. He pumped the handle a few times, not really expecting anything to happen.

Eldridge relaxed his grip. He had done all he could. It was time to pack up and go home to Martha. Then, without warning, the screwdriver was nearly torn from his grasp. He heard the rasp of moving tumblers and a metallic squeal as the lever lifted. To his astonishment, the entire door shook and suddenly popped open an inch or so, the hinges screeching like a woman in labor. A gust of cold air enveloped him, chilling him to the bone.

"My word!" the locksmith exclaimed, and glanced at the mongrel. It was in full flight toward the farmhouse, and he couldn't blame it.

Yanking the screwdriver out, Eldridge slowly stood. Both knees popped. He gripped the door with one hand and attempted to swing it all the way open, but it barely moved. Placing an eye to the crack, he peered within. Something scuttled along the floor and squeaked. A mouse, he figured. Or maybe a rat.

Eldridge couldn't understand how the door had popped open like it had, unless the air had built up behind it over the years and forced it open, much as the pressure in a wine bottle would pop the cork when it was loosened enough. Shoving the screwdriver into a pocket, he took hold of the edge with both hands, dug in his heels, and pulled.

Grinding noisily, the door reluctantly gave way. Eldridge huffed and puffed, refusing to give up until it had gone as far as it could go. Daylight pushed the darkness back, revealing a floor made of large flat stones and mortar, a floor layered thick with dust. Cobwebs dangled from the ceiling, so many that they prevented the locksmith from seeing more than a few feet into the building.

The door was halfway open when it jarred to a stop and would swing no further. Eldridge put his shoulder against it, to no avail. He glanced up the hill and thought of shouting to let the Grants know he had succeeded. As he cupped a hand, a low cry fell on his ears, a cry totally unlike the snarl he had heard earlier. It sounded for all the world like the coo of an infant. Flabbergasted, he whipped around.

Eldridge had no intention of going in. He'd

done his job. Mr. and Mrs. Grant would take care of the rest. Yet when that soft cry fluttered again, he couldn't resist taking a few steps inside. He had to swat cobwebs aside with every stride he took. Halting, he brushed more from his shirt and beard.

Something moved deep in the springhouse. The locksmith heard a rustling noise clearly, but could not identify the source. He stepped to the limit of the light, then produced his flashlight. Flicking the switch, he stabbed the beam into the wall of darkness. In front of him the cobwebs were thicker than ever, as if all the spiders in Spook Hollow had held their last convention there.

Eldridge waited for the cry to be repeated so he could pinpoint the direction. When a minute had gone by and only silence filled the cryptlike structure, he decided enough was enough and pivoted to leave.

As if on cue, the coo warbled from the very rear of the springhouse. On its heels, as distinct as could be, someone whispered. Eldridge gave a start. "Who's there?" he demanded. "Show yourself."

Silence descended, total, utter silence. A shiver coursed through Eldridge as the air around him became as frigid as a polar iceberg. He could see his breath when he exhaled. The sight so stunned him that he did not react right away when his pants leg gave a slight tug, as if someone or something had plucked on it. But when the tug turned into a hard jerk, he glanced down.

Nothing was there.

"What in the world?" the locksmith declared. He'd definitely had enough. This was all too spooky for his tastes. It stirred memories of certain stories he had heard over the years, wild tales too improbable to be taken seriously by any sane person.

"I'm getting out of here," Eldridge said, and turned to do just that. Or tried to. His right leg was wrenched out from under him so viciously that he cracked his hipbone when he smashed onto the floor. Panic rising within him, he gaped in blatant disbelief as something started to drag him into the recesses of the springhouse.

"No!" Eldridge yelled. He still held the flashlight and he pointed it at his leg. His ankle was being held a good foot off the floor—*but no one was holding it!* He kicked out with his other leg, and felt the sole of his shoe connect with something which had the consistency of a sponge. Something invisible. "Dear Lord!" he cried.

A howl rent the springhouse, a howl both human and bestial, a howl unlike any ever heard by mortal ears. The locksmith shot across the floor as if fired from a cannon. He had time to cry out once more, and then he bumped over the lip of a large hole. Clammy liquid closed around his legs and he realized, to his horror, that he was being pulled into the spring.

Eldridge opened his mouth to scream. Instead, icy water poured down his throat, and a moment later the surface closed over his head.

Chapter Four

It grew dark early in the mountains. Once the sun sank below the peaks, a mantle of darkness swiftly shrouded the remote valleys. For the small town of Spook Hollow, caught in the very shadow of towering South Mountain, nightfall came swiftest of all. The shadows lengthened dramatically by the middle of every afternoon, almost as if they were eager to spread out and blight the land.

Kip Grant had only lived there for a few months, but he had grown accustomed to getting out of school at three and having it seem like five or six. On this particular day, Kip hurried to the bus. Settling into a back seat, he flipped open his math book to study—when who should get on but the girl he couldn't get out of his mind no matter how hard he tried. He was mildly surprised. Usually Amy Westbrook attended band practice on Mondays. He promptly closed the book and prayed she would sit near him. To his delight, she scanned the seats, then slowly made her way toward the back and sat directly in front of him. She had her eyes on the floor, and did not appear to notice he was there.

There would never be a better opportunity, Kip decided, for him to ask Amy to the dance. He leaned forward to tap her on the shoulder, then froze, paralyzed by the thought that she might turn him down. The humiliation would be terrible.

Kip had never asked a girl out before. Where some of the boys in his class spent every waking moment thinking about the opposite sex, he had never really had much interest until recently. He'd always been content to immerse himself in science fiction books and movies and models.

Some of his friends back in Philadelphia had liked to tease Kip about that. Even his own sister poked fun at him, claiming he must be either a zombie or from another planet if he didn't like girls. This from the school sexpot.

Kip had taken all the abuse in stride. Unknown to anyone, he'd had a secret talk with his dad. His father had gone into a long-winded fatherly spiel about how some boys were "late bloomers" and not to get uptight if he didn't notice girls until later on. For once, the advice had made sense.

Spook Night

Then came the big move to Spook Hollow. And Amy Westbrook.

The very first time Kip had laid eyes on the girl, a strange knot had formed in his stomach and a lump in his throat. It had been mondo weird. He'd gawked at her like a little kid at his first ice cream sundae. Her braces, her freckles, her ski-slope nose, none of her flaws mattered. In his eyes, Amy Westbrook was the prettiest thing on two legs.

Of late, Kip had taken to having the most fantastic dreams about her. Bizarre dreams in which she would be in mortal danger and he would charge to her rescue as some sort of knight in shining armor. Usually they were on a distant planet, being menaced by hideous monsters. Or in spaceships, eluding the force of an enemy empire.

When Kip thought about the dreams, he would laugh at how stupid they were. Inwardly, though, it tickled him to think of himself as her mighty defender. He'd always had a passion for playing the hero when he had been younger, and he assumed his childhood fascination was spilling over into his teen years.

Now, his hand inches from Amy's shoulder, Kip blanched and debated whether to forget about the Halloween dance. He was a hair away from chickening out when his heart's desire unexpectedly turned.

"Why, Kip. I didn't know you were there," Amy said.

61

Kip lowered his arm and nervously shifted, his brain acting as if it had been zapped by a bolt of lightning. "Amy," he responded, unable to think of anything wittier to say. It occurred to him that he had to be the biggest boob this side of Alpha Centauri.

"How did your day go?"

"Okay, I guess," Kip answered. "I thought you have band practice every Monday and Wednesday."

"Mrs. Williams was gone today for some reason, so it was postponed until tomorrow."

Williams was the school's music teacher and band leader. A hefty woman, she had a voice that could shatter a brick at 20 paces. At least, that was the rumor. Kip had heard her sing once, and been reminded of snatches of opera he'd accidentally caught on the tube. "You play the clarinet, don't you?" he asked, simply to have something to say. He knew full well that she did.

Amy frowned. "It's my mom's big idea. Since she was in band when she was in school, I have to do the same. It's supposed to build my character, but all it does is bore me to tears."

"Parents!" Kip commiserated. "Do you ever get the idea that they're from another dimension?" Her light laughter relaxed him, and he found that he could think clearly again. "You should hear my dad sometime. He goes on and on about how things were when he was our age. In his time kids had to hike ten miles to school, even in blizzards. And when they acted up, their teachers laid into them with bullwhips."

"Your father too?" Amy said, grinning. "Mine likes to tell how he always had at least five hours of homework to do each night, so I have no reason to complain about the little I get."

"It must be something in their blood," Kip quipped. "A biological clock, maybe. Once they get a certain age, they turn into airheads and get all wrapped up in their past."

"Do you think the same thing will happen to us?"

"Never," Kip declared. He was growing more confident, and mentioned, as if out of the blue, "It's hard to believe Halloween is this Saturday. Just five more days." He paused. "And Friday is the dance, isn't it?"

Amy averted her gaze. "Yes," she said rather quietly.

Here it was. Kip's moment of truth. He fanned his courage, and was going to take the big step when someone called his name and a crew-cut figure scooted down the aisle and plunked down beside him.

"I didn't see you, buddy," Tommy Lee Harper said. "What the dickens are you doing, hanging back here by yourself?" He nodded at Amy. "You have to watch this guy. He gets all squirrely every now and then and likes to be by his lonesome."

"I do not," Kip protested, although his friend was right.

"Don't take it personal," Tommy Lee said. "We

all have quirks. I like to howl at the moon every now and then just for the hell of it. And my pa and ma traipsed naked back in the hill country a few times when they were liquored up on shine."

Kip was appalled that Tommy Lee would talk about naked people with Amy sitting right there. "They did not," Kip declared, without much conviction. He wouldn't put anything past the Harpers, who prided themselves on being the "wildest and woolliest clan in all creation," as his friend's dad had once phrased it.

"Have I ever lied to you?" Tommy Lee retorted, miffed. "It's no big deal anyway. I saw this magazine once just chock full of naked people. They all lived at a nudist hive, or some such, and were vacuuming and mowing the lawn and doing all the things we do every day, only without no clothes on."

Kip wanted to throttle his friend. He was sure Amy would be offended, but to his amazement she simply smiled and said, "A nudist colony, you mean. My mother told me all about them. There are people who think it's unnatural for anyone to wear clothes."

"You wouldn't catch me living at one of those places," Tommy Lee said. "Can you imagine sitting in a class with a bunch of bare-assed kids? I don't hardly see how anyone could get any studying done."

Kip had heard quite enough about nudists, so he brought up the first thing which popped into his head, the subject they had talked about that morning on their way to the bus stop. "Forget about that. I've been waiting all day to hear more about the Headless Horseman."

Tommy Lee snorted. "It's called the Headless *Horror*, rocks-for-brains. You're thinking of that other goblin, the one some famous guy wrote about. Irving somebody-or-other."

"Washington Irving," Amy clarified. "And if you had read the story, you'd know that it wasn't really a goblin. It was Ichabod Crane's rival."

"Who's he?" Tommy Lee said.

"The main character, a schoolteacher. He fell for a woman named Katrina, but she already had a boyfriend. And it was the boyfriend who followed Crane home and scared him into thinking he had been attacked by a goblin." Amy paused. "I remember it so well because I always thought it was a mean trick to play on poor Ichabod. I always felt sorry for him."

"Not me," Tommy Lee stated. "Any dork with a name like that deserves whatever he gets."

"It was common back then."

"Really? Then thank God I was born in this day and age. If my folks had called me that, I would have run away from home in shame."

By this time the bus had unloaded a third of the students. It bothered Kip that Tommy Lee had messed up his chance to pop the question a second time, but all wasn't lost. The day was not yet over.

Tommy Lee propped a knee on the back of

Amy's seat. "Where did that take place anyhow? Maine, wasn't it?"

"New York, I believe," Amy said.

"I was close." Smirking, Tommy Lee lowered his voice so only they could hear. "Wherever, it can't hold a candle to the goings-on in our valley. The word is that over twenty people have been killed by the Spook since the whole business began way back when."

Kip very much doubted that anyone had been slain. While he was perfectly willing to believe in life on other worlds, the notion of ghosts and goblins was downright ridiculous. No one in their right mind believed in such nonsense. He would have said so too if Amy had not commented before he could.

"Oh, I doubt there have been that many. It's more like five or six."

Amazed, Kip bluntly asked, "Do you believe in this fairy tale?"

"It's a legend, not a fairy tale," Amy corrected him. "And many of the people who have lived here a long time swear it's true. My grandfather actually saw the thing, but he would never talk about it much to me. He died two years ago or you could ask him yourself."

Tommy Lee was all interest. "Really? Damn, that must have been neat. What did the goblin look like?"

Amy pursed her lips. "It was just like everyone says. A headless spook on a horse. That's all I know."

66

"Did it go after him?"

"I think so. But I can't say for sure. He was always secretive about it around me. I guess he was afraid it would upset me too much."

"Maybe he just imagined seeing something," Kip speculated, thinking of all the times when he had been smaller and thought that he saw a monster lurking in the dark, only to have it turn out to be a coat rack or a bookshelf or some other equally mundane object. He figured that Amy would agree with him.

"Are you calling my grandfather a liar?" she responded resentfully. "Because if you are, I'll have you know that he was a sweet, honest man who couldn't tell a fib if his life depended on it. I loved him with all my heart."

Crestfallen, Kip lapsed into silence. He listened with half an ear as Tommy Lee quizzed Amy some more about her grandfather's experience. It troubled him that they were getting along so well, until he reminded himself that they had known one another for quite a while. Suddenly a devastating idea struck him: What if his friend asked her to the dance before he could? Would she go? Were they closer than they let on? He couldn't wait to be alone with her again.

As always, since the three of them lived the farthest from town, they were the last ones off the bus. As it rattled away, they headed across the Monongahela Bridge. Tommy Lee chucked a few stones into the creek. Amy was lost in thought.

Kip plotted his strategy. On reaching his driveway, he paused and stared off through the trees at the farmhouse. A yellow van was parked out front so they must have company, but it was no one he knew. "I think I'll tag along with you two a ways," he announced. His hope was that Tommy Lee would leave so he could be alone with Amy.

"I have a brainstorm! Let's hunt for crawdads and such in the creek," Tommy Lee proposed excitedly. "The three of us."

"I don't know," Kip hedged. Racking his brain to come up with an excuse to get rid of Tommy Lee, he commented, "I doubt that Amy is very much into crayfish and salamanders."

"Are you kidding?" she said. "I'm a country girl, remember? I was catching frogs when I was six. It's been a while since I did, but I don't think I've lost the knack."

Tommy Lee whooped. "Follow me!" he hollered. "I know this pool crawling with critters."

Amy ran after him, giggling, so Kip had no choice but to tag along. He knew that if he dirtied his clothes his mother would be mad, but he didn't care. He was bound and determined to stay close to Amy until an opportunity arose to pose his question.

Blackgap Road paralleled Monongahela Creek so closely that at times the edge of the road formed the rim of the creek's north bank. At one time the county commissioners had briefly considered erecting guard rails, but so few residents lived on Blackgap Road that they had not deemed it necessary.

The three of them passed the Harper place, a double-wide mobile home situated back in the pines, in a wide basin. Tommy Lee motioned for them to keep quiet, whispering, "I don't want my ma to hear us or she'll make me go in and do my homework. She's a real stickler for book learning." He shook his head. "I don't see what all the fuss is about. Pa never graduated from high school and he's doing right fine."

Kip almost made a mistake. He almost said, "You've got to be kidding!" But he caught himself in time.

Tommy Lee's father did odd jobs for a living. One month he drove a gravel truck, the next he helped out at the mill, and another month might find him filling in for the janitor at one of the schools. The man, by his own admission, had never held a steady job for more than six months in his life.

Kip never had understood why Bob Harper was proud of the fact. Many a time he'd heard the man brag to his father about it, invariably adding, "Yes, sir. It will be a cold day in Hell before I get caught up in the nine-to-five grind."

More perplexing was the attitude of Harper's wife. From what Kip had heard, she never objected, never complained about the low pay her man earned or his reckless work habits. She took it all in stride, just as she did the shenanigans of her eight children.

They had no money to spare. The clothes on their backs were often patched and mended. They lived like sardines, crammed into a house deep in the woods. Yet they were the happiest family Kip had ever seen, always laughing and joking, always making the most of the little they had. There were moments when Kip envied them, and wished he had whatever quality it was that made them the way they were.

After sneaking out of earshot of the Harper home, Tommy Lee led Amy and him to a shaded pool bordered by the road and a grassy glen. They forded at a shallow point below the pool. Depositing their schoolbooks on the grass, they removed their shoes, hiked their pants to their knees, and waded in.

Under the first rock Kip flipped over was a large crayfish. He made a grab for it but the crustacean streaked into deeper water as if jet-propelled. Amy laughed. He returned the favor minutes later when she scooped up a slippery salamander. It fell. She caught it with her other hand, but she couldn't hold on. Again she clutched at it. Again it slid loose. Her hands flailing like a juggler's trying to keep several objects in the air at one time, she kept catching the creature and losing it. Seven, eight times she lost her grip. The salamander finally splashed into the water and swam off, and Amy just stood there and watched it.

"I can take a hint," she remarked.

Spook Night

"Hey, look!" Tommy Lee had noticed an empty pickle jar at the water's edge. "My brother brought this here a while ago," he informed them. "Now we can get serious."

Kip lost all track of time. He was having too much fun. It was like being a kid again, with no cares, no worries. An added bonus was being close to Amy, who turned out to be better at snaring frogs than either of them. She had quick hands, so quick that if she could slink close enough, no frog in the world could get away from her. He imitated her technique, but caught only one.

Tommy Lee stuffed the frogs into the jar. After he had six in there, he held them aloft and smacked his lips. "Boy, won't Ma be tickled with these beauties."

"What do you mean?" Kip asked. "Will she let you keep them as pets?"

"Pets, nothing. She'll roast some frog legs tonight. I can hardly wait. Next to possum meat, there's nothing like a juicy frog leg."

Kip looked at him, certain Tommy Lee had to be joking. But the boy was licking his lips in anticipation and eyeing the jar of bullfrogs as if it contained the tastiest delicacies known to mortal man.

After that, Amy missed every frog she tried to catch.

It could not have been more than half an hour later when Kip glanced westward and was taken aback to see the sun about to dip below the mountains. "It's getting awful late," he noted. "Maybe we should call it quits."

"Oh, my gosh!" Tommy Lee blurted out. "My pa will be home soon. I'll get grounded for a month of Sundays if I'm not there." Striding out of the water, he jerked his pants down, scooped up the jar and his books, and was off like a greyhound out of the starting gate. "It was fun, guys!" he yelled over a shoulder. "Let's do it again real soon." As an afterthought he added, "And thanks again for the frogs. I'll bring you both a leg tomorrow if you want."

"No, thanks," Amy said.

Kip smiled and shook his head. "I like cereal for my breakfast." He waved, but Tommy Lee was scrambling up the bank and never looked around. In no time his friend was a mere shadow among shadows.

Amy coughed. Kip suddenly became acutely conscious they were alone. With her hair windtossed and her pants hiked almost to her thighs, she was magnificently beautiful. The gathering twilight lent her skin the pale hue of alabaster.

"I'd better be going too," she mentioned. "My mom will be worried and might come looking."

"I'll walk you home," Kip offered. Wading onto the shore, he collected his books and handed Amy hers after she tugged her pant legs down. Not saying a word, she took them and forded the creek. All afternoon she had been carefree and happy. Now she was quiet, almost somber. The transformation bewildered him.

He suspected she was uncomfortable in his company, that the only reason she had tagged along was to be with Tommy Lee.

Side by side they walked westward. Her house was the last one on Blackgap Road. Before reaching it they had to pass one other, an enormous, sprawling place with eaves and gables and shutters and gutters four stories high. Kip had gone by it a few times before in the daytime and never given it a second thought. But with the murky veil of encroaching night shrouding the countryside, the darkened house, poised near the road, reared up out of the encircling forest like a primeval beast about to spring at them.

"That's the Jackson place," Amy remarked. "The kids at school say it's haunted."

"Have you met the people who live there?"

"Only one person does. Alva Jackson. She keeps pretty much to herself. In all the years she's been our neighbor, I can think of only one time she's ever paid us a visit."

An older-model car sat in the driveway, so odds were that the woman was home. Kip scanned the inky windows. "You'd think she would put on her lights at this time of day."

Amy edged a bit closer to him. "The house is always dark at night. I don't even know if she uses electricity."

Their shoulders brushed, and Kip forgot all about the spooky house. He spotted the lights of the Westbrook residence in the distance. Soon they would be there. His mouth suddenly went dry. He debated how best to phrase his request. Should he be cool and say something like, "Hey, babe. Treat yourself to a rad time and go to the dance with me." Or should he be sincere and say, "I would be honored if you would accompany me to the Halloween dance." Which would impress her the most?

Kip was so caught up in his musing that he did not notice she had stopped until she touched his elbow. "What?" he asked.

Amy bobbed her chin toward her house. Her mother's strident voice cut the cool air like a knife, calling her name. "I have to hurry. If you're going to do it, do it now."

"Do what?"

"Ask me to the dance."

Flabbergasted, Kip gaped. "How did—?"

"Yes, I'll go with you," Amy said, and pecked him on the cheek. In a lithe bound she sped homeward. "Talk to you about it more in the morning."

For the longest while Kip Grant stood in the middle of Blackgap Road, marveling at the mysterious workings of the female mind. He was half convinced Amy must be telepathic. How else had she known? Delirious with joy, he bent his steps eastward. Grand images of Amy and him swirling about the dance floor filled his head. He paid no attention to his surroundings. So he was all the more petrified when, on hearing a flutter and the pad of feet to his left, he glanced up and saw a tall white apparition billowing across the lawn of the Jackson house.

It was coming straight toward him.

Chapter Five

John Grant leaned back and stretched to relieve a kink in his lower back. Working with a computer might seem like easy work to some, but sitting in a chair for hours on end, day after day, was bad for the human body. Muscles needed exercise or they atrophied, and he sometimes fretted that if his atrophied any worse, he'd turn to mush.

It seemed as if he would never solve the glitch in the system he was developing for the Packmeyer Corporation. Time for a break, he reflected. Then he would come back fresh and tackle the problem anew.

Swiveling his chair toward the office window, John was surprised to see it so dark outdoors. He consulted his watch, rose, and went to the kitchen, where his wife was on her hands and knees scrubbing around the base of the stove. For a few moments he watched her, admiring the shapely figure she worked so hard to maintain and thinking of happier times when they had been able to get through a single day without going at each other's throat.

It was no mystery what had gone wrong. He had been a senior consultant at Industrial Systems Incorporated, spending six days a week at the firm, often working 12 to 14 hours daily. She had worked a rotating shift at St. Joseph's Hospital. They'd hardly seen one another for weeks at a stretch. Their only contact had been exchanged notes clipped to the refrigerator.

Gradually, they had drifted apart. They'd lost that special sense of intimacy so crucial to any marriage. They'd become virtual strangers.

Somewhere along the line, hostility had set in. John had been stressed by his work and his guilt over being away from his family so much of the time, and he suspected that his wife had felt the same. The next thing he knew, they'd been on the verge of divorce.

The final straw had been when Laurie hit him. It had been over a trifle really. She had wanted him to take Kip to the dentist and he had been unable to because of a meeting at work. One thing had led to another. They had shouted and cursed. And in the heat of their argument, Laurie had done something she had never done in all the previous years they were together; she had slapped him across the cheek.

Spook Night

It had been more than a physical blow. It had been a wake-up call, as it were, making John realize as nothing else could that his life had unraveled to the point where he stood to lose all he held dear if he didn't take drastic measures. So he had.

John had spent the first 18 years of his life in Gettysburg. He knew the area well. Although his father and mother no longer lived there, when he'd decided to bail out of the rat race to save his marriage, he'd returned to his roots.

Laurie and the kids had protested. His wife had implied that he was going through some sort of midlife crisis. She'd taunted him about "going off the deep end." But for all her bitterness, he'd noticed that she'd gone along with the idea once she'd realized he was committed to it. And she had backed him up when Shery and Kip had raised a fuss about giving up all their friends and leaving their schools.

Shery had been the worst. She'd thrown a few temper tantrums, and when that hadn't worked, she'd bawled her brains out in front of them, and when the blubbering had had no effect, she'd given them the silent treatment. It had lasted until after they'd moved in.

Through it all, *Laurie had stood by him*. Those words echoed in John Grant's mind as he stepped into the open and asked, "Have you heard anything from the locksmith yet? It's getting late."

About to dip a sponge into a bucket, Laurie let

go of it and glanced at the clock on the wall. "Almost six. And he said he had to quit by five or so."

"I'll go see how he's doing," John offered.

"I'll join you," Laurie said. Stripping off her rubber gloves, she stepped to a cupboard and took out a large flashlight. "We might need this."

John held the door for her, and she gave him a funny look as she passed by. He caught a whiff of her perfume, the same tantalizing scent that had always kicked his hormones into overdrive when they had been younger. A powerful yearning seized him, a hunger he hadn't experienced in so long that he had forgotten what it felt like.

Laurie Grant flicked on the flashlight and glanced back at her husband. For a second there, as she'd passed him, she'd glimpsed a spark in his eyes, a spark she had believed long since extinguished. Could it be? she asked herself. And almost shook her head in denial.

The springhouse was little more than a black blob against the background of inky night. John walked toward it. "Mr. Eldridge?" he called. The van was still there, so the locksmith had to be as well.

Laurie swept the beam over the lawn to the front of the stone building. She gasped on seeing the door open. "He did it! He picked the lock!"

"But where is he?" John asked. He thought the locksmith would have rushed up to the house to give them the good news.

"Maybe he went in there," Laurie suggested.

She remembered the loud pounding on the door that morning, and a secret dread came over her that perhaps something awful had happened.

"I hope not," John said. "These old spring-houses can be treacherous. When I was a boy, a man we knew slipped on a wet step and cracked his skull on a rock."

Laurie's anxiety grew. The locksmith's case and tools were right where she had seen them last. In the glare of the flashlight she saw foot-prints outlined in the thick dust on the floor, leading within.

John stooped to poke his head past the jamb. "George? Are you in here?"

A gust of wind shook an adjacent maple, and Laurie jumped. It was childish, she knew, but the springhouse seemed oddly ominous. A bad case of nerves she figured, and commented, "I hope he's all right. He's such a sweet old man."

John held out his hand. "Let me have the flash-light and I'll have a look."

Not too keen on staying there alone, Laurie said, "We'll go together."

The door was wide enough for the two of them to enter at the same time. As they did, a sudden rasping noise fell on their ears. It sounded to John as if a small chain were being whipped back and forth on the floor. To Laurie, it sounded more like the rasp of large reptilian scales. She envisioned an enormous snake slith-ering toward them, and her skin crawled.

"What the hell?" John exclaimed.

The next instant a violent blast of cold air buffeted them, slamming into them so hard that they were knocked aside and nearly bowled over. Laurie's spine struck the door jamb with a resounding blow. Something scraped against her left hand. She jerked it up and saw a thin red line. The skin had been cut, as if by a razor.

John balled his fist, ready to lash out. But there was nothing to lash out at. The blast of air died as inexplicably as it had arisen. He swatted at a cobweb, then stepped forward. "I wonder what caused that."

"Let's find Mr. Eldridge and get out of here," Laurie said. "This place gives me the creeps."

Just then, a frenzy of vicious barking and snapping broke out up the hill. Both of them whirled and stepped outside.

"It's Buck!" Laurie declared. "What on earth has gotten into him?" She swept the beam at the rear of the farmhouse and framed the mongrel in its glare. He was crouched a score of feet from the back door that led to the kitchen, the hair on the top of his neck bristling, his teeth bared.

John was more interested in the door itself. It hung open, yet he distinctly remembered closing it after he went out. "We'll tend to that dumb mutt later," he said. "Let's find George first." Going back in, he pointed at the tracks. "We'll follow them. They should lead us right to him."

Laurie nodded. For some reason she didn't feel as scared as she had a while ago. Holding the light at her waist, she glued herself to her husband's elbow. The cobwebs were as thick as curtains. They made slow progress, with John swiping the clinging webs aside so they wouldn't get on her.

The springhouse was longer than it appeared to be from the outside. It was a while before John detected the dank scent of water. The tracks led toward it, toward a far corner, the same corner where he had first felt the cold sensation the day before when he had been searching for another way in.

The beam encountered another wall of cobwebs. John tore at them and they clung to his hands, his wrists, his clothes. As he wiped a strand from an arm, a small brown spider scuttled up his sleeve toward his neck. Instinctively, he recoiled and slapped it, smashing it to a pulp.

Laurie pointed the flashlight into the opening in the cobwebs he had made. She saw a dark cavity which had to be the spring. Then the beam shimmered on water—and something else, something she mistook for a log poking up out of the spring. On bending forward, she made out the outline of a human foot. Raw fear knifed through her insides, rooting her to the spot. "It can't be!" she breathed.

"What?" John asked, taking another step. He saw the spring. Dashing to the edge, he dropped to his knees, grabbed the protruding leg, and heaved. It was like trying to lift an anchor. The locksmith's body, encased in waterlogged clothes, was impossibly heavy. "No!" he cried, straining harder. "Please, no!"

Laurie rushed to help. Setting the flashlight beside her, she wrapped her arms around Eldridge's leg to add her strength to John's. United, they were able to lift the locksmith high enough to get both legs out of the water, which splashed around their knees. Gasping from the effort, they paused, but only for a second or two.

"Again!" John directed, breaking out in a cold sweat as he applied his sinews to the herculean task of raising the man the rest of the way. He could see the face now, pale and distorted by the water, the eyes and mouth locked wide open. "If only it's not too late!"

Planting both feet, Laurie threw all she had into levering the locksmith out. Just when she thought she would collapse under the weight, the body slid onto the stone floor. Immediately she bent to administer first aid. As a nurse, she had taken courses in resuscitation, and had once saved a small child using mouth-to-mouth. She probed for a pulse. There was none. "Call for help! I'll do what I can!"

John spun and raced from the springhouse. Buck still barked at the screen door, but he paid the animal no mind. There were two phones, one in his office, the other in the living room. He made for the latter since it was closest to the back door. As he lifted the receiver there was a loud thump overhead, from one of the bedrooms upstairs. Assuming one of his kids was home, he hollered, "Shery? Kip? Get down to the springhouse! Your mother might need your help!"

There was no dial tone. John jabbed the plunger a few times and listened again. Still nothing. Of all the rotten times for the phone to go dead! he fumed. Slamming it down, he sped to his den to try the other one. This time he lucked out. Punching 911, he breathlessly told the operator his address and reported a possible drowning victim. She was brisk and professional. Taking his name and number, she hung up.

John bolted for the back door. The stupid dog had finally stopped yapping. He ran past it, on down the hill, and into the springhouse. Heedless of spiders, he crashed through the cobwebs to the spring.

Laurie heard him coming, but did not look up. Mouth-to-mouth had proven useless, so she had rolled George Eldridge onto his stomach and was applying the back-pressure arm-lift method of emptying the lungs of water and inducing respiration. "He won't respond!" she said, resisting tears. Laurie did not give up, though. She rolled him over and began chest compression, alternating with more mouth-to-mouth. She knew that most people could live for five or six minutes after their breathing stopped. Some had gone much longer.

A lot of water had seeped from the locksmith's mouth, but his lungs refused to work. Over and over Laurie tried the best techniques, yet no matter what she did, no matter how hard she strained, those lungs would not respond. *Come on!* she mentally screamed. *Live! Live!*

The cycle tired her rapidly, but Laurie persisted. Simultaneously, she warded off the shock that nipped at her senses, threatening to render her too weak to do any good. Dimly, she was aware of her husband at her side, of him speaking.

"The police and emergency personnel are on their way. Do you want me to take over for you?"

Laurie merely shook her head. Saving lives was her livelihood, not his. She repeated the cycle, her shoulders aching, her arms leaden. "Come on!" she urged aloud, her desperation mounting. "Revive, damn it!"

John Grant stared at the man's pallid features, at the puddle of water which had formed under Eldridge's face. With a sinking feeling he knew beyond a shadow of a doubt that they had lost him, that the kindly gentleman's devoted wife would soon be receiving a visit from authorities bearing the bad tidings. He scanned the spring, unable to comprehend how so grievous a tragedy could have taken place. No rocks or wood littered the surrounding floor. There was no debris Eldridge could have tripped over. Yet that had to be the only explanation. The locksmith had tripped and fallen in, banging his head on the side.

A wavering howl split the night. John straightened and turned. The police were on their way. Then he listened closer and realized the howl wasn't the electronic wail of a police siren. It was Buck, up on the hill.

The mongrel was wailing as if the world were coming to an end.

Kip Grant couldn't move. He could scarcely breathe. Riveted in his tracks, he gawked at the billowy specter floating toward him. Overcome by rising panic, he was convinced that he was seeing the unthinkable: a real ghost. Kip threw up his arms in front of his face to ward off its attack, and would have screamed had the specter not halted and addressed him.

"You there, boy! Come over here."

Kip did a double take. It wasn't an unearthly apparition. It was an elderly woman, her face as white as the dress she wore, her long hair the color of burnished silver.

"Didn't you hear me, boy? Come here."

"Ma'am?" Kip croaked. She had to be Alva Jackson, he guessed, the crackpot Amy had mentioned. Well, he didn't know her, and he wasn't about to budge.

"We need to talk, boy."

Kip didn't like being talked down to by someone who traipsed around at night in her bedclothes. For those were exactly what Alva Jackson had on, loose-fitting pajamas and a long robe which whipped in the rising wind. "Talk all you want, lady. But if you don't mind, and even if you do, I'm staying right where I am."

"Uppity thing, aren't you," the woman said,

tilting her head to regard him as if he were something which had crawled out from under a rock. She had a nasal twang and a drawl to her words, much like the Harpers did.

"I know who you are, lady," Kip tried to impress her. "You're Alva Jackson, right?"

"Think you're smart, do you?" the woman retorted. "But what you know doesn't amount to a hill of beans, Kipland Albert Grant."

Dumbfounded, Kip took a step back. No one other than his parents and sister knew his full name because he never used it. He hated the name Kipland, even if it had been his grandfather's.

Alva Jackson cackled, a dry, insane laugh devoid of real mirth. "Yes, I know who you are, boy. I know a lot of things that would surprise you. If you need answers, I have them. But that's not why I came out here. I need to warn you, youngster, you and your whole family. Beware, boy. Evil's time is due. And those you love are on its doorstep."

"What?" Kip said, confused by her rapid-fire prattle.

The woman advanced to the gutter. Up close, her face bore more wrinkles than a dried prune. Her eyes, though, sparkled with vitality. Or something much worse. "I've been keeping my eye on you, boy. Watching you in the crystal. You're not like those squabbling folks of yours, so wrapped up in themselves they can't see the forest for the trees. And you're a far sight different from that vain sister of yours. She's let all that TV nonsense and those fool movies go to her head, boy. She thinks the sun rises and sets on her account."

For a crazy woman, Alva Jackson was remarkably perceptive. Kip listened intently.

"You have a good heart, youngster," the woman continued. "If you don't get lost in the maze of your own imagination, you might even make something of yourself one day." A bony hand raised to stab a gnarled finger at him. "Provided you live long enough. You and your kin." She glanced over a stooped shoulder at the gloomy woods, then spoke in a whisper. "I'll give you the secret. Pay heed, boy. What do you get when you add one and one?"

Kip was lost. Her babbling made no sense. But her warning disturbed him, so he replied, "What else? Two."

"Wrong!" Alva Jackson practically shrieked. Tossing her head as if distraught, she shook a fist at him and railed, "I thought you would be smart enough to understand. I thought you could make the others see."

"One and one *is* two," Kip insisted. "Everybody knows that."

The woman snorted. "Everybody believed the world was flat at one time too. Were they right then? I know folks nowadays like to put the common herd on a pedestal, but that's not the natural order of things."

Kip was becoming more confused by the moment. He wanted to be on his way.

As if Alva Jackson could read his mind, she rasped, "Don't run off on me, boy! I want you to see the light before you go." Pivoting, she stared at South Mountain, a gigantic monolith which gave the illusion of towering to the stars. "It's the least I can do. I don't want more innocent blood on my conscience. I don't want to have to attend your funeral, boy, and those of your blood kin."

"Our funerals?" Kip said, alarmed.

The woman nodded. "One and one makes one, boy. Remember that. Plan accordingly and you just might have a prayer. If not, there isn't power on this Earth which will save you when the night of the demon spawn is upon us. Heed me, boy."

Kip had about had enough. He had never met anyone so positively loony. "I've got to be going, lady. My parents are probably worried sick."

Alva Jackson tittered. "Oh, they're sick, all right. But not with fretting over you. They made a big mistake today, boy. A mistake they'll come to regret." She clasped her hands and held them over her head. "As the Lord is my witness, I would have warned them if I thought they would have listened. But they'd only brand me loco, as so many have."

Kip couldn't blame them. He edged eastward, anxious to get out of there. Suddenly the tall woman speared a finger at the base of South Mountain and cried out in triumph.

"There, boy! See for yourself!"

All Kip saw were trees and the black mass

which formed the mountain. "What am I—?" he began, then stopped, perplexed by a faint green glow which had materialized. It glimmered, flared, faded, and flared again. As near as he could tell, it was on South Mountain, on one of the lower slopes. Exactly where was impossible to gauge in the dark. "What is that?" he asked breathlessly.

"It's started, boy. As I knew it would. As it did all those other times."

"What has?"

"Satan's spawn is among us again, boy. Beware the night, for that's its element. Beware the serpent, for that's its power. But most of all, beware All Hallows' Even. The portal is open then."

As if a switch had been thrown, the green light blinked out. Baffled, Kip lingered in the hope it would reappear so he could identify it. A fire was out of the question since no fire he had ever seen burned bright green. Nor could it have been a flashlight beam. A flare maybe? he wondered.

The woman in white faced him. "There. You've seen with your own eyes. So riddle me this, boy. What makes a door important? Is it what lies outside or what lies inside?"

Tired of her games, Kip quipped, "Neither. It's whether the door will open." He'd meant it as a joke, but to his astonishment she screamed with glee and pranced in circles, the whole while jumping up and down and clapping her hands in wild abandon.

"He understands! The Lord be praised, the boy understands!"

That was the final straw. Kip ran, half fearing she would give chase. Alva Jackson, lost in her demented rapture, danced off across her front yard. The last he saw of her, the woman had stopped, knelt, then bowed her forehead to the ground.

"What a ditz," Kip said, and concentrated on putting as much distance behind him as he could before he tired and had to stop. He passed the Harper place, where country music blared from a window. Farther on he came within sight of the Monongahela Bridge and the gravel drive. Up on the hill, near the farmhouse, police lights flashed. He broke into a sprint at the sight. As he did, from the direction of South Mountain, came a sound he did not pay much attention to since there were a number of farms in the area.

It was the whinny of a horse.

Chapter Six

The new day dawned crisp and clear, but John Grant was in no mood to appreciate its beauty. Seated in a wicker chair on the front porch of the farmhouse, he stared out over the tranquil valley and took a sip of scalding black coffee. He was so tired that he could hardly think straight. His eyes hurt, his body ached, and he could feel a headache coming on unless the caffeine counteracted it.

The Night from Hell. That was how John regarded the 12 hours he had just been through. It had been, without exception, the single worst night of his entire life. Taking another swallow, he reviewed the sequence of events.

The police had arrived within five minutes of his phone call. The ambulance, housed at the Spook Hollow Fire Station and manned by personnel who were on call after six and had left for the day shortly before his call came through, had taken longer to get there. The medics had promptly taken over and tried their best to revive the locksmith, without success.

More police had shown up. Four of the five Spook Hollow officers had been on hand, including their heavyset chief, Larry Bogartus.

John had figured their investigation would be cut-and-dried. Obviously George Eldridge had slipped, hit his head, and drowned. But the police had insisted on quizzing him for hours, going over every little detail again and again and again. Finally he'd had enough. At well past two in the morning he had demanded that either they arrest him, if they were really dumb enough to think that he had murdered Eldridge, or leave.

Chief Bogartus had apologized for raking him over the coals. Bogartus had claimed it was standard procedure, and that he certainly didn't suspect them of any crime. Nor did he feel foul play was involved.

But, now that John thought about it, the chief had asked some very strange questions during the interrogation. Questions John had dismissed at the time as par for the course. Were they, though?

John mentally ticked them off: Had any strangers been hanging around the place? Had he and his wife seen anyone lurking near the house after the sun went down? Had they heard any odd noises? Had there been any unusual happenings inside the house? Things they couldn't explain?

John had figured the police were trying to learn if any transients had been in the area. He'd attributed their interest to an event a few years back, when a hobo had been arrested for a series of burglaries and for beating up an elderly woman who'd caught him in the act.

Now John wasn't so sure. The longer he pondered, the more convinced he became that Chief Bogartus had had an ulterior motive for asking all those questions. But what it might be eluded him.

The sound of a door closing upstairs let John know that one of the kids was up. It also reminded him of the tiff he'd had with Shery when she'd had the gall to sneak into the house at three in the morning. She had expected Laurie and him to be in bed, but they'd been in the kitchen recovering from their ordeal, the police having left about 2:30.

In all the confusion, John hadn't noticed that Shery wasn't home. If not for Eldridge's death, he would have turned in at his usual time, about 11, and been none the wiser. Laurie always let the girl stay out too damn late, and then made light of it.

But last night John had been in no mood to let it pass. He'd insisted that Shery tell them where she had been. She'd refused. He'd gotten mad and grounded her for a month. Shery had gone into her typical indignant act and, true to form, Laurie had leaped to her defense.

John had almost punched the wall in frustration. The nightmare of the locksmith's death had drawn his wife and him closer than they had been in years. Until Shery showed up, they had been talking quietly, actually listening to one another for a change, sharing their thoughts as they used to do. Then along had come their spoiled brat, who had ruined everything.

Laurie had refused to ground Shery, with the big Halloween dance so close. John had pointed out that unless they started cracking down on her, Shery would think she could get away with whatever she liked, that it might already be too late to instill any discipline in the girl. But Laurie wouldn't change her mind. She'd merely scolded Shery and made her promise never to come home that late again, then sent her off to bed.

John had tried to control his temper, but couldn't. "I may not be very religious," he'd said, "but I seem to recall something in the Bible about sparing the rod and spoiling the child. At the rate you're going, our daughter will be pregnant before she's eighteen and probably have to drop out of high school. Is that what you want? I know I don't. But don't worry. When it happens, I won't say I told you so." He'd risen, stepped to the doorway, and glared at her. "But I *will* have told you so."

So much for their special moment. So much

for reconciling and getting their marriage back on track. John quaffed the rest of the cup and sighed. He should have known it had been too good to be true. Nothing ever worked out the way it should.

Something wet and soft suddenly touched John's other hand. His nerves were so frazzled that he half jumped out of the chair before he realized it was Buck. The mongrel had disappeared when the police arrived and not shown up since. "Well, hello there, big guy," John said, rubbing the dog's neck. "Where did you get to last night? Do you have a special hiding place?"

Buck grunted and rubbed against John's leg.

"You don't like this place much, do you, boy?" John remarked. "Here I thought you'd love having all this room to run around in. But what do I know, eh? Apparently not a damn thing, according to my wife. Sometimes I wonder why I bother anymore. If no one else cares whether this family stays together or not, why should I?"

"I care, Dad."

Kip Grant emerged. He had risen early so he could use the bathroom before his sister, and was all set for school. Troubled by his father's comments, he walked over and laid a hand on his dad's arm. "I don't like to hear you talk like that. Whatever is wrong, I know Mom and you will work it out eventually."

John had not meant for his son to overhear him. "I was just letting some steam off," he said.

"We had another fight last night when your sister came home late."

Kip frowned. He hadn't kept count, but if he had to make a guess, he would say that over half the arguments his parents had in the past two or three years were caused by his sister. And each and every one had made him unbearably miserable. He couldn't stand to hear his folks quarrel. Back in Philly it had gotten so bad that he'd often buried his head under a pillow and plugged his ears with his fingers.

Kip was no fool. He knew their marriage was shaky. So he made an extra effort not to do anything which would make matters worse. His sister liked to tease him about being a "goody two-shoes," but he didn't care. He would be the perfect son, if that's what it took to help save the family.

"You're up a little early, aren't you?" John said, recalling how upset his son had been when he heard about Eldridge. "Did you have trouble sleeping?"

"Some," Kip admitted. He stared at the springhouse. The door had been propped open with a two-by-four so it couldn't swing shut and lock someone inside. By noon the news of the locksmith's death would be all over school, he suspected, and he would be pestered with questions all afternoon.

"Try not to let it get to you," John said. "Accidents happen. That might sound cold, but it's a fact of life." He slowly stood. "I only knew Mr.

Eldridge a short while, but I liked him a lot. He was a decent human being. His poor wife must be heartbroken."

Seeing his father so downcast, Kip decided to cheer him up. "I wanted to let you know," he said. "I have a date for the dance next Friday."

"You do?" John said, genuinely surprised. His son had never shown an interest in girls before. "What brought this on? Do I know her?"

Kip explained about Amy briefly. The Grants had met the Westbrooks once. Shortly after they'd moved in, Todd Westbrook had brought his family over to welcome them to the area and extended an invitation to get together sometime. As yet, his father had been too busy with his work to take Mr. Westbrook up on the offer, but Kip hoped they would soon. It pleased him immensely when his dad smiled and clapped him on the shoulders.

"Well, well, well. So my son is becoming a man. I'll drive the two of you there and back if you want."

"What about your work?" Kip asked. His father frequently stayed in the office until quite late.

"You're more important," John said proudly.

Their tender moment was interrupted by the squeak of the screen door. Laurie had on a robe and her hair had more spikes than track shoes. She had barely slept, she was so upset by the drowning. The sound of voices had drawn her downstairs. Now, tightening the robe, she yawned and said, "Kip, I'll fix you some breakfast. You shouldn't start the day on an empty stomach."

"I'm sort of in a hurry, Mom," Kip said.

"To get to school? Who do you think you're kidding?" Laurie persisted. "Come on." She held the door open for him.

"I can't," Kip replied. "There's someone I want to talk with before the bus shows up."

Laurie caught her husband giving her a peculiar look. Still stung by his comments about her failure to exercise discipline, she elected to prove him wrong by sticking to her guns. "I won't take no for an answer, young man. Get inside and I'll whip up a plate of eggs and bacon. It won't take long."

"Please, Mom," Kip begged.

"No."

John Grant had heard enough. He could guess who his son wanted to see, and it rankled him that his wife would stand in the way of their son's first true romance. "If the boy isn't hungry, he doesn't have to eat," he said. Giving Kip a friendly shove, he added, "Off you go. Have a good day."

"Thanks, Dad."

Simmering at having her decision overridden, Laurie waited until Kip was halfway down the hill before she said, "Don't you ever interfere like that again! When I tell him to do something, I expect him to do it."

"You're a fine one to talk about interfering,"

John reminded her. "Look at what you did last night."

"That was different," Laurie grated, and went into the kitchen, slamming the door behind her.

John Grant sighed. Another day was off to a wonderful start.

Shery Grant was with Bryce Harcourt. He had driven her to the local lovers' lane in his shiny new Corvette, and they were parked on a ridge overlooking Spook Hollow. The full moon hung overhead, and a warm breeze blew in from the southwest. She had on her short skirt and a blouse which showed more than it concealed. Bryce leaned toward her. His mouth was about to cover hers, when all of a sudden there was a stinging pain in her left foot.

The pain was so sharp that Shery sat up, only to find herself in her bed. Stray shafts of sunlight filtered past the edges of her closed curtains. It was morning, an hour before school.

"Just a dream," Shery said aloud, and went to stretch. Quite abruptly, she felt the same pain in her left foot that she had felt in her dream. Drowsy from not getting enough sleep, she winced as she bent down.

Her right leg was under the covers. But her left had poked out during the night and hung over the edge, bent at the knee. Taking it for granted that she had bumped her foot while tossing and turning, she raised it onto the bed.

There was no bruise. Instead, just below her

big toe, her skin bore an oval indentation, as if something that shape had gouged hard into her flesh. She rubbed her eyes, then bent lower. It couldn't be, yet it looked exactly as if something had *bitten* her without breaking the skin!

Stupefied, Shery got out of bed and knelt to examine the mattress and the frame. No protrusions were evident. None of the springs were exposed. And none of the bolts which held the frame together were anywhere near where her foot had dangled. In short, there was no explanation for the mark below her toe.

The pain was subsiding, so Shery put the indentation from her mind and hustled to the bathroom to beat her brother there. A damp towel lying on the floor told her she was too late, but at least he was already gone, so she had the tub all to herself. Unfortunately, she had to rush in order not to be late for the bus, so she showered instead of bathed.

The hot water soothed her. Shery leaned against the stall and let it cascade over her shoulders and down her body. Her breasts were still tender from the night before. She grinned at the recollection, and said under her breath, "Bryce, you devil, you."

From beyond the shower curtain came a noise. Shery glanced up and listened, but it wasn't repeated. "Is someone there?" she called. "Mom? Is that you?"

When no one responded, Shery parted the curtain, careful not to expose herself in case it was only her dorky brother. No one was there, but the door, which she had shut as she always did, hung open a few inches. "Was that little creep trying to cop a peek?" she said in disgust, and stepped over the rim of the tub to close it again. For just a moment she saw the hallway, and thought she saw something small race down it, something about the size of a cat, something pale gray in color.

Since they didn't own a cat, Shery was taken aback, and pulled the door open to see better. But whatever she had glimpsed had disappeared. She made sure the door was secure before she stepped back into the shower to finish washing.

It didn't surprise her, seeing an animal in the house. It was a *farm* house after all, and although she didn't know a whole hell of a lot about farms, she did know they were overrun with animals, things like chickens and cows and pigeons and God only knows what else. Sure, the place had supposedly not been used for farming in years. But that didn't mean a few cats or whatever weren't still hiding out on the property.

Shery hated the house. She hated the springhouse. She also hated the ramshackle barn, the old woodshed, and the empty chicken coop. She hated everything and anything about the place, and if she could, she would have taken the next bus back to Philadelphia rather than go on living in a hick town where the most popular pastime was watching the grass grow.

It was all her father's fault, Shery believed. He

was the one who had decided to leave Philadelphia. He was the one who had announced clear out of the blue that he had purchased a small farm and they were all going to go live in the country. Even her mother had been caught by surprise. Shery had seen it in her mom's eyes, had witnessed the resentment her mom felt. And since Shery always took her mother's side in all their squabbles, Shery had sided with her on this as well.

There were times when Shery wished the two of them would say that enough was enough and agree to a divorce. They had been squabbling for so long that it seemed the only logical thing to do.

Then there were other times when Shery recalled the loving home they used to have, and she secretly wished it could be like that again.

Until about her tenth birthday, their life had been ideal. Her parents had been hugging and smooching all the time, and never, ever fought. The family had spent a lot of time together, going to places like the zoo and the art museum and the Jersey shore. She had been so much happier then. She and Kip had gotten along just fine, a minor miracle in itself.

Now those days were so long gone as to make her think she must have dreamed them.

Shery turned off the water and climbed out. She spent fully half an hour drying and styling her hair and doing her eyebrows and nails. For a change of pace she applied pink lipstick rather than cherry red. Then, donning her robe, she hurried to her room to get dressed.

She took a step, and halted in consternation. While she had been gone, someone had yanked all the blankets and sheets off her bed and dumped them in a pile. Worse, her jewelry box had been upended on top of the heap. Livid with outrage, she sped to the top of the stairs, but there was no sign of her brother.

"Damn him!" Shery growled. In a huff she dressed and marched down to the kitchen, where her mother sat drinking tea. "That brat has done it again!" she complained, and told about the mess. "When you have time, go up and take a look at it. I think I'll wring the little turkey's neck."

Laurie Grant had been reviewing the clash on the front porch. She had about decided that she had let her lack of sleep cloud her judgment and was going to go talk to John, when Shery had stomped in. Suddenly her son's behavior made sense. Kip had wanted to get out of there before his hijinks were discovered.

"Fix yourself some toast. I'll be right back," Laurie said, standing. She didn't offer to make eggs and bacon for her daughter since Shery never ate a big breakfast. Or any big meal, for that matter. Shery was a fanatic about keeping her slim figure.

John had gone to his office. Extremely tired but too upset by all that had happened to sleep, he was wrestling with a systems design problem which had plagued him for days when Laurie walked in.

"Do you know what your son has done?"

"No," John said, and was given an account. It shocked him that Kip would do such a thing. The boy wasn't above pulling a practical joke now and again, but they were largely harmless.

"Now you see why he was in a big rush to leave for school," Laurie chided. "So what do you have to say for yourself?" She expected an apology. To her added annoyance, her husband didn't offer one. His brow knit and he pondered a few moments.

"Something isn't right here," John said. "How can Kip be to blame? I'm positive he left for school before Shery dragged her lazy carcass out of the sack. He couldn't have done it."

Laurie couldn't credit her ears. "Well, Shery certainly didn't. And it wasn't either of us. So who else could it have been? Buck?"

"There's no need to be sarcastic."

Laurie's self-control teetered. "Excuse me for living, mister. But you're wrong and you're too stubborn to admit it. Kip took advantage of us. He got away with it because *you* were soft on him." She shook her head in disgust. "Last night you made a federal case out of my doing the same thing with Shery, but now that you're to blame, you want to make excuses for your son and justify your own mistake."

John shot out of his chair. "I'm doing no such thing," he objected. "I honestly don't see how he can be at fault. Maybe Shery did it herself just to get him in trouble."

"What?" Laurie exploded. "You're blaming her now? Well, that's just great." She was furious that her husband would stoop so low rather than confess his own glaring blunder. "I won't tell Shery what you've said because I don't want your own flesh and blood to know what a low opinion you have of her." Backing to the doorway, she added, "I'm beginning to question why I even bother anymore. It's abundantly clear that you don't care for me half as much as you used to, and now I doubt you care for your daughter all that much or you wouldn't be unjustly accusing her. Maybe it's high time we faced facts. Maybe it's time we called a lawyer."

"But I do care," John said. But Laurie just spun on a heel and whisked down the hall. He took a few strides to go after her, then changed his mind. Why bother? he asked himself. Perhaps she was right. Perhaps it was high time they accepted the handwriting on the wall and went their separate ways.

Slumping in emotional defeat, John Grant sank back down into his chair, crossed his arms on top of the computer monitor, rested his forehead on them, closed his eyes, and gave in to the rising despair that had been gnawing at him for so many months.

A person could only take so much, he reflected. He had done all he could, he had given it his best shot, and it wasn't enough. He and his wife were no closer than they were when they'd left Philadelphia. If anything, they were farther apart, balancing on the brink of marital oblivion.

John was not a man prone to tears, but they moistened his eyes now. An almost irresistible urge to bawl like an infant came over him. He suppressed it. Crying over spilt milk, as the old saying went, would serve no purpose.

John made up his mind to have a talk with his son when Kip came home. He would get to the bottom of the affair, and if Kip was indeed to blame, he would do the right thing and apologize to his wife for acting like a jerk. It might not appease her, but his effort had to count for something.

"I won't give up yet," John said to himself. "I want to save my marriage." He leaned back to resume work, and as he did, keys on the keyboard clicked as if he had brushed them with an elbow, although he was sure he hadn't. Letters appeared on the screen. He looked at them and froze, totally confounded by the inexplicable.

Somehow, by a sheer fluke, he had typed a word. He couldn't see how his arm had bumped that exact combination of keys, yet there the word shone, as bright as day. He touched the screen, hoping that the word would disappear as mysteriously as it had appeared. But it didn't.

As if the computer itself were taunting him, the screen blazed the challenge: "NEVER!"

Chapter Seven

It had been one of the best days of Kip Grant's life—until school ended, at any rate.

That morning he had waited for Amy Westbrook at the bridge, but she had not shown up until a minute before the bus arrived. There had been no time to talk to her. He had climbed on and taken a seat, then been giddy with excitement when she got on moments later and sat right down beside him as if it were the most natural thing in the world for her to do.

His blood had set to racing, his corpuscles holding their own version of the Indy 500. She had looked so radiant, with her hair done up differently than he had ever seen and a new shade of lipstick she had never worn, that he had mumbled a greeting in dazed awe.

Kip had hardly noticed when Tommy Lee

Harper snickered and made some crack about Romeo and Juliet. It hadn't really registered when his sister, late as always, bustled on board, glowered at him as she passed, and remarked, "You're in for it when you get home, you little twerp!"

Amy had asked him what Shery meant by that, and Kip had replied that he honestly didn't know, that she was always raving at him about one thing or another, and that it wouldn't surprise him if she were declared legally wacko one day.

The morning went by in a blur. Amy was in many of his classes, so they were together most of the time. They made small talk, Kip not even remembering half the things he said.

At noon Kip was jolted off cloud nine when several acquaintances came up to their table and badgered him about the locksmith. He'd been so wrapped up in Amy that he had completely forgotten the man's death, as well as his bizarre encounter with Alva Jackson.

After eating, he and Amy slipped out of the lunchroom and snuck off to a cluster of trees that bordered the football field. Kip told her all he knew about George Eldridge, and was going to mention his run-in with the recluse when the bell rang.

His afternoon classes were a drag. Amy was only in one, and they sat far apart. He could hardly wait for school to end. At the last bell of the day, he dashed to his locker for the books he needed, and was out on the sidewalk in front of the junior high before anyone else. But Amy never showed up. It wasn't until the rest of the students were flocking out that he remembered she had band practice. He wouldn't see her again until morning.

"Damn," Kip said aloud.

"What's bugging you, good buddy?" Tommy Lee asked, materializing at his side. "Has your main babe dumped you already?"

"Get off my case. We're just good friends," Kip said defensively.

"Bull-pukey. Everybody saw the two of you making cow eyes at each other all day long. You're in *love*, friend. And just as soon as I latch onto a spray can, I'll let the whole world know it." Smirking, Tommy Lee regarded the building behind them. "What do you think? Should I write it on the front wall or the back?"

"You do and I'll break both your arms," Kip warned, only partly in jest.

Tommy Lee put a hand on Kip's brow as if checking his temperature. "Yep. Just as I thought. You've got a bad case. Better get to a sawbones while you're still breathing."

The timely arrival of the bus prevented Kip from grabbing his friend and wrestling him to the ground. On the way home Tommy Lee bragged about the tasty frog legs his mom had cooked and asked if Kip wanted to catch more. Kip was going to decline until he recalled his sister's remark that morning. He couldn't think of anything he had done wrong, but if he was in hot water, as she'd claimed, he'd rather face the music later than sooner. "Sure, I'll go with you," he answered.

The bus was empty save for the two of them and Mr. Kimble when it braked just shy of the Monongahela Bridge. Kimble worked the handle that activated the door and said, "Have a good day, boys. See you bright and early."

"Don't remind us," Tommy Lee responded.

Kip followed his friend down the steps and along the road toward the creek. He heard the bus growl as Mr. Kimble shifted gears, and the crunch of its big tires as it backed onto the strip bordering Blackgap Road. Then he heard a tremendously loud thump and the grating creak of metal under stress.

Mr. Kimble had backed up too far. The rear of the bus now jutted into high weeds which grew rank along the creek. There, the ground was soft, much too soft to support the heavy vehicle. Both rear tires had sunk in, as if into quicksand.

"Look at what that old clunkhead did!" Tommy Lee laughed. "He must not have been watching what he was doing."

"It's not funny," Kip said.

The door swiveled open and Mr. Kimble stepped out. He walked with a slight limp thanks to an injury sustained when he fell down a flight of stairs several years ago. On seeing the rear wheels he drew up short and groaned.

Kip went over. "Is there anything we can do to help?" he offered.

Mr. Kimble did not seem to hear. Moving to the nearest wheel, he bent and ran a hand down the tire to where the earth encased it. He groaned again. "Oh, Lordy. Ike Taylor will be fit to spit nails when he finds out."

"Who?" Kip asked.

Kimble looked up. "My supervisor. He has the personality of a piranha. You'd think these buses were flesh and blood, the way he carries on when one of them is damaged."

"Maybe it's not damaged," Kip said. "Maybe you can rock it out of there. My dad did that once when we were stuck in the snow."

Tommy Lee had squatted to peer underneath the bus. "Never happen, dude. This puppy is buried clear up to the axle. It will take a humongous tow truck or a crane to get it out."

Mr. Kimble groaned a third time. "I have to try, boys," he said rather pitiably. "You step back now. I don't want either of you hit by flying dirt or stones."

Kip did as he was told. Tommy Lee walked down the bank to the creek and commenced chucking stones in the water.

The bus lurched forward when Mr. Kimble pressed on the gas, the tires spinning round and round. Clods of earth flew out from under the wheels, peppering the grass like buckshot. For a while Mr. Kimble floored the pedal. Then, shifting, he threw the bus into reverse. The bus lunged rearward and the tires started to come up out of the ground.

"You're doing it!" Kip shouted.

But he was premature. Dirt flew every which way. The bus tilted. Both rear wheels slowly sank until they could sink no further. Mr. Kimble shifted several more times, always with the same result. Presently he emerged.

"Well, that's that. I might as well call it in and wait for help to arrive."

"You're welcome to use our phone," Kip said, indicating the farmhouse at the top of the hill.

"Thanks, son," Mr. Kimble smiled, "but I think I'll walk back to Jake's and call from there."

Jake's Country Market was half a mile or better down the road. Kip couldn't understand why the man would want to walk so far, and said as much.

Mr. Kimble gave him a sly wink. "I might as well make the best of the situation. You see, I get overtime for something like this. The longer it takes them to pull me out, the more I'll make. It's not much, mind you, but when you're on a fixed budget like I am, every penny counts." He chuckled and gave the bus an affectionate smack. "Why, I might even make enough this week to treat myself to a movie. They say the new thriller by that Carpenter fellow is a real humdinger. And I've been partial to monster movies ever since I was a kid and first saw *The Creature from the Black Lagoon*."

Kip would never have guessed. "I can go along

with you if you want," he said. It was a long hike, and kindly Mr. Kimble wasn't in the best of health.

"That won't be necessary," the man said. "You run along with your goofy friend. I'll be all right." Turning, he hiked off down Blackgap Road, moving briskly despite his limp.

It was no secret that a lot of kids at school looked down their noses at old people. Gimps, they were called. Or cobs or geeks or granola gumbies. Kip had lost track of the number of lame jokes he'd heard about the librarian and the science teacher, both of whom were over 60. He never laughed at any of them because he didn't see how having wrinkles and gray hair automatically made a person worthless. Quite the contrary.

Kip's great-grandmother had had gray hair and wrinkles, and she'd been one of the kindest, most caring people he'd ever known. Whenever they'd visited her, she'd always had fresh cookies or cake on hand. And she'd never missed his birthday or neglected to send him money for Christmas. Her death, when he was ten, had been one of the most profoundly disturbing events of his childhood. In memory of her, he would never poke fun at the elderly. They were people too.

"Hey, bud!" Tommy Lee hollered. "Get your butt down here and tell me what you make of these."

Kip took one last look at the retreating figure

of Mr. Kimble, then stepped to the rim of the bank. His friend was on one knee at the water's edge. "What did you find?"

"See for yourself, doofus."

Kip had no real desire to go down there. The bank was steep and slick. If he fell, he'd make a mess of his clothes and his mother would be royally upset. But at that very moment the metallic growl of an approaching car alerted him that someone was coming down the driveway. He went over the side so he wouldn't be spotted.

Raising his head high enough to peer over the top, Kip saw his mom turn her car onto Blackgap Road and roar toward town without so much as giving the stuck bus a sideways glance. Her features were pinched in anger. He felt an urge to wave to get her attention, but felt a stronger impulse not give in to it. When she was in one of her moods, it was best to keep his distance.

"Are you going to look at these, or what?" Tommy Lee impatiently wanted to know.

Kip lingered long enough to see his mom flash past Mr. Kimble, who was almost out of sight. Stepping carefully to the bottom, he set eyes on a long row of large oval tracks. Hoofprints, by the look of them. "So a horse was here? So what?"

"Look again, genius."

Surveying the bank, Kip discovered the tracks were everywhere, running in erratic lines which frequently crossed one another. Several led into

116

Monongahela Creek. On the far bank were scores more, zigzagging back and forth, up and down, from side to side. There were so many that he asked, "Do you think they were all made by the same animal?"

"No doubt about it. Tracks are like fingerprints. No two are ever the same." Poking a thumb at those near his leg, Tommy Lee said, "These were made by a stallion, a huge sucker too. See these marks here? It's been shod, but the shoes are old and worn." He studied the maze of prints. "Unless I miss my guess, the rider was hunting for something."

"How do you know the horse wasn't just wandering around by itself?" Kip inquired.

"Because horses don't wear boots," Tommy Lee said, extending his arm.

Clearly imbedded in mud within inches of the flowing water were a pair of footprints. Evidently the rider had dismounted and stood there a while as if peering under the bridge. Kip placed his right foot down next to the corresponding boot print, and was astounded at the difference in size. The man's track dwarfed his.

"Big son of a gun, ain't he?" Tommy Lee said. "I wonder what the dickens he was searching for?"

"Who knows?" Kip said. He didn't see where it was any big deal. Riders were a common sight in the country around Spook Hollow.

Tommy Lee was studying the tracks again, moving closer to the bridge. He crouched at the

117

bottom of the bank, did a double take, and whistled. "This can't be. Take a gander for yourself."

"What now?" Kip griped, no longer really interested. The tracks were nothing special; he had no intention of staying there any longer. But Tommy Lee was his best friend, so he walked over to see what had him so excited.

They were almost in the shadow of the covered bridge. At that point the bank rose sharply to a height of nine or ten feet. Tommy Lee pointed at a set of hoofprints at the bottom of the bank, then at another set nine feet up, just under the crest.

"And?" Kip prompted.

"Don't you see?" Tommy Lee asked breathlessly. "The horse *jumped* to the top from this very spot where we're standing."

Kip studied the two sets of tracks again. "You're crazy," he said. "No horse alive can leap almost ten feet straight up into the air. It's physically impossible."

Tommy Lee was offended. "Tracks don't lie. My pa taught me how to read sign when I was knee-high to a grasshopper, and while I'm not in his league, I'm not bad, if I do say so myself." He tapped a print with his sneaker, then nodded at those above. "I'm telling you, good buddy, that the damn horse jumped up onto that bank just as neat as you please. With that huge rider on his back, no less."

"Supersteed," Kip joked. "I suppose next you'll

be claiming that it wore blue tights and a red cape."

"Poke fun all you want," Tommy Lee said, retracing his steps to the incline they had descended, "but I know what I know. And I know I sure as hell don't want to run into that horse or that man, if I can help it."

"Why? Afraid they'll eat you?"

Tommy Lee paused. "Do you see me flashing teeth? This is serious, friend. Spook business always is."

"Spook business?" Kip blurted, and burst out laughing. He chopped his mirth off when Tommy Lee scowled and stomped to the top of the bank. "Hold on! I didn't mean to hurt your feelings." Kip scaled the slope in long strides, but Tommy Lee was already on the bridge, crossing rapidly. "Wait up, darn it!"

The boy from Virginia had no intention of complying. Kip had to jog to overtake him, and even then Tommy Lee kept on walking, treating him as if he weren't there.

"You're being silly," Kip protested. "And you're too old to go around believing in spooks and goblins or whatever."

Tommy Lee stopped so abruptly that it caught Kip off guard. "What are you saying?" Tommy Lee challenged. "That I don't know what I'm talking about because I'm from back in the hills? That us country boys are dumber than bricks? That we're all a bunch of superstitious hayseeds who don't know any better?"

"I'd never insult you like that."

Tommy Lee brushed by Kip with a curt wave of his hand and resumed walking, his spine as stiff as a broom handle. "I've got news for you. You just did. And here I thought you were different from most city boys!" He encompassed the woodland on both sides of the creek with another gesture. "There are things out there in the wild that ain't fit for a body to talk about, let alone see. Just ask my ma and pa. You've never lived in the sticks or you wouldn't be such a smart-ass about it. Truth is, you don't know diddly."

"Maybe so," Kip conceded, grabbing his friend's arm and bringing him to a stop, "but I'm willing to learn. So chill out. I meant what I said about not meaning to upset you."

Tommy Lee was still not mollified. "Listen to me, Yank. Country folks have been seeing things that city people never see for more years than either of us can count. And there's a reason for that. The things that live in the deep woods, the things that like to come out after dark, are just like the wild animals they live among. They don't care for people much, and they sure as hell don't care for crowds."

Kip did not for a minute take Tommy Lee seriously. But he let his friend have his say without interrupting for the sake of their friendship.

"When was the last time you heard of a bear waltzing around the middle of a town or city?" Tommy Lee had gone on. "Or of a cougar living in an alley somewhere? You never have and you never will because bears and cougars like to hide out in the wilderness. It's the same with the creature of the night, as my pa calls 'em. They avoid us when they can and kill us when they can't."

"Were there many spooks back in the hills where you were born and raised?" Kip had to ask.

"A few. There was the ghost of Granger's Mill which came out to scare neckers every now and then. And over on Possum Ridge there was a cave which the old-timers said was home to a werebeast, as they called it. No one would go near that place after dark for love or money. Then there was the bogeyman I told you about, but it was a whole different critter."

Kip gazed past the rail at the hoofprints on the north bank. Why did people believe in such nonsense? he mused. Science had proven that so-called demons and sundry monsters were no more than figments of overworked imaginations. Yet science was largely ignored by the very ones it sought to enlighten. Which made no sense to him.

"Yes, sir," Tommy Lee concluded. "Us country folk know what we know, and no amount of fancy words will make us think that we don't."

Much to Kip's relief, they dropped the subject and went on to the pool where they had caught frogs with Amy. For two hours they tried to catch bullfrogs and crayfish, but failed to get their hands on one.

Kip's problem was that he couldn't keep his mind on the task at hand. Repeatedly he rose on tiptoe and scanned Blackgap Road in the hope of spotting the brown car owned by Amy's mom, who was picking her up after band practice. But the car never appeared.

"What a waste," Tommy Lee said about the time the lower half of the sun had sunk below the mountains. "I reckon we'd better call it a day. My ma will be awful disappointed, though. She was looking forward to frying up another mess of frog legs tonight."

They parted company. Kip took his sweet time, stalling in case Amy should yet appear. Darkness reigned when at last he came within sight of the Monongahela Bridge. Lights were on up at the farmhouse, but none were evident near the bus stop, so he assumed that a tow truck had long since freed the vehicle.

As Kip drew abreast of his driveway, he gazed across the creek, and was surprised to note the dull glint of yellow metal. The bus was still there. He figured that for some reason or another the tow truck operator had been unable to haul it out and they would try again in the morning. Mr. Kimble, he reasoned, had long since left.

Then, as clear as could be, Kip heard the sound of the folding door being opened. He thought he saw someone climb on. Puzzled, he moved closer to the covered bridge, hugging the shadows so whoever it was wouldn't spot him.

No cars were parked on the shoulder of the

road or near the bridge. None were in sight for as far as Kip could see. So the person on the bus had to have come on foot. Kip halted behind one of the wide upright timbers at the corner of the bridge to listen.

Suddenly a side window opened, sliding down with an audible snap. A few seconds later the vehicle squeaked, as it might if someone were moving down the aisle toward the rear.

Kip wondered if it might not be Mr. Kimble. Maybe, he reasoned, Kimble had been unable to catch a ride back into Spook Hollow and was stranded there for the night. He was tempted to go see, but he couldn't bring himself to do it.

Up the creek, there was a loud splash. Then a second. And a third. Kip pivoted, his heart hammering wildly. It sounded as if something were wading downstream toward him. The splashes grew louder. At the limits of his vision a vague form took shape, an enormous form which in his rising terror he deduced must be a roving black bear. A low nicker proved him wrong.

It was a horse.

Kip thought of the hoofprints and the huge tracks of the rider. The man had come back. Why, he had no idea. But he did know he didn't want to be there when the giant reached the covered bridge. Call it silly. Call it a hunch. Blame it on Tommy Lee's talk about spooks and were-beasts. But he felt that if he stayed, he was in grave danger.

He had two choices. Either he ran to the

David Robbins

gravel drive and tried to reach the farmhouse before the rider overtook him, or he dashed to the bus. It wasn't a difficult decision to make. Outrunning a horse on a hill was impossible, and the bus was so much closer than the farmhouse.

Another wavering whinny wafted on the wind. Kip could see the pale spray of water displaced by the animal's heavy hooves. In another few moments the rider would spot him.

Taking a breath, Kip darted across the Monongahela Bridge. Under the bridge's roof it was pitch black. He experienced the illusion of running in a vacuum, of his legs pumping empty air. Only the hard smack of his feet on the boards told him otherwise. Bursting into the open, he angled across the grass toward the bus. To his rear hooves pounded. He glanced back, but didn't see the horse.

Kip reached the bus. Leaping onto the second step, he drew up short at the sight of someone slumped over the steering wheel, as if resting. He recognized the cream-colored sweater Mr. Kimble had been wearing. "Mr. Kimble, wake up," he said, grabbing the driver's arm. "I think there's someone out there."

The man made no answer. Kip tugged to awaken him, and suddenly Mr. Kimble slid off the steering wheel and started to pitch forward. "Mr. Kimble!" Kip cried, dropping his schoolbooks to catch hold of the driver before Kimble's head could hit the floor.

Spook Night

"Wake up!" Kip repeated, giving the man a shake. He shifted so he could see Kimble's face, and as he did he could feel all the blood drain from his own. His stomach churned. His senses swam.

The bus driver no longer had a head.

All that remained atop Kimble's shoulders was the severed stump of his neck, still spurting his life's blood.

Chapter Eight

There was a gremlin in the computer.

Or so John Grant thought testily as he leaned back in his chair and angrily regarded the monitor. All day the computer had been giving him problems, problems it had never given him before, unusual quirks and glitches that in and of themselves were annoying enough, but that taken as a whole constituted an extremely frustrating series of delays that had put him at least six hours behind in his work. For two cents, he told himself, he'd take a sledgehammer to the damn thing and go out and buy a new one.

Only they couldn't afford a newer model. Money had been tight since the move, and would continue to be so until they paid off a few credit cards and socked away a little in the bank.

John had a habit of talking to himself while

he worked, and he did so now while tapping his fingers in irritation. "Bad command or file name! How the hell can that be when I've used it a zillion times without a hitch?" He speared the proper key to retry the command, but again the computer refused to cooperate.

"What the hell is going on?" John addressed the screen. "Is your hard drive going out? Is that what this is all about? You're about to crash on me, aren't you. Hit me with another big bill I can barely afford. I'll bet that's it." He pushed the chair back and stood. "Murphy's Law strikes again."

Picking up his coffee cup, John walked to the kitchen. The house was quiet. His wife had gone shopping after another tiff over the mess made in Shery's room. Laurie wanted to ground Kip for a month. John would rather question the boy before they handed out any punishment. He still felt the time frame was all wrong. Kip couldn't have done it.

Neither of the children were home at the moment. John figured that Kip was either over at the Harpers or maybe visiting Amy Westbrook. As for Shery, there was no telling who she was with or where she might be. The girl did as she pleased when she pleased, and she had made no secret of the fact that she didn't care one iota whether her parents liked it or not.

She was more frustrating than the computer could ever be.

John sighed as he stepped up to the counter.

He had tried his best over the years, but every time he had made a serious effort to impose any discipline on Shery, Laurie had intervened in her behalf.

He would ground Shery for a week, and Laurie would reduce it to two days. He would refuse to spend money for designer jeans and other outrageous clothes, and Laurie would go out and get them behind his back. When he refused to let Shery date certain boys who might as well have had "Sex-Crazed Morons" tattooed on their foreheads, Laurie had let Shery go provided she was home by a "decent hour," which in Shery's book invariably turned out to be midnight or later.

"Why do I bother sometimes?" John asked the walls as he raised the pot to pour. A whine at the back door gave him pause. He set both the cup and the pot down and went over.

Buck sat outside, wagging his tail and grinning like the adorable bundle of affection he was. John laughed. "There you are, you big coward. Where have you been keeping yourself all day?" He opened the screen door. "Come on in and I'll feed you. You must be starved."

The mongrel rose. He sniffed the air, then whimpered and pawed at the ground.

"What's the matter?" John said. Ordinarily the dog would rush right in. Mealtimes were his favorite times of day. "Now don't you start acting up on me too. It's bad enough the stupid computer has been giving me headaches."

Buck started to enter, but promptly backed out again, tossing his head and sniffing.

"Look, birdbrain," John grumbled. "I'm not putting up with this nonsense. Either get your hairy butt in here or you can go hungry tonight."

As if the mongrel understood, he took a step over the threshold. Suddenly he bristled and went rigid, his lips curling up over his teeth. Staring balefully toward the far side of the kitchen, he let out with a ferocious snarl.

John had never seen the dog behave that way. Startled, he spun, and out of the corner of his eye he glimpsed something flash into the hallway. He couldn't tell what it was, but he did hear a scraping sound as the thing sped off.

"What the—?" John blurted out, and ran to the hall. The thing was nowhere to be seen. Judging by its size and speed, it had to be a small animal of some kind. He hurried toward the living room, peering into rooms he passed along the way, flickering on all the lights as he went.

The front room, as was customary in old farmhouses, was the largest. It contained a sofa, chairs, a coffee table, and an entertainment center, as well as several planters. There were plenty of places where a small creature could hide.

John moved toward the heavy drapes that flanked the picture window, but stopped when the raucous blaring of a car horn rent the night. It came from the bottom of the hill and was becoming louder by the second. As he opened the front door to investigate, a car roared up the driveway. His wife's car. She was pounding the horn like a madwoman and going at least 60. When she braked, the car sloughed sideways. Gravel pelted John's legs as he dashed down the steps.

Someone else was in the car with her.

John bent to see who. His wife threw her door open and the overhead light came on, revealing their son. Shock riveted John Grant in place. His legs went weak. He reached out and gripped the car for support. "It can't be!" he exclaimed.

Yes it was. Kip was covered with blood from his shoulders to his toes. He sat as one dead to the world, his face as blank as an empty slate, his skin like a sheet, his eyes the size of half-dollars.

Laurie Grant slid out and dashed around the front of the sedan. She was practically beside herself, on the verge of hysterics.

Not five minutes ago she had been on her way home after grocery shopping in Spook Hollow. She had still been simmering over her last spat with John, and thinking that she couldn't wait to quiz Kip about the dirty trick she just knew he had played on his sister.

Then, when she approached within a few hundred feet of Monongahela Creek and the covered bridge, a walking figure had been caught in the glare of her headlights. Someone had been shuffling down the middle of the road toward her. Automatically, she had slowed and veered to one side to go around.

As Laurie drove closer, she recognized her son. Slamming on the brakes, she rolled down her window and called out, "Kip? What in the world do you think you're doing? Get in the car this instant, young man. We have something to discuss."

He didn't answer. Arms limps, eyes unblinking, he shuffled on to the south as if he had no idea she was there.

"Kip?" Laurie said, getting out. Mushrooming anxiety replaced her anger. Only then did she note the dark stains on his clothes and realize that something was terribly, dreadfully wrong.

Laurie darted over and stood in front of him to block his path. He halted, but there were no recognition in his eyes, just that awful blank stare. "What's the matter?" she asked, gripping his arms. "What's wrong with you?"

Kip didn't respond. When Laurie lowered her hands, her palms were sticky with whatever drenched his clothes. She held her hands out so she could see them in the glow of her car's taillights, and a thunderbolt of sheer horror jolted her entire body. Her palms were covered with blood.

It took less than a minute for Laurie to guide Kip into the front seat. He didn't appear to be hurt, but all that blood meant that someone somewhere had to be. She leaped to the conclusion that something must have happened at the house. Flooring the accelerator, she raced up the hill, leaning on the horn without really knowing why she did.

Now, grabbing John by the shoulders, Laurie nearly screamed, "What's going on? What happened here? Why is he like that?"

The sudden contact galvanized John Grant. Shrugging loose, he replied, "I have no idea. He never came home after school." The panic and fear her features betrayed aroused feelings long dormant. He impulsively clasped her to him and said softly in her ear, "We have to stay calm, honey. We have to get to the bottom of this."

Laurie nodded, her mind in a whirl. She looked at the house. All appeared normal. "I don't understand. Where did that blood come from?"

"I don't know." John opened the door and leaned in. "Kip? What happened to you?" His son made no effort to answer, and when he touched Kip's cheek it was like touching a block of ice. "We have to get him into town so the doctor can look him over. And the police will have to be notified."

"The police?" Laurie said, struggling to dispel her confusion.

"Something terrible has happened," John said. "They'll need to know." He moved aside. "You sit next to Kip and I'll drive."

Buck came around the corner of the house as the two of them piled in. He sat at the edge of the porch, watching as the car wheeled onto the lawn, backed up with its tires gouging furrows in the grass, and sped down the hill.

The mongrel whined, then reclined on his belly, his head erect. His sensitive ears told him that the four people he cared for were gone. He settled down to wait for them, knowing they would return sooner or later, as they always did.

Time went by. Buck let his head droop onto his paws. His eyes started to close, and he was about to doze off when there was a faint grating to his right. Instantly alert, Buck leaped erect.

The inner door hung open, but the outer door was closed—and something was pushing against it. The door moved outward a little. Both hinges squeaked, as they had since the day the family moved in.

Growling, Buck circled to the left. On the other side of the screen door something clawed or gnawed the wooden frame. Buck crouched, prepared to bolt if the door opened any farther. It suddenly shook violently.

The dog sprang off the porch. He would have fled had a car not appeared below, winding slowly up the hill. Loud music blared, mixed with feminine laughter.

As if by coincidence, the door stopped shaking.

Buck moved closer to the driveway and stood wagging his tail. A wreathe of blond hair framed the face of the passenger. He wagged harder, trying to please her by showing his devotion.

Once, when she had been much smaller, they had been the best of friends. She had taken him into her room every night and helped him up onto her bed so he could sleep cuddled at her side all night long. Their days had been spent playing together. At meals she had slipped him tasty scraps. Life had been grand.

And then the change had taken place. Buck had not known why, but she no longer wanted him in her room. She no longer took him for long walks or wrestled with him. She'd shut him from her life, and it had hurt.

About that time the boy had taken an interest in him, and the two of them had become inseparable. Buck had looked after the boy as he had the girl. Once, in a trash-littered alley, he had held another dog at bay so the boy could escape without being bitten.

But now the boy had grown. Like the girl, the boy no longer was very interested in him. Now and then they would go for walks, but it wasn't the same as the old days. The boy left him pretty much on his own.

Buck straightened. The car was long and sleek. It ground to a halt and the girl got out. Buck greeted her by pressing his nose against her leg, as he had done in the old days. Instead of a pat, he received a slap on the head and a stern rebuke.

"Quit slobbering on me, mutt," Shery Grant said. She bestowed her sexiest smile on Bryce Harcourt, and leaned over to trace the outline of his square jaw with a polished fingernail. "Sorry about this, lover. But my dad laid an egg last night when I got in so late. So tonight I'll be the dutiful daughter and shock his tootsies by showing up before ten."

"No problem, babe," Bryce said. "I need to brush up on my playbook anyway. The coach about had a coronary when I blew a few drills at practice today."

"Adults!" Shery declared. "They're a pain in the butt, but what's a person to do? We can't live with 'em, and we can't live without 'em." She had to stretch in order to lightly brush her lips against his. "As for that brushing up you're going to do, just make damn sure it's not up against Deb Coker."

"Deb who?" Bryce said impishly. He winked as she stepped back, then shifted and peeled out, following the drive as it looped around past the ancient barn and the chicken coop. The horn beeped twice; then he was off like a bat out of hell, wheeling the Corvette around the turns below with smooth precision. Once he hit the straightaway beyond the covered bridge, his car was a blur.

Shery watched until he was out of sight. "That's my guy," she said proudly, the throb of the Corvette's powerful engine still drumming in her ears. "Coker, eat your heart out, you bimbo."

Stepping onto the porch, Shery noticed that her mother's car was gone. It made her hesitate. She counted on her mom to back her up if her father got out of hand. Squaring her shoulders, she grasped the door handle and began to pull it open. Without warning Buck was there, sliding between her and the door, preventing her from going in.

"What do you think you're doing, you dumb dog?" Shery scolded. "Get out of my way."

The mongrel didn't budge. He pushed against her, forcing her back a step.

"Didn't you hear me?" Shery said, attempting to push him out of the way. "I don't have time to play." She shoved, but Buck sidestepped, causing her to nearly lose her balance. Her temper heating up, she drew back a foot and kicked him in the ribs. Buck yelped while retreating to the grass. He bowed his head as if in shame.

"You should feel guilty," Shery said. "I don't know what's gotten into you lately, but you've been acting really weird." She giggled at an idea. "Go out and find a lady dog to bang and you'll feel more like your old self in no time."

Flinging the door wide, Shery walked into the living room. "Dad! I'm home!" she announced to insure her father was aware of the fact. She didn't want her noble sacrifice to be in vain.

When there was no reply, Shery ambled to the kitchen, passing her father's office along the way. He was nowhere to be found. The coffee maker was on, so she helped herself to a cup, then closed the back door and carried the cup to the foot of the stairs.

"Dad? Kip? Are you two up there?"

Other than the tick-tock of the grandfather clock in the living room, the house was as silent as her shadow. Shery remembered to shut the front door before climbing slowly to her bedroom, sipping as she went.

Of all the dumb luck! She'd gone to all the trouble to make a good impression and no one was there to see it. Her parents must have gone off together, and her brat of a brother was probably off with one of his equally bratty friends.

The only consolation was that now Shery had the place to herself. It meant she could treat herself to a rare luxury, a nice, long bath, without having to worry about anyone barging in on her.

In the bathroom Shery started the water running full blast. After placing the cup on top of the toilet tank, she stepped to her bedroom. Switching on the light, she stood in front of the full-length mirror to undress. Her blouse went over the back of a chair. Her short skirt wound up lying on the floor next to her bed. She primped her hair, then sat at her vanity to file a nail down.

Almost too late, Shery remembered her bath. Clad in her bra and panties, she threw the robe over her shoulders, selected a magazine, and hastened back to turn off the water before the tub overflowed. She had taken no more than a few steps when she saw the bathroom door was closed. Yet she distinctly recalled leaving it open.

The knob turned easily enough, but when Shery pushed, the door wouldn't open. She tried again with the same result. Puzzled, she twisted the knob to the right and the left. There was no telltale click. "Oh, great," she muttered. "Just what I need. The damn latch is broken."

All the while the water continued to run. Shery could tell by the sound that it was close to the top. Jerking on the knob with all her strength, she threw her shoulder against the panel. She might as well be trying to move a concrete slab.

"Why is it always me?" Shery addressed the thin air. If the tub spilled over she would be in big trouble. Her parents had warned her a dozen times about going off and leaving it unattended when water was running. She would have to put up with them saying, "I told you so!" for next to forever.

Growing desperate, Shery slammed into the door again and again. Convinced it would take dynamite, she stepped back to ponder. Think, girl! she scolded herself.

There was only one other way into the room, through the window. Since it was two stories up, Shery had no means of reaching it. Or did she?

Swiftly donning the robe, Shery looped the belt around her slim waist and hurried downstairs. Buck was gone when she stepped outside and hastened to the east side of the house. A grin of triumph lit her face. Lying where her father had left it when he cleaned the gutters was a long aluminum ladder. She hefted it to test the weight, which was negligible, then carried it around to the west side and propped it against the wall. The top rung wound up well short of the windowsill. She would never reach it unless she sprouted wings and flew.

Shery remembered being outside when her father adjusted the ladder's height so he could reach the highest gutters. But she hadn't been paying much attention and had no inkling of how he had done it.

The ladder was in two sections. Logic dictated that one or both sections must slide upward. Shery attempted to lift each in turn, and learned they were locked in place. "There must be a release button or something," she speculated, running her hands up the side rails.

It was then Shery noticed a pair of braces or prongs which were attached to one section and clamped against the rungs of the other section. It took some fiddling, but she managed to figure out that by hiking the braces she could free half of the ladder and hike it high enough to reach the window. Realigning the braces so the ladder wouldn't collapse on her, she jammed the red plastic shoes into the ground, tested the bottom rung with a foot, then quickly climbed.

Shery imagined water gushing over the rim of the tub. To her vast relief, she gained the top and saw that the water was nipping at the edge but had not yet overflowed. Wedging her palms under the middle sash, she heaved.

Nothing happened. The window wouldn't

move. Shery checked the frame, seeking a lock. So far as she knew, there was none. A second attempt to raise the window proved more rewarding. It screaked upward, but less than an inch before grinding to a stop. She couldn't understand why at first. As she jiggled and pushed, the reason became apparent. The frame was warped.

"Just frigging great," Shery groused. Drops began spattering onto the polished wood floor inside. Soon there would be a torrent. "I don't need this damn aggravation!"

She gave the sash a halfhearted push. To her utter astonishment, the window flashed upward as if fired from a catapult. For a few moments she gaped in disbelief. Then, thinking that Lady Luck was finally smiling on her, she climbed one rung higher on the ladder so she could hook a leg over the sill.

At the base of the ladder something growled.

Shery jumped, and nearly lost her grip. Buck was staring up at her, the hair at the nape of his neck forming a stiff ridge. "What the hell are you up to now?" she demanded. "Go chase a rabbit or something." Easing her left leg inside, she shifted to duck under the upper part of the window, but to her dismay the ladder shook violently. In reflex she caught hold of the sill with both hands and sought the cause.

Buck had clamped his jaw on the left side of the ladder, and was shaking it as he might the neck of a feral rival. Exhibiting unsuspected strength, he actually lifted the bottom off the ground.

"Stop that!" Shery shrilled. "Do you want me to fall and break my neck?" She gestured, but the mongrel paid her no heed. Afraid that in another instant he might upend her perch, she bent at the waist, pushed off from the rung, and dived into the bathroom.

Shery landed on her shoulder, jarring the bone. Shaken but safe, she rose and poked her head out. Buck had backed up and was gazing intently at the window. "I'll shoot you tomorrow!" she railed, then slammed it shut.

The splatter of water reminded Shery of her first priority. Lunging, she spun both taps. Other than a few puddles, no harm had been done. She leaned on the tub and exhaled loudly. Thank God! she reflected. That had been much too close for comfort.

Straightening to undo her robe, Shery was scared out of her wits when the bathroom door unexpectedly crashed inward behind her. Before she could whirl, something slammed into the small of her back, ramming her into the tub. Her knees smashed against the rim. She flapped her arms to retain her balance, but she slipped on a slick puddle and the next thing she knew, she was sunk to her waist in the water with heavy pressure on her shoulders.

Someone was trying to drown her!

Chapter Nine

Doctor Horace Syms gently pushed Kip Grant's right eyelid up with his thumb. Flicking on a pencil flashlight that he had removed from a drawer, he examined the pupil, noting its reaction. As he had done over a dozen times since the examination began, he said softly, "Hmmmmmm."

John Grant could not take any more. He had stayed calm on the mad race to town because he knew that if he didn't, he might run the car off the road. He had contained his escalating fear while pounding on the physician's door and waiting for ages for Syms to answer. And he had stood silently to one side while the doctor poked and prodded his son. But now his nerves snapped and he stepped forward to demand, "Well? What's the matter with him?"

Horace Syms was a portly man who liked to hide his balding pate with an old baseball cap he had picked up at a flea market. That cap spoke eloquently of the man's character. Where younger physicians went in for fancy suits, he always wore casual clothes that could only be described as frumpy. And instead of polished oxfords, he went around in a pair of beat-up tennis shoes.

It was said that nothing ever rattled him, that he had delivered breach babies and amputated limbs with the same unflappable poise he now displayed as he turned to thoughtfully regard John, Laurie, and Chief Bogartus. "I would say the boy is in shock, Mr. Grant."

Laurie sat perched on the edge of a chair with both arms clutching her chest. For many minutes she had been rocking back and forth while waging an intense inner struggle to control a rising wave of panic.

She was a nurse, Laurie had reminded herself over and over. She had handled plenty of emergencies before, so she should be able to take the crisis in stride. But it was one thing to minister to perfect strangers without being personally affected, quite another when the victim was her own flesh and blood.

Now, on hearing the doctor's comment, Laurie snapped erect. "We already know that! Give him something to bring him around so we can find out what caused this!"

Old Doc Syms came over to rest a hand on her shoulder. "Everything will be all right, Mrs.

Grant," he said softly. "In cases likes this, you know as well as I do that it's best if the patient comes out of it on his own." He pointed at a cot against the far wall. "Why don't you guide him over there while I fetch some blankets and a cup of tea?"

"Sure," Laurie said. It got to her, the way he was using the same soothing beside manner she ordinarily used when dealing with distraught patients or their families. It made her realize that she had to get a grip on herself. "But I doubt he'll drink anything."

Doc Syms grinned. "The tea is for you." Motioning at the chief, who in turn beckoned John, he left the examination room, in reality one of several on the bottom floor of his house, which was also his office. He quietly closed the door.

A patrolman by the name of Simmons was reading a magazine in the waiting room. As Grant, Bogartus, and the doctor appeared, he tossed it down and stood. "What's the verdict, Chief?"

Bogartus was staring at the physician. "That's what I'd like to know."

John Grant didn't see why the chief wanted him out there. He'd rather be with his wife and son, and he was going to go back in when the doctor's next words gave him pause.

"No one can lose as much blood as was on that boy, Chief, and still live. There's at least one body out there somewhere, maybe more. My guess is that the youngster saw what happened and it traumatized him so severely, he went into shock."

"So much for my night off." Bogartus sighed, then jammed his hat onto his head. "We'll be back, but I can't say how soon." Curling a finger at John, he said, "All right, mister. Let's go. You're coming with us while we conduct our investigation."

"What?" John responded in surprise. "Why?"

"Because your son is involved somehow. Because whatever happened, happened out near your place. Because if the doc is right, two people have died out there in as many days." Bogartus grinned, but there was no warmth to it. "And because I said so."

"But George Eldridge's death was an accident," John protested. "Right now my family needs me."

"The doc will take real good care of them," Bogartus said. "I really must insist."

John resented the chief's attitude. He doubted the man had the legal right to force him to go along against his will, and he was half tempted to call a lawyer. Doing so, though, would only anger Bogartus, and if he intended to live in Spook Hollow the rest of his life, it wouldn't be very smart to antagonize the local representatives of law and order. "Lead the way," he said.

"After you."

A patrol car and Bogartus's converted four-wheel-drive truck were parked out front. They piled into the latter, with John in the back. No one spoke until they had traveled several blocks.

"Listen, Grant," the chief said. "I know how hard this must be on you, but you'll have to bear with me. One possible homicide on my hands is bad enough. I sure as hell don't need another."

"There's been a murder? Why wasn't it in the paper or on the radio?"

"I'm referring to Eldridge."

John was dumbstruck.

"I heard from the county coroner late this afternoon," the chief disclosed. "The official word is that George drowned. But there were no bumps or bruises on his head, as there should have been if he slipped and fell. The only marks on his whole body were down around his ankle, of all places. The coroner can't explain them, and frankly, neither can I."

"What kind of marks?" John asked, uncertain the chief would tell him and not really sure he wanted to know.

Chief Bogartus glanced back at him. "They were teeth marks, Mr. Grant. *Human* teeth marks."

Shery Grant was so stunned by the savage on-slaught that for all of five seconds she was par-alyzed with fright. Whoever was pressing against her pressed harder. Her stomach gouged into the top of the tub. Her feet swept up off the floor.

Hot water rushing up into her nose and down into her ears electrified Shery into acting. Wildly

147

flailing her arms, she caught hold of the faucet with her left hand and the back of the tub with her right. She pushed against them, using them for leverage, but whoever held her would not let her rise.

Shery had managed to suck in a little air before she went under. Enough to last a minute, maybe more. She battled fiercely, fighting for footing, which the slippery floor denied her. The waterlogged robe impeded her movements, hampering her. In desperation she kicked out, trying to connect with her assailant's legs, but she missed each time.

Her lungs began to ache terribly. Shery resisted an urge to open her mouth and gulp for air that wasn't there. She started to feel light-headed. Instead of giving up, though, instead of submitting to the weakness that was spreading through her, Shery did as she always did when things didn't go the way she wanted; she got mad. A sudden surge of newfound strength enabled her to raise her head high enough to take a single breath before she was pushed under again.

She had bought herself some time, but not much.

Think, girl! Shery's mind shouted. If she didn't use her wits, she was dead meat! Somehow, she had to break loose. The only problem was that she couldn't turn to grapple with whoever had jumped her. Or could she?

Inspiration sparked Shery into suddenly tugging at the belt to her robe. Since it wasn't knotted, she unfastened it in a twinkling. Then, twisting, she pulled at the left sleeve and slid her arm free. The water churned, spilling over the brim, but a soaked floor was the least of her worries. She pushed at the loose portion of the garment, keeping it between her and her assailant. It billowed inward, as if the person were trying to seize her, but she jerked aside. With a sharp yank, she freed her right arm, as well. Spinning, her back to the wall, she tucked her legs up under her and surged out of the water, ready to rip into her attacker.

Only no one was there.

Shery blinked in amazement. Gulping in air, she peered over the outer edge of the tub in the belief that her assailant had crouched beside it. All she saw was the drenched wood. She glanced behind the door, then flung the bunched shower curtain aside. Apparently, the person had fled.

Gripping the rim, Shery swung her legs out of the tub. More water went every which way. She slipped as she landed, and would have fallen had she not held on. The floor was so slick that she had to use the wall for support as she dashed to the doorway.

Shery thought that she could catch a glimpse of her attacker before he reached the stairs. The hall, however, was empty. She started to give chase, stopping when she realized that whoever it was might see fit to finish the job. Backing into the bathroom, she noticed that her wet footprints were clearly defined on the otherwise dry hall floor. No others were evident.

That couldn't be, Shery told herself. Whoever had jumped her had been standing in the water which spilled. There should be other prints.

Time enough to solve the mystery later. Shery ran to the cabinet above the sink. On the top shelf, in a slender box with a painted peacock on the lid, was a straight razor which had belonged to her grandfather. Her dad never used the thing, but kept it there as a keepsake with strict orders that no one else was to touch it.

Shery snatched hold of the box. Her hands were shaking so badly that she lost her grip and it toppled into the sink, cracking the lid. The razor popped out. She pried the blade from the recessed groove in the ivory handle. The edge was sharp enough to split a hair, and she could well imagine what it would do to a human being.

There was still no sign of her attacker, but Shery wasn't fooled. No doors had slammed and there had not been any sound of a car driving off, so the person might still be in the house.

Her best bet, Shery reasoned, was to stay put until her parents returned. The only flaw in that plan was the shotgun her father stored in the master bedroom. If her attacker found it, the razor wouldn't do her much good.

Shery decided to make a try for one of the phones downstairs. She took a step, and then it dawned on her that her assailant might be waiting for her to make just such a move. He could be in any one of the rooms along the hall, coiled to pounce when she came by.

Well, she'd outsmart the bastard! Shery grinned as she closed the door and crossed to the window. The ladder leaned at a dangerous angle, almost out of reach. Extending herself out over the sill as far as she dared, she snared the top rung with her fingernails and slowly pulled it close enough to grip.

Buck was gone.

The house was eerily silent.

Fearful of making any noise which would give her away, Shery carefully aligned the ladder. She winced when it rattled slightly. Necessity demanded that she back out of the window legs first, which she did as gingerly as if she were lowering herself onto broken glass. She applied her weight bit by bit rather than all at once. When both feet had solid purchase, she warily descended.

A cool breeze wafted from the northwest, raising goose bumps all over Shery's flesh. She shivered, then froze when the ladder rattled again, louder than the last time. Anxious not to be caught high up where she would be helpless, she lowered herself three more rungs, then pushed off and dropped.

In her haste Shery neglected to bend her knees as she hit. As a result she staggered backward, tripped, and sprawled onto her backside. She forgot about the razor and nicked her thigh, drawing blood.

About to push to her feet, Shery froze on seeing a shadow flit across the living room window. Her attacker was definitely in there. The curtains rustled, as if he were going to look out. She darted to the wall to keep from being seen, and huddled there as a pool of light washed over the lawn. It winked out moments later. Craning her neck, she verified the curtains were closed before she crept toward the front of the house.

Shery had changed her mind. Rather than risk running into the killer by venturing back indoors, she opted to make a break for Blackgap Road. There she would lay low, hiding in the trees until her parents showed up.

In a crouch, Shery reached the corner and paused. A sweep of the front porch revealed the coast to be clear. She listened but couldn't tell where her attacker was. Hoping the S.O.B. was at the back of the house or else upstairs, Shery bolted. Skirting the porch, she slanted across the yard toward the gravel driveway.

In her eagerness to get out of there, Shery forgot about her bare feet. The instant her soft soles crunched down on the hard stones, she inadvertently cried out. Not loudly, but loud enough for the person in the farmhouse to hear.

Wanting to kick herself for being so stupid, Shery moved to the edge of the drive where the soft grass permitted her to pour on the speed. She had covered perhaps 20 yards when the pad of rushing feet to her rear let her know that she was no longer alone.

Clutching the straight razor close to her side,

Shery flew around the first bend. It was a long way to the bottom of the hill, but she believed that she could make it if she didn't stumble over something in the dark. Or if her attacker didn't overtake her first.

Another bend loomed in the night. Shery was going to cut across it and enter the line of dense vegetation beyond, but as she abruptly changed direction a black mass materialized as if out of nowhere. With no time to stop, Shery was at the mercy of her own momentum. They collided, and in the blink of an eye she was flat on her back with her attacker on top.

"What the hell is that, Chief?" Officer Simmons exclaimed.

The question derailed John Grant's train of thought. He had been mulling over the chief's revelation about the teeth marks and wondering if maybe Bogartus suspected him of slaying George Eldridge. The very idea was ludicrous, until he put himself in the chief's shoes. He was, after all, new to the area, so Bogartus knew next to nothing about him. For all the man knew, he might have a criminal record as long as the chief's arm. Talk about an ideal suspect.

"It looks like a school bus," the chief was saying as he applied the brakes and veered the truck toward the right side of the road.

John was as mystified as they were to see the bus parked off on the shoulder. Their headlights, playing over the rear of the vehicle, revealed why. "That must be the one my son and daughter take every day," he commented. "It looks to be stuck."

"That it does," Bogartus concurred.

Simmons cranked down his window and leaned out for a better view. "School was over hours ago. You'd think someone would have pulled it out by now."

"Wouldn't you, though?" the chief said with an air of suspicion. Coasting to a stop, he shifted into park, but let the engine idle. From under his seat he produced a small spotlight designed to work off a vehicle battery. Popping out the cigarette lighter, he inserted the spotlight's adaptor, switched the light on, and climbed from the truck.

The beam was intensely bright. It lit up the front of the bus as if the sun were directly overhead. No one was inside, but the door hung partially open.

"Want me to go have a look-see, big guy?" Simmons asked.

Chief Bogartus glanced in at John, then at the darkness around them. "We all will," he said. Clipping the spotlight to a rack on the roof, he stepped around in front of the grill, drew his service revolver, and checked the cylinder.

"You act as if you're expecting trouble," Officer Simmons said, punctuating the statement with a nervous laugh.

"Didn't you see how much blood was on Grant's kid?" Bogartus responded.

154

Simmons pulled his own gun out.

John hadn't moved. In his estimation they were wasting their time. A stranded bus was hardly out of the ordinary. He'd much rather head on up to the house so he could check to see if Shery had made it home yet. Which he doubted. She seldom showed up before 11, even on school nights.

"Let's go, mister," Bogartus prompted, wagging the revolver. "I'm not letting you out of my sight."

"Because you think I'm a dangerous criminal?" John joked as he obeyed.

"No, because you're still alive."

John would have asked what the chief meant by that remark, but the two officers advanced on the bus with their weapons leveled. He trailed them, his attention fixed on top of the hill. It appeared as if every light in the house were on, yet when he'd raced off to town earlier only a few had been.

"Hey, look there!"

Officer Simmons was referring to the partially open bus door. Dribbling through the gap and trickling down over the final two steps was a darkish liquid. John did not need to get any closer to identify it.

"Blood," Chief Bogartus said. Cautiously, his thumb on the hammer of his gun, he inched to the door, gripped it, and heaved.

John didn't know what he expected to happen, but it certainly wasn't a headless body to come tumbling down the steps and plop onto the grass at the chief's feet.

Bogartus recoiled and trained his gun on the corpse before he realized what it was.

Simmons sucked in a breath, then staggered backward. Blanching, he caught himself. "Oh, God!" he declared. "Oh, sweet Jesus, Joseph, and Mary!"

The bloody stump of a neck fascinated John Grant, strips of ragged flesh and the severed spine all that remained. It looked as if someone had literally ripped the man's head from his shoulders, which was patently impossible.

"Now we know where all that blood came from," Chief Bogartus commented while sliding to the door and peeking in.

"So you think the kid did this?" Simmons asked, aghast.

"Not unless he's Hercules in disguise," Bogartus retorted. "Keep me covered, ding-a-ling." In a rush he went up the steps, dropping into a combat stance at the top.

John Grant's stomach was doing flip-flops. A delayed reaction had set in. He worried that he might be sick. Tearing his eyes from the body, he covered his mouth and backpedaled toward the truck. Was this what Kip had seen? Or had Kip witnessed the crime itself? No wonder his son was in shock. He reached the vehicle and leaned against the front quarter panel.

Bogartus did not stay in the bus very long. On exiting, he rummaged in the pockets of the dead man and found a wallet. With Simmons at his elbow, he hastened back, saying, "We need to radio this in. Have Deever and Malcolm haul their asses out here pronto. And tell them to bring flashlights. I couldn't find the damn head anywhere."

"Yes, sir," Officer Simmons replied.

Just then, from up the hill, fluttered a piercing scream that prickled the short hairs at the nape of John Grant's neck. Whirling, he bleated, "That sounded like my daughter!" and started to run off.

Chief Bogartus grabbed him on the fly. "Think, man! How fast can you get there on foot?"

John was shoved into the backseat. The chief buried the gas pedal and the truck peeled out, sliding sideways until the tires found traction on the asphalt. They shot across the Monongahela Bridge doing over 60. Bogartus took the turns like a pro, whipping the steering wheel right and left.

All John could think of was his daughter suffering the same fate as the man on the bus. He leaned forward to tell the chief to increase their speed. Suddenly a pale figure reared up in the middle of the drive, directly in front of them. Bogartus cursed and spun the wheel like a man possessed. The truck's tires squealed. John was thrown against the side as the vehicle slid to the right, digging furrows in the drive. It bounced over a shallow drainage ditch into the bordering brush, flattening weeds and churning up small bushes. He saw a wide tree trunk rush toward them. At the last moment, with barely inches to spare, they lurched to a stop.

"Oh, God! Oh, God!" Simmons cried, his familiar refrain.

John was the first one out. He sprinted to the road, swatting limbs that nipped at his face. As he stepped into the open, Shery hurtled into his arms. He was so taken aback at finding her in her underwear that he stood there with his arms outstretched, too embarrassed to hug her. "Are you all right?" he croaked. "We heard a scream."

Shery, exasperated, stabbed a finger at Buck, who stood a few yards off. For a second there she had thought her number was up, until the mongrel had commenced licking her. "That damn mutt! I fell over him and thought he was the guy who tried to kill me!"

Bogartus had joined them. "What was that, miss?" he asked.

"Up at the house. I think he's still there," Shery said. Now that she was safe, she felt more anger than anything else. She wanted to see the bastard pay for what he had done. To that end she urged, "If you hurry, you might catch him." She thought the officers would rush off by themselves, but her father and the chief both took an arm and whisked her to the truck.

Moments later they were speeding on up the hill.

Chapter Ten

Laurie Grant sat on a chair next to the cot on which her son slept and watched the rhythmic rise and fall of his chest. In repose his features were serene. She tenderly touched his arm, then shifted as the door opened and in walked Doc Syms bearing a silver tray.

"He's sleeping? Good," the physician said softly as he placed the tray on a counter. "The rest will speed his recovery." He gave her a cup of steaming tea balanced on a saucer. "It's Raspberry Supreme. Supposed to calm frazzled nerves."

"You didn't have to go to all this bother," Laurie said, resting the saucer on her thigh.

"I didn't," Doc Syms said. "My better half made it. She's a regular fussbudget about not letting me anywhere near her kitchen. I made the mistake of leaving a mess once about thirty years ago, and she's never let me hear the end of it."

Despite herself, Laurie laughed. The tea tasted delicious, and she welcomed the comforting warmth which spread through her.

Doc Syms sank onto a stool. "If you mind the company just say so and I'll leave you be."

"No, not at all," Laurie said, grateful to have someone to talk to. It had galled her to learn her husband had gone off with the police instead of staying by her side, where he belonged. Once again he had shown how insensitive he could be when she needed him the most.

The physician sipped his tea while regarding her with his brow furrowed. "If I recollect correctly, your family is the one that moved into the old Helstrom place."

"If you mean the farmhouse on the hill north of town, yes, that's us," Laurie said, absently adding, "I've never heard it called by that name before."

"Most of the old-timers refer to it that way," Doc Syms said. "In honor, you might say, of Arkady Helstrom, one of the most colorful characters ever seen in these parts."

Kip shifted, and Laurie was immediately attentive. But he didn't open his eyes. "Was this Helstrom person the original owner?" she asked.

"Oh, no," Doc Syms said. "He bought the farm a few years before the Civil War broke out, and wound up living there until pretty near the turn of the century. His son took over after that, but met a tragic end. Since then there have been about nine or ten owners." He paused. "None ever stay there very long."

"Why would that be?"

"People say the place is haunted."

Laurie glanced around. "You're joking, right?"

Syms did not look as if he were. His expression, normally so pleasant, was somber to the point of being grim. "No, Mrs. Grant, I'm afraid not. Local legend has it that the whole area up there is the Devil's playground, you might say. Blackgap Road, Monongahela Bridge, even South Mountain figure prominently in a lot of stories spread over the years."

"No one ever takes them seriously, do they?" Laurie asked.

The doctor did not seem to hear her. "It all started, as near as I can tell," he went on, "way back when this area was home to the Susquehannock Indians, before the first white man ever set foot in this part of the country. They called South Mountain by a different name, Monongahela Mountain."

"The same as the creek," Laurie noted.

"Yes. And they avoided both as if their lives depended on it."

Intrigued, Laurie inquired, "Does anyone know why?"

"In their tongue *monongahela* meant serpent. The tribe believed that Monongahela Mountain was home to a huge evil serpent that wriggled up from the bowels of the earth from time to time to drink in the creek."

"You know," Laurie said, "I just saw a show on TV the other week about Indians in Ohio who also believed in some kind of wicked serpent being."

"Many tribes did," Doc Syms said. "Most whites scoffed, of course. But the Indians stuck to their guns. I knew an Indian once, when I was a boy growing up here, and he used to say that there are places on this earth where evil can flourish when conditions are right, places we'd best stay away from if we know what's good for us."

Laurie wondered why the physician was telling her all this. "Do you think these silly superstitions have any bearing on why no one ever lives at the farm for very long?"

Syms's mouth twitched—whether in a grin or a frown, it was hard to say. "I take it you've heard all the tales about the Headless Horror of Spook Hollow?"

"The what?"

For a few seconds the doctor's face reflected dismay, which he quickly concealed. "I took it for granted someone would have told you by now. Reports of the Headless Horror date back from 1870 or so. He always appears at about this time of year, but there's no other set pattern. Sometimes he's sighted two or three years in a row. Then he might not show up for another ten or twelve."

"And what does this Headless Horror do? Pop out of nowhere and scare people half to death?"

Doc Syms locked his eyes on hers. "No. He rips off heads."

Chief Bogartus could not hide his disappointment. "Nothing," he declared gruffly. "We searched from the basement to the attic. No one is in there."

John Grant exhaled, feeling some of the tension drain from his body. Beside him on the porch Shery sat, bundled in a heavy coat of his which he had taken from the living room closet. The chief had refused to let either of them go up to her room for some clothes before the house was thoroughly checked.

Shery sniffled. Her damp hair was plastered to her head and her feet hurt where she had scraped them on the gravel. The cut on her thigh stung terribly. And to top off her misery, she felt grungy, in dire need of the bath she had been so long denied. "Finally!" she said, rising. The coat parted and Officer Simmons's eyes almost bugged from his head. "A girl could catch pneumonia waiting for you guys to do your job," she snapped.

"Shery!" John said sternly, flustered by her lack of gratitude. Not to mention her complete lack of modesty.

"That's all right, Mr. Grant," Chief Bogartus said. "Your daughter is entitled to speak her mind." He gazed toward town. "The rest of my

163

men should show up any minute now. Simmons and I will check the barn and the outbuildings in the meantime."

"We will?" Simmons said.

Shery sashayed to the doorway. "Thanks ever so much for everything, Officers," she said playfully, enjoying how flustered the younger policeman became when she smiled at him.

"Not so fast, young lady," Bogartus said. "I'll expect you at the station first thing in the morning to file an official statement."

"But I've already told you all I know," Shery pointed out. She wasn't keen on the idea of being late for school since it would put a crimp in her desire to hang out with Bryce for a while before classes began.

"It's just a formality," Chief Bogartus explained. "We need to document everything you can tell us about your attacker."

"Which is zilch," Shery reminded him. "I never got a good look at the bozo, remember? Hell, I don't even know if it was a man or a woman. It could have been Frankenstein or Dracula, for all I know."

To John Grant's surprise, the chief stiffened and took an involuntary step toward her. "What made you say that, young lady?"

Shery chuckled. "Jeez, Louise. It just popped into my head. Chill, dude, before you have a coronary." Tittering, she pranced off across the living room, then ascended the stairs two at a time.

Bogartus turned. "That's some girl you've got

there, Grant. Most women would be in hysterics after what happened. Does she always take things in stride like this?"

John had never given it much thought, but now that he did, he had to admit that, yes, Shery did have a knack for not getting flustered in a crisis. Hardship rolled off her like water off a duck's back. But that didn't stop her from bitching to high heaven when things didn't go the way she wanted them to go. "Most of the time," he confirmed, standing.

The chief walked to the end of the porch, Simmons reluctantly dogging his heels.

John Grant fingered the closed razor in his right hand. His daughter had given it to him when they raced up the drive. It shook him to think of how close she had come to being murdered. A core of rage formed deep within him, an urge to see justice done, to make the bastard responsible pay. "Hold on and I'll go with you," he said. "I know the layout of the buildings."

"Do you have any flashlights?" Bogartus asked.

Nodding, John made a beeline for the kitchen door, which he verified was locked. Then he opened a kitchen drawer and removed a large flashlight given to him the previous Christmas by his wife. He had rarely used the thing.

Hurrying down the hall, he recalled the many gifts she had bestowed on him during the course of their marriage: a camera, a VCR, a set of tools, and much more. For his last birthday it had been tickets to an Eagles game. On the 50-yard line, no less. It made him realize that for all their bickering in recent years, she had never stopped loving him.

Chief Bogartus was impatiently waiting. He took the flashlight, snapped it on, and strode toward the barn, his hand resting on the butt of his Smith and Wesson.

John locked the front door to guarantee Shery would be safe. He stayed a few yards behind the officers in case they were lucky enough to find the suspect. The last thing he wanted was to be caught in the line of fire.

Built decades ago, the barn was three times the size of the farmhouse. Walls once painted white were chipped and peeled with age. Both wide double doors were closed, as were the smaller hayloft doors above. From within rose the musty scent of hay and straw and other less easily identifiable odors, not all of them pleasant.

The real estate agent had told John that the previous owner had tried to raise horses and hogs. As a result, dry manure littered the stalls where the horses had been housed, while the floor of the hog pen was inches-thick with excrement. One day John intended to get around to cleaning the place out, but the chore wasn't high on his list of priorities.

Bogartus pulled the right-hand door open. Hinges long neglected squeaked loud enough to raise zombies from their graves. Dust hung suspended in the air. Cobwebs decorated the rafters over their heads.

"This place is spooky," Officer Simmons muttered.

John had to agree. He could count the number of times he had been inside on one hand, and he had never gone in after the sun went down. Since the few tools he owned were stored in the basement of the house, he rarely had a reason to be there. In addition, the barn had a peculiar oppressive atmosphere which he tried to chalk up to his imagination but couldn't.

The place just didn't feel right. That was the only way John could describe it. Laurie had once mentioned that the barn gave her the creeps. And Kip, whose boundless curiosity had prompted him to explore every square inch of their new property, remarked at supper one evening that he couldn't understand why the barn was always so warm and muggy inside.

Chief Bogartus prowled down the center aisle, sweeping the flashlight into the stalls on either side. He also ran it over the straw-covered floor and the huge timbers above.

Suddenly, to their right, something scuttled in the shadows. Claws scratched on a rough surface and a frenetic chittering broke out.

Officer Simmons spun, his revolver leaping from its holster. The gun boomed once, the blast reverberating back and forth like an echo in the Swiss mountains.

"Hold your fire, damn it!" Bogartus roared.

"What the hell were you shooting at?"

"I saw something!" Simmons declared, as if that were justification enough. "I thought it was coming at us."

The chief roved the light over the east wall. It revealed the sprawled form of a raccoon lying on its side in a spreading puddle of blood. Limbs twitching, it worked its mouth, but no sounds came out.

"Oh, just swell!" Bogartus growled at his subordinate. "What if it had been their dog?" He stepped closer, then shook his head in disgust. "Even if it had been the suspect, we can't shoot him unless he resists arrest. I don't know what made you pick a career in law enforcement, Simmons. You'd be better off as a banker or a store clerk."

Stung by the rebuke, Simmons hung his head. "I'm sorry, Chief. I truly am. But you know what they say about this old place."

John's interest perked. "What do they say?" he interjected.

Chief Bogartus forestalled an answer by rasping, "We don't have time for a bunch of old wives' tales. Wait for us outside, Simmons. We won't take long."

The young patrolman, crestfallen, departed. John couldn't help but feel sorry for him. Being jumpy was understandable, given that they were after someone who presumably had torn the head off a grown man and tried to drown his daughter. "Aren't you being a little too hard on him?" he asked.

"No harder than I am on myself," was the chief's response. "I expect my men to keep a level head at all times, Mr. Grant. Our lives may depend on it. Anyone who can't keep a rein on his nerves doesn't deserve to be wearing a badge, in my book."

"Even so," John said, but got no further. From out front rose Simmons's voice in a harsh crackle.

"You there! I'm a police officer. Hold it!"

"Now what?" Bogartus snapped. and beat John to the entrance by a few steps.

Officer Simmons was peering westward, toward the springhouse, his hand resting on the butt of his holstered gun. "I saw someone!" he exclaimed.

"Oh?" the chief replied, in a tone which implied it was more likely Martians would invade the Earth in the next five minutes. "What was it this time? A marauding cow?"

"No. A big guy on horseback."

John would never forget the look that came over Bogartus. The man acted as if he had just been zapped by a lightning bolt. Astonishment—and something else—rippled his features.

"I couldn't get a good look at his face," Simmons continued, "but he seemed to be watching us from beside that building over there."

The next moment they all heard the steady

clop of heavy hooves as the rider moved off at a brisk walk through the trees. John glimpsed a large form that was promptly swallowed by the vegetation.

"Come on!" Chief Bogartus bellowed, streaking in pursuit like a sprinter off a starting block. For a big man, he could move extremely fast. Officer Simmons was hard pressed to keep up.

Apprehending the suspect, if it really proved to be the suspect, was their job, not John's. He had no real business joining in the chase. Yet he did, his legs pumping seemingly of their own accord. The policemen plunged into the undergrowth ahead of him and vanished in the gloom. He slowed to get his bearings, heard one or both of them smashing through the brush like a bull in a china shop, and homed in on the sound.

"Police! Halt!" John heard Bogartus bellow. A shot shattered the brisk air, but whether it had been fired by the chief or Simmons, he couldn't say. The horse nickered loudly, as if stricken.

John did his best to catch up. But years of little exercise had reduced his stamina to a pathetic level. Soon he was huffing and puffing while the crash of fleeing figures grew fainter and fainter. The rider appeared to be bearing due west, toward South Mountain.

Presently John halted and leaned against an oak to catch his breath. A glance revealed that he had gone much farther than he figured. The lights of the farmhouse were a good hundred yards distant, if not more.

From the racket being raised by Bogartus and Simmons, they were prepared to follow the rider deep into the wilderness if need be. John felt they were wasting their time. Try as they might, they could never overtake a horse.

Grasping a low limb, John pulled himself to his full height and shuffled home. With all that had occurred since finding the bus, he hadn't given much thought to Kip. A call to the doctor was long overdue.

Lost in thought, John weaved through the maze of wide trunks, avoiding dense thickets and logs. In the light of his son's ordeal and the attempt on his daughter's life, it was clear that moving to Spook Hollow qualified as the worst decision of his life. He'd hoped and prayed it would save his marriage. Instead, it had put his two children in jeopardy.

John toyed with the idea of calling it quits, of packing up everything and moving back to Philadelphia before the week was out. He had friends who would gladly help his family find a place to live.

Laurie's sister lived in Philly too, and even though she was the biggest snoop alive and took perverse delight in antagonizing him, Martina Brewster would do anything for Laurie if asked.

The snap of a twig brought John Grant up short. It had come from off to his left, well back in the trees. Since he could hear Bogartus and Simmons yelling somewhere to the west, someone or something else had been responsible. "Who's there?" he called out, but didn't receive an answer. "Buck, is that you, big fella?"

A gust of wind fanned John's cheeks, chilling him. He bustled on, anxious to get out of there before he started jumping at every shadow. Urban paranoia had been supplanted by that most primal of human instincts, raw, unreasoning dread. A feeling came over him that he was being spied on, which was absurd.

Then the undergrowth rustled to the passage of a large form and an ominous nicker sent a shiver down John Grant's backbone. It was the horseman. The rider had eluded the police and circled around.

John ducked low. He debated whether to stay where he was in the hope that the man would move on, or to make a mad dash for the house.

Shouting to alert the police was out of the question. It would enable the rider to fix his exact position if the man hadn't done so already.

Easing past a bush, placing each foot down with the utmost care, John focused on the light above the front porch, then hurtled toward it heedless of the brush which snatched at his legs. Almost immediately the horse whinnied again. The ground drummed to its hoofbeats. John risked a look and beheld a huge man astride a gray steed of equal size. Heavy shadow hid the man's features.

The rider had seen him! The horse thundered closer, plowing through a thicket as if it were not there. John faced front just in time to see a low log and vaulted over the obstacle. Landing awkwardly on the ball of his left foot, he nearly took a tumble.

Meanwhile, the rider narrowed the gap.

John fairly flew, concentrating on the front light to the exclusion of all else. It was his beacon of hope, a promise of sanctuary. The killer might think twice before venturing out into the open. He had to reach it before the horseman reached him.

Ahead was the tree line. Beyond, a strip of lawn led past the springhouse and on up the slope. John burst from the forest. The pounding of hooves hammered in his ears. He swiveled to see the rider, and could not believe his eyes. Bewildered, not thinking clearly, he slowed to get a better look, to prove that he was wrong. But he was right.

Horse and rider materialized out of the woods like ghostly specters out of a fog. The man was as gray as his mount, only in his case it was due to a gray uniform: gray pants, gray coat, a short gray cape, and gray gloves. Both the rider and his steed were caked with dust, the animal more so than the man.

The truly remarkable aspect about the rider wasn't the color of his clothes, though, or his size, or the superb skill with which he rode, or the long saber which clanked at his side. It was the fact that on his broad shoulders rested a short stump of a neck, and *nothing more*! The rider had no head!

John Grant was so shocked that he came to a stumbling halt and turned. At first he thought that it must be some sort of trick, that the man wore the coat pulled up over his head with holes cut in the fabric so he could see out. Yet John saw no holes. He saw nothing to indicate the man on the horse was anything other than what the rider appeared to be—a *headless horseman*.

The macabre vision bore down on him, slowing as the rider grasped the hilt of the saber and started to draw the blade from its scabbard.

The horse was so close that John could see its nostrils flare, could smell its sweaty hide. Part of his mind screeched at him to keep on running, to get out of there before he suffered the same fate as the man on the bus. Another part assured him that none of what he saw could be real, that he was hallucinating, that if he faced his delusion squarely it would evaporate into thin air right before his eyes.

That was when the saber swept on high, then whistled toward his neck.

Chapter Eleven

Laurie Grant stared at her sleeping son and prayed he would be fine once he woke up. Her stomach rumbled, reminding her of the supper she had missed, but she was in no mood to eat.

She glanced at the door, wondering why in the world the doctor had seen fit to tell her that drivel about the nature of evil and the Headless Horror of Spook Hollow. If she didn't know better, she'd swear that in an oblique fashion he had been trying to warn her of something. But what? And if that were the case, why hadn't he simply come right out and told her what was on his mind?

It was a minor mystery, one meriting scant attention. She had too much else to worry about: her son, her marriage, her whole life. As she had done several times recently, she pondered whether it was best to try to ride out the hard times in the hope things would improve, or whether a trial separation from John and a whole new life were in order.

Abruptly, the door opened, framing Doc Syms. He wore a haunted expression and opened his mouth twice before he could bring himself to speak. "I just got off the phone with Deputy Malcolm. It seems I'm needed out near your place. The chief found a body in a bus close to the Monongahela Bridge. Its head is missing."

Laurie's breath caught in her throat.

"That's not all. Malcolm told me that there has been an attempt on your daughter's life. He didn't know all the details, but she's unhurt. Your husband is with her now, so you needn't worry."

"Shery!" Laurie declared, rising. Her first instinct was to rush out to the farm, and she took a step before the sight of her son brought her to her senses. She couldn't leave Kip alone, not in his condition.

"I'm terribly sorry to have to leave you alone," the physician was saying, "but it can't be helped. Bogartus will need some idea of the time and cause of death, and I'm the closest thing to a big-city coroner that Spook Hollow has." He gestured over a shoulder. "I'll tell Candice to check in on you from time to time. If you want more tea or anything else, you just say the word."

"I will," Laurie said. As the doctor pivoted, she had to ask, "You don't think there's any connection, do you? I mean, between the headless body and those stories you told me?"

Doc Syms hesitated. "I'd never go on public record as claiming I believe in the supernatural, but I've been around a long time, Mrs. Grant, and I've seen more than my share of strange happenings. Many of them involve your property, and the people who have lived there at one time or another."

Laurie had a dozen questions she wanted to throw at him, but he left in a rush, shutting the door. She sank down again, emotionally shattered, feeling as if her entire world were crumbling around her, unraveling at the seams, as it were.

It was all her husband's fault. It had been John's bright idea to move to Spook Hollow, his brainstorm to move into the old farmhouse. And now look!

"Mom?"

The croaked word brought Laurie around so swiftly that she nearly slipped off the chair. Her son gazed wearily at her, then studied the room in evident confusion. "You're in town, at the doctor's," she explained, clutching his cold hand in both of hers. "You've been in shock. No one knew exactly why . . ." She stopped herself, thinking of the headless corpse.

Kip stared at her, struggling to remember. The last he seemed to recall was walking toward the stuck school bus. He had climbed on, hadn't he? And Mr. Kimble had been in the driver's seat, hadn't he? Kip had reached out, had touched him.

Like a bolt out of the blue, everything came back to Kip in a gush of horrid detail. As if he were standing on the bus again, he saw the driver slump, saw the pumping blood and the gory stump. He had screamed and let go, staggering backward, almost losing his footing on the slick floor. The creak of a seat behind him had made him turn.

Icy fear had ripped through him, fear so potent it had deadened his limbs and brought a lump to his throat. For rising from one of the seats had been a huge hulk of a man, a grayish figure wearing a short cape and holding an oval object tucked under one arm.

Kip remembered yelling, "Who are you, mister?" And getting no response. He had started to back up, convinced the man must be responsible for Mr. Kimble's death. Not watching where he was going, he had bumped into the driver's legs and fallen onto his backside. As he put both hands flat to shove upright, the hulking figure had taken two long strides and loomed above him.

That close, Kip had clearly seen the oval object. He had seen the ragged ring of flesh at the bottom, seen the ruffled hair on top and the drooping eyelids and the mouth locked eternally in what must have been Kimble's death wail.

But the grisly severed head hadn't been the ghastliest sight. No, by far the most terrifying element had been what lay on top of the huge figure's shoulders. Or, rather, what *wasn't* there. Because as the killer bent and extended a gloved hand toward him, Kip had plainly seen that the figure did not have a head of its own.

Something had snapped deep within him. Kip recalled experiencing fright so potent, it was indescribable. Vaguely, he remembered spinning and scrambling over the driver's body. On his belly, he had bumped down over the steps and landed in the pool of blood forming on the ground. Dimly, he recalled pushing to his feet and stumbling off into the darkness. After that, his memory was blank.

Until now.

Kip looked at his mother, and shivered.

Laurie hugged him, alarmed by his sudden pallor and the gleam of unbridled terror she detected in his eyes. "You're safe now, son," she soothed him. "Everything is fine. Whatever happened is behind you."

Kip didn't believe her for an instant. Nothing would ever be the same again. By every rule of science, the same science he had always thought had all the answers to man's existence, the horror he had seen could not exist. By every dictate of logic, it should not exist. Yet it did. And knowing that fact, he'd never again view the world as he had before he'd entered that bus and reality had run amok.

"Your father would be here, but he's home with your sister," Laurie felt compelled to say. "I don't know all the details yet, but someone tried to harm her. Doc Syms told me she's all right."

Kip thought of the monstrous nightmare he had confronted, and another shiver racked him. His father had to be warned, if he didn't know already. "How soon can we go, Mom?"

"We should wait for the doctor to give his okay," Laurie said, although she really wanted to rush home to confirm Shery was indeed safe.

"I'd rather go right this minute," Kip said, sitting up. "All of us need to sit down together and have a long talk. It's important."

Laurie needed no further prompting. "I suppose Doc Syms won't hold it against us. I'll let his wife know." She tapped the white gown he wore. "The only thing is, you can't wear your own clothes. You'll have to go home dressed as you are."

Once, Kip would have balked at the idea. Once, he would have shunned the embarrassment of being teased by his sister. But now it hardly mattered.

"I don't care. Let's just go."

John Grant's limbs were leaden, his mind spinning like a child's top. Mesmerized by the apparition bearing down on him, he made no attempt to ward off the blow the headless wraith aimed at his neck.

John fully expected the abomination to vanish at any instant. Even when the figure raised the saber, he could not accept the testimony of his own eyes. Headless horsemen did not exist. Therefore there could not be one in front of him. It was as simple as that.

The saber had started its downward sweep when behind John a car engine roared and headlight beams speared across the lawn, impaling him and the apparition in their glow.

The moment the light struck the rider, the figure recoiled, twisting away from it. The blow never landed. Instead, in the blink of an eye, the unearthly specter wheeled his steed and plunged into the forest, the two flowing as one in a literal blur.

Dazed, John Grant stayed where he was as footsteps approached from the rear. A flashlight was trained on his face, making him blink.

"Mr. Grant, isn't it? I'm Officer Deever. Who the hell was that? Was he holding a sword?" Deever turned the light on the wall of trees. "I didn't get a good look."

John had to force his vocal chords to work. "Neither did I," he lied.

"Where's Chief Bogartus and Simmons? I was told to meet them here."

"Out there somewhere," John said, nodding. "They were chasing someone the last I saw."

Deever was a muscular man whose service revolver sported pearl grips. "Damn!" he complained. "Something finally happens around this two-bit burg and I miss out on all the action. Just my luck." He tapped John's elbow with the flashlight. "You look a little peaked, mister. Why don't we go up to the house and you can tell me what the hell has been going on?"

Briefly, John did as they walked toward the front door. Deever left him when he slumped into a chair on the porch to go place a call on the cruiser radio. Seated there, staring out over the benighted valley and the stark mountains to the west, John Grant clenched the arms of the chair and gritted his teeth as, belatedly, the full impact of his encounter hit him with the force of a physical blow.

It had really happened. If Officer Deever had seen the rider, than the apparition had not been a figment of John's imagination. He had nearly been killed by a flesh-and-bone madman riding around in the dead of night in an outlandish costume. There was no other explanation.

John had never been so close to dying before. Like most people, he'd always tended to dismiss the possibility by not thinking about it. Death afflicted others, not him, not until he was good and ready.

Only that wasn't how life worked. Death might strike at any time, invariably when a person least expected. It was a shattering revelation, made more so by the bizarre appearance of the man who had almost beheaded him. And since it was doubtful two lunatics roamed the night, the same demented soul must have tried to drown his daughter.

Why? John mused. Was it a personal vendetta? Doubtful, since he had no enemies to speak of. Had they just happened to be in the wrong place at the wrong time? More to the point, would the psychotic try again? Should he pack up the family and get the hell out of there first thing in the morning?

Absorbed in reflection, John merely grunted when Chief Bogartus eventually showed up and informed him the rider had gotten away.

"We'll be at the bus for the next three or four hours if you need us," the lawman also mentioned. "Doc Syms is there now." He began to walk off, but stopped. "You might be interested in knowing that the dead man has been identified. He was the bus driver. So there's a good chance your son saw something. I'll need to talk to him as soon as he comes around. Will you bring him to the station?"

John nodded. The chief got into his truck and executed a U-turn on his lawn, then sped down the drive. No sooner was it out of sight than a low whine let him know he had company. Buck sat at the edge of the porch, tail wagging like a berserk metronome. John held out a hand and the mongrel came over to be petted.

"What does it all mean, big fella?" he speculated aloud. "And what do I do?"

It wasn't all that long before another vehicle crawled up the hill. John was out of the chair and at the end of the walk before it came to a stop. Without saying a word he warmly embraced his son and turned to do the same to his wife as she went by. But Laurie held a palm out

183

to prevent them from making contact and walked to the front door.

"Mom's ticked off at you, Dad," Kip disclosed. "She told me on the way home that she blames you for what happened. I tried to tell her it's not your fault and she ignored me."

"I understand," John said. All too well. The signs were unmistakable. Laurie was spoiling for another fight. All it would take was one wrong word on his part and she would explode like a human grenade.

Fate spared him momentarily. As they entered the living room, the phone rang. Laurie scooped the receiver to an ear, squealed, "Tina!" and moved to a recliner in the corner where she could talk undisturbed.

John decided to make himself scarce. His sister-in-law had never been one of his biggest admirers. Once Martina heard the latest, she'd be screaming for his manhood on a platter, garnished, preferably, with "whatever passes for his brains." She had openly doubted that he had any several times since they'd met over 20 years ago.

Taking it for granted his wife would be tied up a while, John escorted his son upstairs. Humming from the bathroom told them where Shery was.

"I never thought I'd be glad to hear that foghorn she calls a voice," Kip joked. He had so much he wanted to tell his father, and remarked as much, adding, "Maybe all four of us can get together in the kitchen in a bit to compare notes."

"I'll spread the word while you dress," John proposed. Going on, he rapped on the bathroom door. "Shery, I'd like to see you downstairs in about five minutes," he announced.

"Wonderful. What did I do now?"

"Your mother and brother are home," John revealed. "Meet us in the kitchen for a family meeting."

Years ago they had made it a point to get together at least once a week. It had been Laurie's inspiration. What with the kids wrapped up in school and the two of them putting in long hours at work, they'd hardly spent any time as a family.

John sometimes wondered if their marriage would be in the sorry state it was if they were still sitting down together regularly to air mutual gripes or discuss anything else they deemed important. Without an outlet, bitter feelings were often pent up until they reached the boiling point.

As if on cue, Laurie appeared on the landing. She noted that her husband appeared haggard. For a few seconds tenderness replaced the anger she had nursed on the ride from town, and she was going to ask if he was all right when he posed a question which she automatically assumed was calculated to provoke her.

"Off the phone already? Usually that flaky sister of yours keeps you jabbering for hours on end."

"For your information, Tina is as levelheaded as I am," Laurie said stiffly. "And I didn't stay on long because I wanted to see how Shery is doing. Doc Syms told me there was an attempt on her life."

John nodded. "I'll let her tell you about it. We're holding a family meeting in the kitchen in a few minutes. In the meantime, I have something to do." He sensed that she wanted to say more, but he went to the master bedroom, to a closet in the corner where his clothes were hung. Behind them, propped in a corner, was the shotgun Laurie had bought him five years ago for his birthday.

It had long puzzled him. John was no hunter and only rarely went fishing. At the time, they had been living in the heart of Philadelphia, where no one in his right mind would traipse down the street with a shotgun in hand unless he wanted every cop in sight to use him for target practice.

Eventually he'd deduced that he owed his possession of the gun to a news special his wife had seen. A ratings-hungry reporter had raved on and on about the dangers of urban living, citing statistics skewed to show that the average Philadelphians had a better chance of being shot in their own home by a criminal than they did of dying from old age. Typical garbage. The reporter's intent had been to brainwash the viewer into believing that all guns should be outlawed to preserve civilization. It had backfired, and

John had wound up with a brand-spanking-new self-defense shotgun. It was a pump-action 12-gauge with an 18-inch barrel. Magazine capacity was five three-inch shells. It came fitted with swivel rings and a sling.

He had fired it maybe ten times, at an indoor range, and been amazed at the size of the holes buckshot made in paper targets. Truth to tell, John had never expected to need it to protect himself or his loved ones. Now he sat on the bed, the shotgun in his lap, and loaded five shells through the bottom port.

When he was done, John took five extra shells from the box and stuffed them into his front pockets. Shrugging the sling over his left shoulder, he went to the kitchen. Given that his wife was mad at him and Shery had a knack for dragging her heels whenever she was asked to do anything, he counted on being the first one there. To his surprise, the others were waiting for him. Three sets of arched eyebrows greeted the appearance of the shotgun, but no one objected. He slid into the chair at the head of the table and laid the weapon down on top with a pronounced thunk.

"I won't mince words," John began. "This family is at a crossroads. As if it weren't bad enough that we're always at each other's throats, now it appears there's a psychopath out there somewhere who is stalking this area. He's a suspect in George Eldridge's death. And tonight he tried to kill Shery and me."

"And me," Kip said.

The news disturbed John immensely. One attempt could be dismissed as a fluke. Two attempts might be a coincidence. But three proved deliberate intent beyond a shadow of a doubt. "Okay. Here's the way we'll do it. Each of us will tell what took place. Then we'll pool the information and decide where to go from there. Agreed?"

Everyone did. Shery went first, calmly relating her ordeal. Kip told of his run-in at the bus, and could not help quaking every few seconds. John sketched his near-fatal encounter.

Laurie listened quietly, her hands clenched so tight the knuckles were white. She was the first to speak when they were done. "Well, I guess we know what we have to do. We pack up and leave. Tomorrow."

No one else commented until Shery cleared her throat and said, "Can't, Mom. The big dance is next week and I can't miss it." She had laid the groundwork for a night she would never forget, and she didn't care to have it spoiled.

"Did I hear you correctly? Someone tried to murder you tonight and all you can think of is a stupid dance?" Laurie said.

"I don't want to go either," Kip made bold to say. He had been thinking it over, and as insane as it sounded, he wanted to get to the bottom of the mystery. His father believed the man on the horse was some nut-case in a costume. Kip didn't agree. He'd seen the man close up, much closer than his father had. And he knew deep down in the core of his being that there was more to the Headless Horror than that.

John surveyed the room. "This is our home," he pointed out. "We've invested a lot in this property. It would be a shame to give it up without a good reason."

"And just what do you call being murdered?" Laurie responded. She looked at each of them in turn and shook her head. The thought of losing any of them, including John, petrified her. "I can't believe I'm hearing this. We all know it was a mistake leaving Philly. I say we cut our losses and get out of here while we still can."

"Maybe we should put it to a vote, like we did back in the old days," John proposed.

Laurie leaned forward. "Are you insane? The lives of our children are at stake here. It's too damn dangerous to stay."

"I won't argue that there is an element of risk," John said, "but if we take a few simple precautions, we should be fine." He ticked them off on his fingers. "We keep the doors locked at all times. We never go outdoors alone. We draw the shades at night. And I'll rig up spotlights at the front and the rear of the house."

"Spotlights!" Laurie declared. "We're talking about a mental case who decapitates people!"

"Wacko or not, he's not likely to show up again any time soon. The police nearly caught him tonight. My guess is they scared him off."

"You hope."

Shery fidgeted in her chair. She did not intend to sit there all night listening to them quarrel. "I agree with Dad," she interjected. "Let's put it to a vote. And I vote we stick around a while yet."

"Me, too," Kip said.

Laurie Grant was too flustered to speak. How her husband would vote was obvious. Since she wasn't about to go off and leave her children to be butchered, she had no choice. "I think this is a major mistake on our part, but I'll go along with it, for now."

John was delighted. "Do you realize that this is the first time in years the four of us have agreed on something? We're working together as a family should. Isn't it terrific?" He beamed at his wife. Plainly, she didn't share his sentiments. Based on the set of her features, he didn't have to worry about the so-called Headless Horror of Spook Hollow. There was a good chance his wife would do him in before the goblin ever did.

Chapter Twelve

John Grant went to sleep that night with a smile creasing his face and contentment in his heart. As the adage went, every cloud has its silver lining, and in this instance the murderous madman on the gray steed had brought his family closer together than they had been in ages.

He would be the first to admit that it was supremely silly of him to make too much of their family meeting, but he couldn't help himself. For the first time in months there was a genuine glimmer of hope, however feeble, that he could mend the rifts which had shattered his family and virtually destroyed his marriage.

As added encouragement, Laurie had turned to him before she drifted off, given him the oddest look, then kissed him the cheek. He had no idea why. But it was the first kiss she had bestowed on him in weeks, and he took it as an omen.

The next morning John bounded out of bed, fired with a zest for life he had not felt in a long, long time. He surprised Laurie by giving her a kiss smack on the lips as she came out of the bathroom. "I'll get breakfast started," he volunteered, and went down the steps whistling softly to himself.

John was almost to the bottom when someone pounded on the front door. He couldn't imagine who would be paying them a visit so early, unless it might be the police.

Chief Bogartus had phoned shortly before they turned in to ask about Kip. John had told him about his son's encounter with the lunatic, and the chief had requested that he bring Kip along when Shery came in to file her report. Maybe, John decided, Bogartus had seen fit to drive out and escort them into town to make sure they got there bright and early.

Chuckling, John opened the door, saying as he did, "You just don't trust anyone, do you?" His grin faded when he set eyes on a sandy-haired woman in jeans and a sweatshirt standing on his porch with a large suitcase in hand and a scowl of greeting on her angular face.

"You're got that right, buster," Martina Brewster said. "And that includes you."

Taken aback, John froze, unable to think of a suitable comeback. His sister-in-law brushed past him and plopped the suitcase down on the sofa. "How rustic," she said dryly while scanning the room. "Your own little farm in the middle of nowhere. You must be in seventh heaven."

John slowly closed the door, his good mood withering as fast as morning dew under a hot sun. "I wasn't expecting it to be you, Tina," he said lamely.

"I'm sure," she responded tartly. "And I can just imagine how happy you are to see me." She gave a toss of her long hair. "Blame that idiot sister of mine. I called last night to see if she had come to her senses yet and contacted a lawyer, and what does she tell me? That she can't talk at the moment because she just brought my nephew home from the doctor's and someone tried to kill my niece. Then she hangs up on me!" Tina unslung her purse from her shoulder and tossed it beside the suitcase. "What else could I do? I gassed up the car and drove half the night to reach this backwater town."

"The kids are fine," John said defensively. "And Laurie has no need for a lawyer."

"Oh?" Tina replied. "Did a miracle happen in the time it took me to get here? The last I knew, your marriage was still on the rocks." She sighed. "Frankly, I don't know why she didn't file for divorce years ago instead of putting herself through all this misery. *I* would have."

John couldn't help himself. He snapped, "Of course you would have. You've been married four times. You treat your husbands as if they're disposable diapers."

Tina placed her hands on her hips. "Is that a dig just because I've never had kids? And is it my fault every Prince Charming I hook up with turns out to be a frog in disguise?"

"We all have warts," John said. "The key to a successful marriage is to look past them at the total person."

"Why, thank you for that insight, Dr. Sigmond Freud," Tina responded. "But it seems to me that you're a fine one to talk when your own marriage has been on the ropes for so long. Can it be that you're more like me than you're willing to admit? Can it be that you can't stand warts either?"

"I love your sister," John said with all the passion in his soul. "I don't care how many flaws she has. She and I are right for each other, and I'll never stop loving her. If it's the last thing I ever do, I'll save our marriage."

Tina rolled her eyes. "How utterly romantic. And how impractical. When are you going to grow up and realize that life isn't a fairy tale? It doesn't always have a happy ending. That applies to marriage as well."

There was a low cough, and they both turned to find Laurie on the stairs, regarding her husband intently.

"Sis!" Tina exclaimed. "Did you hear this nitwit?"

"I heard," Laurie said, inwardly swelling with pride. She had not heard him say anything like that in so long, she had forgotten the last time.

194

After all they had been through, he still truly cared for her.

"Well, how about a cup of coffee?" Tina said, going over as Laurie came down and looping an arm in hers. "You can tell me all that's happened and cry on my shoulder if you want. Then we'll set things right." She gave Laurie a playful shake. "You know my motto."

"Never fear, Sis is here," Laurie quoted.

John watched them go down the hall with dread eating at him. So much for the auspicious omen. His sister-in-law despised his guts, and had done all in her power over the years to bring him nothing but grief. Why, he didn't really know. But he was convinced that a large part of the blame for his crumbling relationship with Laurie fell squarely on Tina's meddling shoulders.

Keenly upset by the turn of events, John went out and sat on the porch. Brilliant sunshine had transformed the murky netherworld of night into a sparkling, pristine Garden of Eden. The grass and trees were a deep, rich hue of green. Songbirds chirped. Colorful butterflies flitted about. Near the springhouse a doe and her fawn grazed. Over by the barn a rabbit nibbled on a morsel.

It was the kind of morning which invigorated most people, but not John Grant. Not this day. In a funk, he rested his chin in his hand and mulled over what to do. He had half a mind to march back in and demand that Tina go back to

Philadelphia, where she belonged. But that would only make matters worse. Tina would stubbornly refuse to leave until she was damn good and ready, Laurie would jump down his throat for even suggesting it, and the kids would be peeved at him since they were fond of their aunt. God knew why.

No, John reflected. It would be best if he didn't overreact. Let Tina have her say. He had to trust his wife to do the right thing.

Stretching, John rose to go upstairs and shave. Suddenly he stiffened. The doe and the fawn had raised their heads and were staring at the open entrance to the springhouse with their ears pricked. The fawn started to back up. At a bleat from the doe, they spun in unison and bounded into the woods, the whites of their tails flashing.

Something inside the springhouse had spooked them. John stepped to the edge of the porch, debating whether to go on down or to fetch the shotgun first. It was unlikely the killer would hang around the property in broad daylight, but on the other hand, the springhouse made an ideal hiding place since no one ever went there.

The near-fatal encounter with the lunatic the night before had taught John Grant a lesson. Quietly opening the front door, he crept up the stairs to the master bedroom. The shotgun lay on the floor on his side of the bed, within easy reach if he heard any strange noises in the middle of the night.

Extra shells were still crammed in his pockets, so John did not bother to get more. He picked up the gun and went down the stairs as stealthily as he had gone up them in order not to attract his sister-in-law's attention. Tina hated guns, and had thrown a fit when Laurie bought him one.

Once outside, John hurried down the slope. Buck appeared beside a maple, but would not come any closer when he beckoned. The mongrel stared at the springhouse and growled, confirming his suspicion.

When John was within ten paces of the doorway, he drew up short. A keening wail had fallen on his ears, an anguished, moaning cry such as the wind might make when howling through a tunnel. Only there was no tunnel in the springhouse—none that John knew of.

Cautiously, the shotgun leveled, John advanced. His shoes made no sound on the carpet of grass. He flicked off the safety as he stepped to the right of the entrance and leaned against the jamb to listen.

The wailing was louder. John glanced at Buck, who whined at him as if to say, "You're making a mistake going in there." John was inclined to agree. The smart thing to do was phone Bogartus and let the police handle it. But then again, this was his property, his home. He had a responsibility to his family and himself to safeguard it as best he could.

The wailing abruptly ceased. John bent at the waist and ducked inside, keeping his back to the inner wall. It took a full ten seconds for his eyes to adjust to the gloom.

There were far fewer cobwebs. Most had been torn down by the police when they went over the springhouse with a fine-tooth comb the night Eldridge died. John could see the interior, if dimly.

Back near the spring a figure was huddled.

Slanting to the right into deep shadows, John slowly closed in. He had gone halfway across the floor when it dawned on him that he might not have fed a shell into the chamber. To do so, he had to work the pump. But if he did it now, the figure was bound to hear and he would lose the element of surprise.

His palms growing slick with sweat, John inched nearer. The person was bent over at the waist, so he could not tell much other than that the figure wore dark clothes and had something pale in its right hand. Swallowing, he planted both feet, tucked the stock to his shoulder, and barked, "Don't move, whoever you are! I'm the owner and I have you covered."

The figure uncoiled and threw up its arms. "Please don't shoot, mister! I didn't mean to disturb anyone!"

John cocked his head. The voice was that of an elderly woman, but not anyone he knew. "Who are you, lady? What are you doing here?"

"I'm Martha Eldridge."

Astounded, John walked up to her, forgetting about the shotgun. She swiveled, gasping when her nose brushed the barrel. "I'm sorry," he apologized, quickly lowering it. "If I had known who you were . . ." Feeling he had made a royal fool of himself, he left the statement unfinished.

"That's all right, young man. I understand. I would do the same thing if I were in your shoes."

The woman stood. She was short and squat, her hair streaked with gray. An aura of gentleness clung to her like a cloak, reflected in the benevolent cast of her features and her compassionate smile.

John glanced at her right hand. It clasped a single yellow rose. "What are you doing here, Mrs. Eldridge?" he inquired, going on hastily. "Not that I mind, you understand. You're perfectly welcome to visit any time you like. It's just that it would have been best if you had let us know in advance. This place is . . ." He paused, seeking the right word, a word that wouldn't remind her of her husband's tragic end.

"Dangerous?" Martha finished for him. "Believe me, Mr. Grant, I know. I dare say I know more about this old farm than you do. A lot more." She touched the rose. "I knew that I should stay away, but I just had to see for myself. I had to see where my dear George met his Maker."

John stared into the dark depths of the spring. "I wish I could impress on you how sorry I am.

If I had known the accident would happen, I would never have asked your husband's help in unlocking the door."

"Accident, Mr. Grant?" Martha said. "Please don't patronize me. We both know darn well that it was no accident. My George was killed by the spooks."

"Possibly," John said, thinking it would be easier on her if she accepted the accident theory. "The police suspect foul play, but it has yet to be proven."

The woman snorted. "Proven! You can find all the proof you need in the Spook Hollow Library. Go there sometimes, Mr. Grant, and check the back issues of the *Spook Hollow Gazette*. You'll be amazed at what you find."

"Maybe I will," John said to appease her. "But in the meantime, how about if I walk you to your car?"

"Afraid I'll suffer the same fate as my George?" Martha said. "Don't fret yourself. The spooks mainly come out at night." Facing the spring, she raised the rose to her lips and gently kissed a petal. "This is in memory of you, my love," she said softly as she dropped the flower into the water. It bobbed a few times, then floated toward the other side.

John said nothing. The poignant gesture moved him deeply, sparking a tidal wave of gushing guilt. He wished there were something he could say or do to relieve the widow's profound grief. But of course there wasn't.

"My George was always fond of roses," Martha was saying. "Especially yellow ones. When he wasn't working on locks, he did so love to putter in his little garden."

As she headed for the door, John fell into step beside her. "If I can be of any help in any way," he offered sincerely.

Martha studied his profile. "That's awful decent of you, Mr. Grant. But you're the one who needs help, you and your family. If you ask me, you should get them out of here. Today. Spirit them back to that big city you came from or anywhere else on God's green earth. But don't stay in that dreadful farmhouse another night. Not if you value their lives."

John patted the shotgun. "You needn't worry on our behalf, Mrs. Eldridge. If that madman on the horse shows up again, I intend to do whatever is necessary to protect us."

"A gun is useless on spooks. Didn't your mother ever tell you that?"

John thought she had to be jesting, but her countenance showed she was in earnest. It would be impossible to set her straight. Her superstitious beliefs were too ingrained. So he didn't try.

"The previous owner thought he could defend his loved ones too," she said. "After his dog and horse were killed, he took to patrolling the farm with a 30.06 rifle. Fat lot of good it did him."

"You knew Mr. Powell?" John asked, extremely interested. "The real estate agent, Miss

Ferguson, told me that he gave up the farm because he couldn't keep up the payments."

Martha Eldridge stepped out into the bright sunlight and halted. "Susie Ferguson would do anything to make a sale, even tell a whopper of a lie like that." She gazed up at the house, trepidation etching her face. "No, Mr. Grant. Powell gave up the farm because he was grief-stricken after the death of his wife."

John's blood chilled in his veins. "Do you know all the details?"

"Most of them. Powell was a nice man. He used to come to bingo at church every Wednesday night." Martha smoothed a wrinkle on her dress which did not need smoothing, as if she were stalling. At length she said, "Some folks tried to warn him, but he wouldn't listen. He was a lot like you. A city boy. He scoffed at the notion of spooks and such. So he learned the truth the hard way."

"What happened?" John prompted.

"Well, as I recall, first he complained of hearing someone pound on the springhouse door late at night. Then he found his dog hacked to bits right about here." Martha pointed at the ground in front of them. "A few days later they found his horse out in the field north of the barn. Someone had cut off all four legs and ripped its tongue out."

"My God," John said. "When did all this occur?"

"About a week or so before last Halloween,"

202

Martha answered. "The usual time." She looked at the house again, and shuddered. "His wife was killed on Halloween night. Someone broke in while Powell was gone. Tore her head clean off her shoulders."

John thought of Laurie and grew even colder. "Someone should have told me," he said angrily.

"Don't blame the folks hereabouts," Martha said. "The Headless Horror of Spook Hollow isn't a favorite topic of discussion. Those who believe would rather sweep the whole thing under the rug, while those who aren't believers think it's too ridiculous for words." She pivoted, peering into the springhouse. "I believe, but my George didn't. Not wholeheartedly. He kept saying there had to be a rational explanation." Clucking to herself, she added, "That's what killed him, Mr. Grant. His failure to believe. So don't blame yourself." Tears dampened her eyes. "That man was too darned pigheaded for his own good."

John started to follow her as she walked off around the corner, but she stopped and held out a weathered hand.

"Please, I'd rather be alone right now, young man. My car is just down your drive a little ways. I'll be all right by myself."

"I don't mind tagging along," John offered, but she shook her head and departed, her body slumped in sorrow. He waited until she was lost in the trees before he turned and climbed the steep hill.

The information Martha Eldridge had imparted gave him much food for sober thought. He began to question if staying was such a bright idea, if perhaps he shouldn't have listened to his wife. Standing up to the lunatic in the costume still seemed like the right thing to do, but not if it meant he would lose the one he cared for most in the world. Her life, or the lives of their children, constituted too high a price to pay for the luxury of defiance.

A shadow fell across his legs. John grabbed for the shotgun, then saw it was only Buck. "Don't sneak up on people like that," he scolded. "The next time I might accidentally blow your brains out."

The mongrel whined and rubbed against him.

"Let me guess. You're hungry." John stroked the dog's neck. Above him, the slam of the screen door served the same function as the shriek of an early warning siren.

Tina Brewster's brow roiled with ominous thunder. She stalked toward him, her fists bunched, her teeth clenched like those of a feral dog about to bite.

John tried to nonchalantly swing the shotgun behind his back but it was too late.

"Don't try hiding your cannon," Tina rasped. "As if that thing will do you any good." Barring his path, she poked a long pink nail into his chest. "She told me everything, and it's worse than I thought. I want all of you ready to leave within the hour. You're coming to live with me until we can find you a place of your own."

Something clicked inside him, an internal fuse tripped by her abrasive attitude. But then, she always had that effect on him. "We'll make our own decisions about where we will live, thank you very much."

Tina poked harder. "I heard all about your decision, buddy boy. A family vote? Don't make me laugh. Your lives are at stake and you indulge in a juvenile exercise in parental democracy."

Not one minute ago John Grant had been willing to leave. If his wife had walked out and asked him to, he would have said yes in an instant. Now, he met his sister-in-law's glare with one of his own and stated out of sheer spite, "Butt out, Tina. This doesn't concern you."

"Like hell it doesn't! Laurie, Kip, and Shery mean more to me than anything. If you want to commit suicide, that's your business. But I'll be damned if I'll let you take them down with you."

"Has Laurie already agreed to go?"

Tina's eyes blazed lightning bolts. "No. I tried my best, but she won't split unless the kids and you leave too." Grabbing his wrist, she dug in her nails. "Listen to me, you bastard. If you don't wise up, you're liable to get all of them killed."

"Is it so wrong for us to stand up for what's ours?" John asked her. Yanking his wrist free, he rose to his full height and said, "Tell me something, Tina. All these years you've hated my guts. I'd like to know why."

She never missed a beat. "Because my sister

deserves better. I knew you'd never amount to much, and I was right." Tina encompassed the farm with a sweep of her arm. "Look at this. The Waltons' mountain all over again." She paused. "What are you trying to prove?"

"I didn't move to Spook Hollow to prove anything," John said. "But now that you mention it, maybe I would like to prove one thing."

"Like what?"

"That it's still possible in this day and age for a family to live the way families should live. Caring, concerned, committed to one another. Is that so bad?"

Tina sniffed in contempt. "You're pathetic, Grant. You're a throwback to the days of fifties sitcoms. Get with the program. Traditional families are a thing of the past."

"Like hell they are."

Whirling, Tina Brewster stomped off, slinging over an arched shoulder, "This isn't over, mister. Not by a long shot." John Grant stared after her, thinking to himself, *What on earth have I just done?*

As if in answer, for no reason at all, Buck threw back his head and howled.

Chapter Thirteen

"You must have had a terrible day," Amy Westbrook remarked.

Kip Grant stifled a yawn in the act of opening his mouth. Giving his head a vigorous shake to dispel clinging tendrils of fatigue, he asked, "Is it that obvious?"

"Afraid so. You look as if you're about to keel over."

"I am," Kip admitted. "It's been a bear." And not through any fault of his. For starters, he'd barely slept a wink all night. Every time he'd started to doze off, he had been jarred awake by a gut-wrenching feeling that the Headless Horror was creeping toward his bed. Several times he had sat bolt upright and surveyed his room in blatant terror, absolutely certain it was really happening. Each time, though, the room mocked him with its emptiness.

Then came morning. His delight at seeing his aunt again soon gave way to irritation when she made a federal case out of his going to school. Aunt Tina insisted he spend the day in bed to recover from his ordeal, and she persuaded his mom to go along with the idea. Repeatedly, he told them that he was fine, that he actually wanted to go, but Aunt Tina refused to listen. "No boy in his right mind *wants* to go to school!" were her exact words.

It didn't help matters any that Kip couldn't reveal his reason. He wanted to see Amy, but he wasn't about to bare his heart to them.

The situation looked hopeless. Then his dad came in and announced that Chief Bogartus wanted to see Shery and him that morning to file reports. Aunt Tina got on his dad's case about "dragging the poor kids off to be interrogated by the local Gestapo when they're still recovering from being severely traumatized."

About that time, Shery waltzed into the kitchen dressed in one of her slinky outfits, merrily humming a rock tune.

So Kip wound up in a stark room at the Spook Hollow Police Station, answering the same questions again and again for two and a half hours. Bogartus quizzed him in person. And while the chief was polite and considerate, there was an intensity about him that Kip had found unnerving. The chief was particularly interested in his description of the headless figure, going over it point by point so many times that Kip grew tired of answering the same questions.

Then came school. Kip didn't arrived until almost noon, so he figured he would skate through the rest of the day with no problem. He was wrong. Somehow, word had already spread. Every last student knew about Kimble's death, and every last one wanted to hear the gory details from Kip's own lips.

Now, the sun on its westward arc in the azure vault of sky, Kip was walking Amy Westbrook home and trying to stay awake at the same time. He was so tired that he didn't mind that Tommy Lee had tagged along. His friend walked along the edge of Blackgap Road, tossing rocks into Monongahela Creek.

They had already passed the Harper place. Ahead reared the Gothic home of Alva Jackson. Kip's stomach balled into a knot. His last encounter with the eccentric recluse had left him anxious to avoid another. He hoped they could slip on by without being noticed.

Suddenly a shadow detached itself from the wide trunk of a willow tree. It was the old woman. Only this time she wore a black dress instead of a white one, and she moved with the prim decorum of a proper lady rather than dancing about like a dervish. "Hello, children," she said to them pleasantly.

Amy stopped and smiled. "Hi, Mrs. Jackson. Haven't seen much of you in a while."

"I've been around, my dear. Busy, but around."

Kip took Amy's elbow to steer her along. "Nice seeing you," he said, "but I promised my folks I'd be home by sunset. So we have to be going."

"Kip!" Amy said.

Alva Jackson tittered. "Oh, that's perfectly all right, Amy darling. Your boyfriend's atrocious manners are understandable. He think's I'm crazy, you see."

"I do not," Kip responded, blushing. Amy glanced at him, her own cheeks tinged crimson, although why that should be, he didn't know. Over at the bank, Tommy Lee stood poised with a rock in hand, gaping at the recluse as if she were a creature from another planet.

Alva Jackson came right up to them. She was even taller than Kip had imagined, taller than his father by at least five inches. "I would be honored, children," she said softly, "if the three of you would join me for a little snack."

"We can't," Kip responded before anyone else could. If that woman thought she could lure them into her house, she had another think coming.

"I won't keep you long," Alva said. "See? I have cookies and milk already set out on my patio." She indicated a small courtyard adjoining her dwelling on the south side. Low brick walls enclosed a fountain, a table, and chairs. "Please. I so rarely have company."

Kip was going to refuse, but Amy thwarted

him by nodding and letting the woman clasp her other arm. Reluctantly, he went along, noticing that the recluse seldom took her piercing eyes off him.

Tommy Lee had bounded over at the mention of food and assumed the lead. "Nice place you've got here, ma'am," he said in his patented drawl. "It reminds me of that spooky house where the Adams Family lives."

"And that's a nice accent you have, young man," Alva responded. "Your family is from the South too, I gather?"

"Virginia, ma'am."

"How fortunate for you. My roots are in Atlanta. A distant relative of mine was one of the founding fathers of that fair city." She proudly held her head high. "Blue bloods, some might call us. Although, of course, no knowledgeable person would ever use that term to describe a true son or daughter of the South." She winked at Tommy Lee, and he laughed.

"Why not?" Amy asked.

Alva peered down her long nose. "Really, child. I expect better from you. Surely you're heard of the War for Southern Independence? Or have they stopped teaching about it in the schools, just like they have everything else of any value?"

"You mean the Civil War," Amy said. "Oh, yes. They still teach it. Mr. Gunther, our history teacher, spent a whole week on the subject."

"One whole week? Mercy me. I wonder he

could spare the time." Alva chuckled and stroked Amy's arm. "Pay me no mind, child. For some of us, the war has never ended and never will. So we take it a mite more seriously than most."

Kip had not intended to say one word, but he couldn't help himself. "After all this time you still hold a grudge?"

Alva halted so unexpectedly that Amy nearly lost her balance. "A *grudge*, young man? The war destroyed our way of life forever. It destroyed the cream of Southern manhood in the prime of their lives. And it gave the Yankees an excuse to lord it over us and rob us blind. So, yes, I suppose you could say that some of us still hold a *grudge*."

"My pa does," Tommy Lee mentioned. "When he has a few six-packs under his belt he likes to talk about the day the South will rise again and teach the blue-bellies a lesson." He grinned at Kip. "No offense to you, bud. You can't help being born north of the Mason-Dixon."

Alva's mirth wafted on the breeze. "I do declare, son! I'll have to invite your entire family over soon so we can swap tales about the glorious days of the Southland."

They reached the courtyard. A pair of steps led up to an elevated patio constructed of flagstone. On the white table sat a full pitcher of milk, a plate heaped high with chocolate-chip cookies, and four glasses, one at each chair.

Tommy Lee took a seat without being asked. "Hey!" he declared. "You've set out just enough for everybody. How did you know we'd all be by?"

"I knew," Alva said enigmatically. She poured milk for each of them, then passed out two cookies apiece. Tommy Lee helped himself to two more.

"So," Alva said, facing Kip, "have you given any thought to our chat the other night?"

"Not really," Kip answered. With all that had happened, he'd forgotten about her cryptic words of warning. Now they came back to him in a rush of clarity, and he paused with his glass halfway to his lips. "You knew, didn't you? You knew the Headless Horror would come after my family."

"Didn't I say as much?" Alva rejoined. "If you'd listened, if you'd warned your blood kin, your sister and your pa might have been spared the nightmares they went through. It's still not too late for all of you." She gazed soberly toward South Mountain. "See the truth, child, and it will set you free."

"What truth? That one-plus-one nonsense you were raving about?" Kip said sarcastically. "All you do is speak in riddles, lady. If you want me to see the truth, quit beating around the bush."

Alva's visage acquired the cast of granite. "It's getting to you, isn't it, boy? You're not as cocksure of yourself as you were the last time we talked. You sense, don't you, that your whole family is doomed."

"I sense no such thing!" Kip stated, so agitated

that he smacked the glass down and spilled some of the milk. Amy and Tommy Lee were shocked, but he didn't care. He was tired of the woman's games. "You claim you know so much! Then tell me how to stop the spook, or whatever the hell it is."

"I already have."

Kip was so mad that he crumpled the cookie in his left hand without being aware of it. "There you ago again. Spell it out in plain English. I'm sure my friends would like to hear. They live on this road too. They're probably in as much danger as I am."

"Only sweet Amy."

"What?" both Amy and Tommy Lee said at the same time.

"I wish it were otherwise," Alva Jackson said. "I truly do. But what's done is done, and nothing I can do can change the past." She bowed her head. "If only you could appreciate how difficult this is for me, Kipland Albert Grant. If my ma were alive, she'd brand me a turncoat to the cause. If my great-grandma were still with us, she'd have me strung up by my thumbs and horsewhipped." Closing her eyes, she uttered a racking sob. "I've already told you more than I should. You'll have to figure out the rest on your own, boy. I'm sorry." Tears streamed down her bony face.

Kip did not know what to say. Amy rose and tugged at his sleeve, so he stood and went with her. Tommy Lee followed, but only after stuffing cookies into both front pockets. None of them uttered a word until they were back on Blackgap Road.

"Will one of you please tell me what the dickens that was all about?" Tommy Lee said, his mouth so crammed that his words were slurred.

"She's not in her right mind," Kip said.

Amy was staring at the patio where the old woman still sat with quaking shoulders. "I don't know," she said uncertainly. "I think she was being as honest with you as she could. To tell the truth, I sort of feel sorry for her, yet I can't say why."

"What was that stuff about the two of you having a talk?" Tommy Lee asked.

Kip gave them the gist of his previous conversation. When he got to the part about the strange green glow, his friend perked up.

"You don't say? Right there on South Mountain?" Tommy Lee scoured the dense forest on the lower slopes. "Now that would be a sight to see. We should check it out. It must have something to do with the spook."

"Say what?" Kip said.

"Not right this minute," Tommy Lee said. "Later this week would be better. Say, Friday or Saturday. None of us have to worry about homework and we can stay out a little later than usual. What do you think?"

"That you're as loony as Alva Jackson," Kip stated. He had learned his lesson on the school bus. Under no circumstances would he traipse off into the wilderness after that monstrosity. Whether it was flesh and blood or something else was beside the point. It *killed* people. His resolve, however, melted like wax under a blowtorch with Amy's next statement.

"I think it's a good idea, Tommy Lee. Count me in."

Kip snatched her hand. "Are you as crazy as he is? That spook, as everyone calls it, killed Mr. Kimble. Maybe Mr. Eldridge too. And if all the tales are true, it's done the same to a lot of others over the years. Do you want to wind up like them?"

"No," Amy said, "but I would like to get to the bottom of this." She headed homeward, making no effort to loosen his grip. "As you just pointed out, this has been going on for as long as I can remember. Every so often the spook appears out of nowhere, terrorizes people a while, then disappears again." She looked at him. "My mom and dad have always laughed at the stories. But after Mr. Kimble's death, they're not so sure. Neither am I. And since we're not moving away any time soon, I figure it's in my own best interests to learn the truth."

"You and me, both, babe," Tommy Lee said. "I'm with you one hundred percent."

Resisting an urge to kick his friend in the shins, Kip made one last try. "I say we play it safe. Let's just lay low until after Halloween."

"And what about the dance?" Amy brought up. "Do we stay home that night too?"

Spook Night

Kip knew a lost cause when he saw one. Tommy Lee was grinning like an idiot at the prospect of their grand adventure. And the girl of his dreams was clearly determined to get some answers. "All right," he sighed in resignation. "We'll pretend we're the Three Musketeers and see this thing through. But don't say I didn't warn you. I can't help thinking that we're making the biggest mistake of our life."

Tommy Lee shrugged. "Hey, bud, what's the big deal? No one lives forever."

"Maybe so, but I thought it would be nice to at least graduate from high school."

Shery Grant couldn't exactly say why she decided to go home before the sun even set. It was so unlike her, it bordered on the bizarre. She had Bryce Harcourt drop her off.

The school's star quarterback was coming along nicely. She wasn't going to let him score until the night of the big dance, yet he doted on her as if she were the Queen of Sheba, dogging her footsteps like an overgrown puppy dog.

Boys were so predictable, Shery reflected as she strolled up the front walk. All a girl had to do was bat her eyelashes, nibble on an ear or two while letting the poor jerks cop an occasional feel, and any boy alive was hers to do with as she pleased. It always gave her a sense of tremendous power when she wrapped a boy around her little pinkie.

The quiet of early evening was rent by her

father's bellow as Shery strolled up the front walk. Mentally crossing her fingers that she wasn't to blame, she went in and discovered him on the sofa with the newspaper in his lap. He looked outraged enough to chew concrete. "Something wrong?"

"They're claiming it was an accident! Can you believe it! After what Kip saw! After what *I* saw!" John Grant shook the paper so hard it ripped at the top. He had gone down to the mailbox minutes ago, curious to learn if any additional information had been learned by the police. Tucking the paper under an arm, he hadn't glanced at the headline until he was on the sofa. At first glance, he'd thought he must be seeing things.

"BUS DRIVER DIES IN FREAK ACCIDENT" was the banner headline. The story went on to relate how the bus had become stuck at the last stop of the day, on Blackgap Road. Samuel J. Kimble, the driver, had walked to a local market and phoned Garth's Towing. But Garth had been off on a prior call. His helper had told Kimble it would be an hour or more before the tow truck could get there. Kimble had agreed to stay with the bus until then.

That had been the last contact the driver had had with anyone. According to the paper, his body had been found by a "local junior high student." Kimble, the account claimed, had apparently opened the hood to "fiddle with the carburetor," against district policy. Why he should do so, the reporter couldn't say. But evidently, as Kimble climbed down, he had bumped the brace. The hood had crashed down onto his neck, its sharp bottom edge shearing clean through and decapitating him. A "freak mishap," the paper called it. A "one-in-a-million fluke."

All this John told Shery, finishing with: "What a pack of lies! A bus hood isn't a guillotine. It can't slice a man's head off, for God's sake. And there's no mention of the man in the costume. Or an explanation of how Kimble managed to crawl back into the driver's seat without his head attached."

Shery had to smile. "Get real, Dad. What else did you expect? That they'd come right out in the paper and admit there is some truth to that old legend?"

John looked at her in blank confusion. "But there is a killer at large. This isn't Philadelphia or New York. The police can't cover something like this up. I won't let them."

"What will you do?"

"Go to the paper. Tell them my version. Tell them I saw the psycho with my own eyes."

"And you honestly think they'll accept your version over the police report?"

John did a double take. He was so accustomed to his daughter acting the part of the perfect space cadet, he tended to forget that she could be shrewdly practical when she wanted to be. In this case she had hit the proverbial nail on the head. If the Spook Hollow police were engaged in some kind of cover-up, the newspaper staff must be in league with them. Or whoever had the last word on what got printed. "You might have a point," he conceded.

Shery walked on, patting him on the head as she went by. Halfway down the hall she heard clashing voices, and halted. Her mother and her aunt were going at it again, exactly as they had been doing when she left that morning.

"—won't leave and that's final," her mother was saying. "Now will you drop the damn subject?"

"Not on your life," Aunt Tina responded. "If you weren't such a spineless jellyfish, you'd do what's right. March out there and tell him to go to Hell. Tell him you're taking the kids to Philly whether he likes it or not. Tell him—"

Shery had heard enough. She liked her Aunt Tina, but there were times when the woman went full-tilt gonzo. And she was in no mood to put up with Tina's constant carping. Retracing her steps past her father, who had his nose buried in the paper and was puffing like a porpoise that had just surfaced for air, she went outside and leaned against a porch post.

Trudging up the drive came Kip. He blinked on seeing her, consulted his watch, glanced at the setting sun, and said, "Are you sick? It's still daylight."

"Good one, twerp," Shery shot back. "Keep at it and we'll book you on the Comedy Network."

Spook Night

Kip set his book on a chair. In order to be home before dark he had jogged all the way from Tommy Lee's. His feet were sore and he was caked with sweat. "What's up?" he asked. "Why are you home so early?"

"Maybe I was worried about all of you," Shery confessed. Realizing the slip she had made, she blustered, "Or maybe the day has just been a major bummer and I wanted to catch up on my beauty rest."

"Then why are you out here instead of in there?" Kip asked, hiding his amazement that she would admit she cared. It was so unlike her that for a few seconds he wondered if she had been dabbling in drugs again, as she had a few years ago until one of her friends died of an overdose and she came to her senses.

"Adult Central in there," Shery said. "Dad is in a huff because he can't fight city hall, and Mom and Aunt Tina are still playing pit bull."

"Just great," Kip muttered. He had been looking forward to crashing out, but he knew if he went inside, he'd be drawn into the debate over whether they should stay or go. To delay the inevitable, he asked, "Have you seen Buck anywhere? We've been neglecting him lately. I'll treat him to a game of fetch."

"Some treat," Shery cracked.

Kip headed around the north side of the house. The shadows were lengthening. Premature twilight shrouded the springhouse, and soon the barn and other outbuildings would be claimed as well. "Buck!" he hollered. "Come here, boy!" Going to the nearest maple, he selected a suitable stick.

Shery watched from the corner. She had nothing better to do, she told herself, and she sure as hell wasn't going inside yet.

When Buck didn't appear, Kip strolled across the lawn in search of him. Sometimes the mongrel liked to lie in the shade between the barn and the chicken coop, but the dog wasn't there. The right-hand door to the barn hung open, as it had since the police checked the property. Guessing that Buck had strayed inside, Kip entered, but only took a few steps. The barn was warm and muggy, as it always had been. "Yo, Buck? Where the heck are you, boy? Come on out and play."

Shery saw her brother go in, but did not think anything of it since she could still see him. She arched her back, and was going to stretch when three things happened simultaneously.

Buck stepped into view near the woodshed.

The sun sank below the horizon.

And with the air so still that not a single leaf fluttered anywhere in sight, the huge barn door swung shut all by itself.

Chapter Fourteen

Kip Grant was on edge the moment he entered the murky confines of the barn. He never had liked being in there. It always gave him a bad feeling, an inexplicable sense of impending danger so powerful that he had to choke down an impulse to whirl and flee.

On this day that feeling was particularly strong. Kip would have jumped at his own shadow, and knew it. So when a different, much more immense shadow enveloped him and spread down the aisle, he yelped and whirled. He was stunned to see the barn door closing, seemingly of its own accord. Then it occurred to him who must be to blame.

"Very funny, Sis!" Kip called out. "Quit fooling around, will you?"

Shery Grant heard muffled words, but could

not quite make them out. She was halfway to the barn, dread gnawing at her heart like a termite on wood.

Common sense told her there had to be a logical explanation why the door had closed. Maybe it was off-kilter. The ground appeared flat at the front of the barn, but maybe it sloped just enough for gravity to come into play. She reached the building just as the door began to swing outward.

Kip had not waited for his sister to open it for him. He had dashed over and pushed. On seeing Shery standing there with a weird expression, he snickered and said, "Nice try, but you didn't scare me one bit."

"I didn't do it," Shery said, embarrassed at how upset she had become for no real reason.

"Sure, and cows can fly."

Shery bristled at being accused of something she hadn't done. "Hey, dork. I'm telling you the truth. If you weren't such a dweeb, you'd know that."

"Uh-huh," Kip said. "Better luck next time." Amused that she would think him so gullible, he moved toward the stalls. "Buck? Where are you, big guy?"

Indignant, Shery took a few steps toward him, intending to give him a piece of her mind. She stopped when he yelled, and laughed. "I rest my case."

"What?" Kip said.

"You boogerhead. Buck is out by the wood-shed. I just saw him."

Kip didn't know whether to believe her or not. As long as he could remember, she had delighted in teasing him or making him out to be the prize chump of the Western Hemisphere. There were times when he thought that they would never be able to hold a conversation without taking digs at each other. He stared at her, trying to determine if she was sincere, and tensed as the door swung shut again behind her. "I'll be damned," he blurted. "I guess I owe you an apology."

A distinct thud made Shery turn. Darkness shrouded her as she stepped forward. "What is it about doors at this place?" she groused. "First the springhouse door wouldn't ever open. Then that bathroom door jammed on me. And now this nonsense." She braced her palms against the wood and shoved. Nothing happened. Throwing her weight into it, she tried the left-hand door. It wouldn't move either. "What the hell?"

Kip laughed. "What a wimp. It's not that heavy." Going over, he joked, "You need to exercise more, Sis. A five-year-old could open this."

"Oh, yeah? Let's see you do it."

Digging in both sneakers, Kip heaved against the right side. Since the door had opened so easily the last time, he assumed it would do so again. To his consternation, it was like pushing against a concrete slab. "Bizarre," he commented, and strained once more. The door did not move so much as an inch. Stepping back, he studied it. "This can't be."

"Duh!" Shery taunted. "Let's try together."

Shoulder to shoulder, brother and sister put their combined muscles into the task. They might as well have been attempting to open a locked bank vault.

"This just can't be," Kip reiterated. He shivered, and realized the air around them had grown as cold as the air inside a deep freeze. On exhaling, he saw his breath. "Hey, look," he said, doing it again for Shery's benefit. "What's going on? The temperature outside is close to seventy."

Shery could feel goose bumps breaking out all over her. "I don't like this one bit," she announced. It gave her a trapped feeling. She hurled herself against the door several times in swift succession, to no avail.

"If we shout, maybe someone will come," Kip proposed.

Dubious, Shery nonetheless cupped her hands to her mouth. "Mom! Dad! Aunt Tina! Let us out of here!"

Kip added his voice. They hollered for over a minute, but no one answered or appeared. "It's hopeless," he said in due course. "They can't hear us. We're too far from the house."

"There must be another way out," Shery said, swiveling around. The lower level of the barn was mired in shadow growing darker by the moment. A musty scent clung to everything. She moved along the aisle, scanning the hayloft to her left and the dim outline of the ladder which led up to it. "I've got an idea," she said. "Let's open the loft door and shout. They're bound to hear us then."

"If they don't, we can always jump," Kip suggested.

"And break a leg? No, thank you," Shery said crisply as she made for the wooden ladder, located at the very rear. A noise gave her pause. From one of the stalls further down issued a scratching sound, as of claws on a rough surface. Her skin prickled anew. "Do you hear that?"

Kip stopped in his tracks. In his mind's eye he relived his nightmare on the bus; he saw the Headless Horror stalk toward him; he saw Kimble's head tucked under one arm. Panic seized him. A scream nearly tore from his throat. Biting down on his lower lip to stifle it, he shook himself and forced his mouth to work. "Probably a mouse," he said without conviction.

The scratching stopped. Shery resumed walking, but slowly, her nerves stretched taut. When something brushed her left elbow, she jumped.

Kip had joined her. "We should stick together," he said, worried for her safety as well as his own. It rattled him to think that the killer might be hiding in there. Whether it was the madman his father claimed, or something far worse, hardly seemed important. In either case, their lives would be on the line. Staying close to her, he took a few more steps.

More scratching broke out, this time from the front of the barn. Both of them spun. A muted whine and loud sniffing let them know who it was.

"It's just that stupid dog," Shery growled. She partly blamed Buck for the fix they were in since he hadn't come when called. The mongrel barked a few times, then launched into a loud, lingering howl. "Figures. We're the ones who can't get out, and he acts as if his paw is caught in a trap."

Kip was inspecting the stalls they passed. He turned to stone on hearing a small animal scuttle across a timber directly overhead. Glancing up, he thought that he saw a pair of reddish eyes staring back at him. He blinked, and they were gone. "Did you see that?" he asked.

"What?" Shery was almost to the ladder. She skirted a bale of hay. A pile of twine lay nearby.

"An animal, I guess," Kip said. But the size of those eyes troubled him. They had been too large for a mouse or a rat.

"Must be a raccoon," Shery guessed. "Dad told me that they found a dead one in here the other night."

Kip had completely forgotten. "That's right," he said, relaxing. "And raccoons don't bother people unless they're rabid."

"There's a comforting thought," Shery said. Gripping the sides of the ladder, she started to lift her right foot. As she did, something constricted around her ankle, holding her leg in place. Perplexed, she looked down. In dawning horror she beheld the twine looping itself around her ankle. It slithered and flowed just like a snake would. "Kip!" she exclaimed breathlessly.

"What?" Kip responded, his gaze on the rafters. When she gasped, he turned. His sister was frozen with fright. On the floor, something moved. He leaned down for a closer look, and suddenly had to spring back as she was yanked violently off her feet. "Sis!"

Shery felt the twine tighten, felt herself being pulled. She grabbed a rung of the ladder and held on. Her right leg jutted into the air. The twine was stretched tight as if someone were hauling on the other end—*only no one was there!* "Kip!" she repeated, bewildered. "How—?"

Before Kip could answer, the twine gave a sharp wrench and his sister lost her hold. He lunged as she went shooting off across the floor, but missed. Straightening, he was aghast to witness her hurtling toward one of the stalls. "Look out!" he warned.

The corner of the stall rushed toward Shery at amazing speed. She twisted, striving to miss it. The twine gave another jerk. She was whipped into the end of the stall with bone-jarring force. Her right shoulder went numb. In vain she clawed at the floor, seeking to slow herself down. Instead, she went faster, the twine lancing through the air as if it were a thin spear. This time whatever was on the other end dragged her toward the door.

"No!" Kip thundered, giving chase. He was so worried for her welfare that he hardly noticed the temperature had dropped even further. If not for his encounter with the spook in the bus, he would have been convinced he was going off the deep end.

Twine did not come to life. Twine did not wrap itself around a person. Twine could not drag someone behind it. Yet that was exactly what the twine was doing.

Or was it?

Kip glanced at the other end. The same pair of reddish eyes were suspended in the air inches from the frayed tip. Again, when he blinked, the red eyes disappeared. But he was sure he had seen them, that they weren't a figment of his imagination.

Shery tugged on her leg with all her might. It was as if her ankle were locked in the jaws of a shark. The twine wouldn't give, wouldn't weaken. Reaching down, Kip clutched at it, but couldn't hold on.

Outside, Buck continued to howl.

Running as he had never run before, Kip Grant gained. Taking two more long strides, he dived. His outflung hands closed on his sister's right arm. He attempted to brace his knees to bring them to a stop, but their momentum was too great. The addition of his weight, though, slowed her down, so that when the twine whipped in an arc as it had done at the stall, the two of them rolled into the bottom of the right-hand door instead of smashing into it. Bruised and scuffed, Kip firmed his hold.

Shery sought an anchor to grab. The twine gave a weak pull, then went as limp as a strand of overcooked spaghetti and plopped to the floor. In seconds she unwound the loops around her ankle. She tossed the coils into the shadows. Rising with her back to the door, Shery swallowed to lubricate her dry mouth. "How could that happen?" she rasped. "What in God's name are we dealing with?"

"You're asking me?" Kip rejoined, barely able to hear her over the mongrel's howls. He eased onto his knees.

No movement broke the stillness. The gloom was now so thick that they could hardly see their hands at arm's length.

"We have to try for the loft again," Kip said.

"Not on your life."

"It's the only way out," Kip insisted. To demonstrate his point, he rammed his shoulder into the door a few times. All it did was make Buck howl louder.

Shery balked. To reach the loft they had to scale the ladder, and she was not about to venture back into the depths of the barn again for any reason. "Mom or Dad or Tina is bound to come eventually," she said. "Let's sit tight until they do."

Her fear was transparent. Under different circumstances Kip might have poked fun at her for being a wuss. But now he was solely preoccupied with getting both of them out of there alive.

In the dim recesses of the barn, something moved. Kip and Shery saw it at the same time. Something as as tall as Kip but as thin as a broom handle. Ever so slowly, it slid toward them as if gliding on thin air.

"What is that?" Kip whispered.

Shery did not know. Nor did she want to stick around to find out. Whirling, she hurled herself at the door, pushing and pounding in a frenzy of frantic fear.

The object moved to the center of the aisle. It hovered a few feet off the ground. Kip's eyes narrowed. A dull glint of metal low down gave him a clue to what it might be. "It's a hoe!" he declared. "Or maybe a rake!"

It can't be, Shery was going to reply. Only in light of the twine attack, doing so would be absurd. The term "reality" no longer had any meaning. It had been rent asunder, casting them into the outer limits of a twilight zone where the unreal became real, where the impossible became possible, where things that went bump in the night came to life with a vengeance.

The thing floated nearer, moving from side to side as if to prevent them from darting past. It had a long handle, just as a hoe or rake would. But it wasn't a hoe or rake. It was much more deadly than that.

"Oh, God!" Kip cried. "It's a pitchfork!"

Shery could see that for herself. She pressed against the door and sucked in her gut to make a less conspicuous target.

The pitchfork coasted to a stop. It rotated on an invisible axis. The long, wicked tines swung up and out so that the four razor tips were pointed at them.

Kip Grant knew what would happen next, and came to an immediate decision. "I'll draw it off," he said. "When I make my move, you hall ass for the ladder and don't look back, Sis. Keep going until you reach the loft door."

"I'll do no such thing," Shery said.

Kip figured that she was afraid but would move once he did, so he skipped to the left. The pitchfork glided a corresponding distance, those nasty prongs trained on his chest. When he stopped, so did the implement.

Shery quit cowering and straightened. As it sank in that her little brother was risking his life to save hers, the fear dominating her was supplanted by rising anger. *She* was the oldest. *She* was the one who should be bailing his butt out of the fire, not the other way around. "We split for the ladder together," she said.

Kip could not afford to take his eyes off the tines. At any moment the pitchfork was going to come at him. He had to be ready. "Don't argue!" he responded. "For once in your life do what I tell you without giving me a hard time."

"No way, moron," Shery said. She took a step, and the pitchfork promptly swung to cover her.

Kip had long wondered if his sister was 50 bricks shy of a full load, and now he had proof. They were in grave peril, up against something beyond their comprehension, and she saw fit to make a federal case out of him trying to save her. "Just go!" he stated, taking another step to the left.

The pitchfork rotated, aiming at him again. It hung in the air as soundlessly as dust, as still as death. No red eyes were visible, but Kip knew as surely as he lived and breathed that they were fixed on him in relentless hatred.

"It can't get both of us at once, so we go on the count of three," Shery said. "One—."

Kip wanted to rail at her for being a pigheaded ding-a-ling, but he knew it would do no good. When she made up her mind, that was it. She would never change it.

"Two!"

As if it knew what they were up to, the pitchfork shifted from one to the other while edging steadily nearer.

"Three!" Shery called out, and bolted, hunching her shoulders as she did. The pitchfork was pointed at her, so she had every right to expect it would zero in on her first, but it did the opposite.

Realizing that he had no choice, Kip bounded down the aisle at the same instant his sister did. He saw that it had turned toward her so he bellowed, "Try me!" to draw its attention. The ruse worked. With a piercing hiss the pitchfork cleaved the air, streaking toward his face. More by accident than design, he ducked low at the right moment. It missed him by a fraction. He heard a thud, and glanced back to see the prongs imbedded in the wall. For a few fleeting seconds he thought it was stuck, that they were safe. Then it shook wildly, as if being wrenched by unseen hands, and sprang free.

Shery was a few yards ahead. She slowed so her brother could catch up. Raw terror spasmed through her as the pitchfork spun, quivered, and then hissed toward her brother's back like a heat-seeking missile toward a programmed target. "Drop!" she screamed.

Kip did. He dived flat, heard whizzing above his head, and looked up to see the pitchfork arc high into the black shadows shrouding the rafters. It vanished. He rolled to the right to be close to the stalls. Hands looped under his shoulders, helping him stand.

"Are you all right?" Shery asked. The tines had come so close that it was a miracle he still breathed. Once, she might have put on an act and claimed she didn't care one way or the other what happened to him. But now she trembled at the thought of his close call. Dork or not, pain in the butt or not, he was still her brother, the only one she had. He was still family.

"Don't talk!" Kip said. "Don't move!"

"Is that any—" Shery began to complain.

Kip clamped a hand over her mouth. "Shut up, will you? I think the thing homes in on

235

movement and sound. If we stand perfectly still, it might not get a fix on us."

Shery was skeptical. They were up against a flying pitchfork, not one of those flying darts in that ridiculous movie her brother liked to watch about a bunch of worm riders on a desert planet. Hugging the stall, she peered up into the inky void above them.

Kip balanced on the balls of his feet, ready to flee at the first inkling of a threat. He listened for the hissing, and heard total silence. Only then did it dawn on him that Buck had stopped howling. He'd hoped the howls would bring his parents, until he remembered that the mongrel had been doing so much of it of late, no one paid attention when he did.

Shery estimated that they were halfway to the ladder, and she was tempted to make a dash for it. She whispered as much, adding, "We can't stand here forever. We're not safe as long as we stay in this damn barn."

She had a point, but Kip was reluctant to put his theory to the test. If he was right, the pitchfork would be on them before they took two steps. He scoured the length and breadth of the huge timbers overhead, tingling all over when he spied the same pair of scarlet eyes blazing at him. They were the fiery eyes of a demon, or worse. He opened his mouth to tell his sister, but the red orbs blinked out yet again.

"Well?" Shery goaded. "What are you waiting for?"

Kip nodded, then gave her a shove to get her in gear. She stumbled, caught herself, and bounded away, a gazelle in full flight, eating up the distance with astounding speed for someone who had never run more than 50 feet in her entire life. He paced himself a yard to her rear, covering her back while trying to watch his own, his head craning every which way.

Hissing like a den of enraged rattlesnakes, the pitchfork flashed out of the blackness, streaking toward Shery. Kip saw it and reacted without thinking. Leaping, he shoved her. She squawked as she was driven to her knees. The pitchfork slashed the narrow space between them, a lower prong gouging a furrow in her back, a higher one nicking his wrist. It smacked into the end of a stall, imbedding the tines.

"Keep going!" Kip yelled. She did, and he seized the handle of the pitchfork. It felt as cold as ice. He held on as the wood vibrated in his grip.

Shery, taking it for granted her brother was on her heels, reached the ladder and started up. On spotting him, she stopped. "What are you doing? Come on!"

"Go!" Kip shouted. "Get the loft door open!" He did not let her know that he had no intention of letting go of the pitchfork until she was in the clear. The handle was growing colder by the moment, so cold that his palms felt frozen clear through. The implement shook madly, nearly jarring him off. He clamped his fingers and braced himself, barely in time. The pitchfork exploded backward, the prongs tearing out of the stall, ripping the wood to splinters.

Kip held on, and was propelled across the aisle. His back struck another stall, but not with sufficient force to make him let go. The pitchfork, or whatever animated it, hissed louder than ever. Suddenly it took off like a rocket, arching straight up.

Kip should have let go, but it happened so quickly that he could not unlimber his frigid fingers in time. He found himself swooping high above the floor, carried aloft as if he were riding a berserk broomstick. His hands began to slip. He would have fallen had the pitchfork not leveled off and zoomed toward the loft. With the cold spreading rapidly up his wrists, he dangled from the middle of the handle.

Shery was sprinting for the small double doors. She vaulted a bale of hay, went around another.

The pitchfork slowed slightly. The tines angled to the left. Vibrating fiercely, the deadly implement picked up speed.

Kip Grant saw his chance. By prying his fingers loose at the right instant, he could drop onto the loft instead of the floor far below. Then he saw his sister. She was near the doors, but not near enough. She also had her back to him, so she was unaware the pitchfork had been aimed at a spot between her shoulders blades and would shear into her flesh in less time than it would take him to yell a warning.

Chapter Fifteen

Kip Grant yelled anyway, and as he did, he wrenched on the handle with both arms while swinging his feet up and over the handle, close to the prongs. It was a desperate gambit, executed in the hope it would cause the pitchfork to veer and miss his sister.

He succeeded, although not as well as he would have liked. The pitchfork lost a few inches of altitude and slanted to the left, but not enough to spare Shery. Fortunately, at that precise instant, she had shifted to look over her shoulder for him. The tines missed her chest by the width of one of her painted fingernails. One prong gashed her forearm.

Then the pitchfork rammed into the loft door, burying the tines. To Kip's amazement, the impact slammed the door open. He wanted to let

David Robbins

go before it swung out all the way, but his hands were virtually frozen to the handle. In a blur, he sailed past Shery, past the edge of the loft, and out over the barnyard.

The second the pitchfork cleared the barn, the cold sensation ceased. Kip's palms were slick with moisture, whether from sweat or some other cause, he didn't know. The result caught him off guard; he could no longer hold on to the handle when he needed to the most. He plummeted like a rock.

Kip had climbed many a tree in his time. Like most adventurous boys his age, on occasion the daredevil in him took over and he would jump from branches ten feet up, or higher. So he knew to relax as he dropped, and to bend his knees on impact to cushion the shock. Even so, he tumbled forward, scraping his left shoulder, banging his right elbow, and cutting his cheek on a small but jagged stone.

Kip came to rest on his stomach, his ears ringing, his chest thumping like a jackhammer. A thud behind him barely registered.

Warm hands gently grasped Kip's shoulders and rolled him over. The worried countenance of his sister shimmered above him before taking definite shape. He mustered a wan grin. "Did you see, Sis? That guy with the red cape and the big S on his chest has nothing on me."

"Who?" Shery said, wincing as she shifted to grope his legs. "Is anything broken?"

"Don't think so," Kip said, propping himself

on his elbows. He glanced at the loft door, at the pitchfork still imbedded in the wood. It didn't shake or shimmy or try to extricate itself. It was an ordinary pitchfork once again. Then he noticed that the main door was still closed. "Wait a second. How did you get down here so fast?"

"How else, rocks-for-brains?" Shery said, keeping her voice brittle to hide her true emotions. "I jumped."

Kip looked into her eyes, and was dumbfounded to find a trace of moisture rimming them. "Oh," he said, for lack of anything better to say. Never in his wildest dreams would he have thought that his sister would be so worried over his welfare. After years of bickering over everything under the sun, of rarely having a kind word to say to one another, it was a stunning revelation to realize she really and truly cared for him.

No less bewildered was Shery Grant. Not an hour ago, if anyone had asked, she would have claimed that her brother was the biggest geek in all creation and that she didn't give a damn what he did or what happened to him. But that was then, this was now.

Shery had been terrified by the thought of losing him. When he had rushed to her rescue to save her from the twine, she had not thought much of it. It had seemed like the natural thing for him to do. Then he had offered to lure the pitchfork off, to sacrifice himself so she could escape, and there had been no denying the depth of his devotion. Her brother loved her. Really and truly. It was a devastating insight, made more so because she had taken it for granted for years that he despised her as much as she pretended to despise him.

Now Shery helped him stand. Her left ankle, sprained in the jumped, flared with pain, but she could walk without too much difficulty. The gash on her lower back and the one on her right forearm hurt much worse. So did some of her bruises.

"We look as if we've been through a war," Kip commented. His clothes were covered with bits of hay and dirt. Blood dribbled down his cheek.

Buck came running up, wagging his tail furiously. He licked both of them and rubbed against Shery's legs.

Kip patted the dog's head. "You tried to get someone to come, didn't you, big guy?"

Shery petted him too, stopping when they neared the back door of the house. Of a sudden, she veered to the right. "Come with me," she said, limping around the corner. A wave of weariness bent her knees and she sagged against the house, clasping her forearm. "We need to talk."

"We do?" Kip said. "Shouldn't we tell Mom and Dad what happened first?"

Shery eased lower and sat. "If we do, how do you think they'll react?"

Kip shrugged. "Dad will rush out to check the barn for himself and probably not find a thing. I guess Mom will hover over us like a mother hen. Aunt Tina will fly through the roof and demand that we move back to Philadelphia right away."

"Do you want to go back?"

Kip thought of Amy Westbrook. "No. I like it here, Sis. Even after all I've been through, I'd rather stay." He sank beside her. "Call me crazy if you want, but I think this country living has city life beat hands down. Haven't you noticed how the pace is so much slower here? How the people are so much friendlier?" Kip plucked a blade of grass and placed it between his lips. In his best imitation of Tommy Lee Harper, he declared, "I reckon I'm just a hick at heart."

Shery smiled. "You know, it's funny. A few days ago I wanted to be back in Philadelphia so bad I could taste it. Now, I don't know. I have a new boyfriend, the richest kid in Spook Hollow. And school isn't half as bad as I thought it would be." She chuckled. "Plus, it's bitchin' being the foxiest babe in the whole town."

"So what's your point? That we shouldn't tell Mom and Dad?"

Rather than answer, Shery posed a question of her own. "Do you remember why Dad insisted we move here?"

"How can I forget? He went on and on about how much good it would do, how it would bring us together as a family again, how everything would be like it used to be when we were small."

"You don't suppose"—Shery paused—"that he knew what he was talking about?"

"He has his moments."

"Boggles the brain, doesn't it? I'm used to thinking that neither of them have any idea what life is all about."

"Things back in their day were so different, they just see things differently than we do."

Shery rested a hand on his arm. "The bottom line is this. Do we want it to work out? Do we want to be a family again?" She gazed grimly at the barn. "After today, I do. I want very much to stay, even if that means fighting for what's ours."

"Fight how?"

Choosing her next words carefully, Shery said, "I have this quirk. When someone tells me I can't do something, I always have to do it to prove them wrong. Don't ask me why. I'm not a nerdy psychiatrist. I just know that no one tells me what to do and gets away with it."

"Like when Dad says he doesn't want you to wear short skirts?"

"Yeah."

"Or when he complains about you coming home too late? And having hickies on your neck? And sneaking off to rock concerts behind his back? And the time you hung out with the drug crowd when he didn't want you to?" And when—"

"Enough, already. I get the idea."

Kip snickered.

"Something doesn't want us here, brother mine. Something is doing its damnedest to kill us or drive us off, just as it did to the people who lived in the house before us." Shery surveyed their farm: the fragrant field of alfalfa and clover to the north, the neat rows of apple trees in the orchard to the east. A myriad of stars twinkled in the heavens, while a soft breeze rustled the maples and willows. "I'm not going to let it. Nothing can make me do what I don't want to do. Ever."

"You want to fight this thing?"

"There has to be a way. Even if we can't lick it, we can outlast the bastard. From what everyone says, the mondo weirdness stops after Halloween is over."

Kip pondered. His sister had never bared her soul to him before. It surprised him to learn they thought so much alike. "Okay. Agreed. We take this sucker on. But it won't be easy. We don't have any idea of what we're really up against."

"We can find out. Someone must know."

The prancing image of Alva Jackson came into Kip's head. "There is someone who claims to," he mentioned. He explained about the recluse and the green light he had observed. "This Saturday, Tommy Lee, Amy, and me are headed for South Mountain to see if we can find what caused it."

"Count me in."

"You?" Kip couldn't help saying. To his knowledge, his sister had never set foot in the wilderness in her life.

"Why not?" Shery slowly rose. "I might even bring a friend or two along. A muscle-head or two would come in handy if we run into that headless whatsis you saw."

"We're not taking the chance of that happening. We plan to be back well before dark."

They walked to the front porch, slowing at the sight of their father, who leaned against the post at the opposite end. He had his back to them and was gazing toward Blackgap Road. Tucked under his left arm was the folded newspaper.

"What do we do?" Kip whispered. "If he sees the shape we're in, he's bound to ask questions."

"March right in. Don't give him time to." Suiting action to her words, Shery lowered her hurt arm and casually ambled to the front door, saying cheerfully, "Is supper ready yet? We're going in to wash up."

"It should be soon," John Grant replied, hardly giving them a glance. "I'll be in shortly." He was preoccupied, thinking about the conversation he'd just had with Chief Bogartus and its outcome. As his son reached the threshold, he partially turned. "Say, did you hear Buck a while ago? What was that all about? I would have come out to see, but I was tied up on the phone."

Kip answered, "Who knows? That mutt keeps getting stranger every day." He slipped inside before his father could notice the state of his clothes.

John Grant sighed and resumed watching the approach from town. He did not have long to wait. Within five minutes headlights flared. The car was moving much too fast to belong to a local resident. Either it was a kid out for a joy ride, or one very steamed chief of police.

John knew that he shouldn't have placed the call. His daughter had been right about not fighting city hall. Yet he couldn't let the matter drop without doing something. His conscience wouldn't let him.

The vehicle roared up the winding drive. It was Bogartus's four-wheel-drive, sure enough, and it braked in a spray of gravel and dust. The big, burly chief jumped out, slamming the door.

Since John did not want his sister-in-law to eavesdrop, he met Bogartus halfway up the walk. "Glad you could come," he said earnestly.

"I don't like being threatened, Mr. Grant," the lawman said, getting right to the point. "And I sure as hell don't like being called a liar."

John hefted the newspaper. "You are, though, and we both know it. That bus driver wasn't killed in a freak accident. Nor was the locksmith. The people of Spook Hollow deserve the truth. For the life of me, I can't understand why you're keeping it a secret."

Bogartus glanced uneasily at the house, then lowered his voice. "Let's examine your allegations a moment. First, we have no conclusive evidence that George Eldridge was murdered. So what if we found teeth marks on his leg? There were no other bruises or abrasions, as there would have been if someone had overpowered and drowned him. Which is why officially his death is listed as an accident."

"And Kimble?"

The chief motioned and led Grant to the truck. Leaning on the door, he said, "All we know for certain is that the bus driver was decapitated and his head was found lying in front of the bus."

"Baloney," John said. "What about the man my son saw? The one in the headless horseman costume?"

"We found no evidence to substantiate your son's claim. There were no fingerprints found at the scene, and believe me, we dusted every square inch of that bus."

"What about footprints?"

Bogartus was slow in replying. "The few we found were inconclusive. Most were those your son made after he stepped in the blood."

"Most, but not all?" John persisted.

Spook Hollow's top law officer frowned. He had bags under his eyes from too little sleep and stubble on his chin from not having enough time to shave. Scratching his jaw, he said, "As I just told you, they were inconclusive. So in light of the facts, we pieced together a plausible scenario and gave it to the newspaper." His tone hardened. "Which is why I won't take it kindly if you run to them with a wild-ass tale about a lunatic in a costume going around ripping people's heads off."

John fought to suppress his indignation. "But I saw him! So did two of your own men!"

"All Simmons saw was somebody on horseback. Deever isn't sure what he glimpsed.

And you were overwrought at the time, so maybe you only imagined the whole thing."

"I know what I saw."

Chief Bogartus puffed his lips, then tilted his head while massaging the back of his neck. "Listen. Mr. Grant. I'm tired and I'm cranky, so you'll have to forgive me if I'm too blunt. But I don't want you meddling in police affairs, and that's final."

"Telling the truth would be meddling?" John countered. "Damn, Bogartus. What sort of man are you? How can you cover up a thing like this?" His queries were reasonable enough, he thought. So he was unprepared when the officer abruptly grabbed him by the front of the shirt and in an exhibition of sheer physical brawn jerked him into the air. He braced for a blow which never landed.

Bogartus glared a few seconds, then eased him down, straightened, and stared at his hands as if he couldn't believe what he had just done. "Please excuse me. I haven't been myself ever since I . . ." He stopped, turned, and rested both arms on the truck.

"Ever since what?" John goaded. Stepping closer, he was startled to see the chief's eyes were closed. Bogartus seemed to be in tremendous anguish. "Are you all right?"

"I'm just fine," Bogartus said.

"Is there anything I can get you?"

"Some sanity would be nice."

"Beg pardon?"

The lawman spun and poked a thick finger into John's chest. "Listen to me, Grant. And listen good. If I were you, if I had a wife and kids, I'd get my butt out of here before something happens I'd regret."

"If it's all in my head, why bother?"

Chief Bogartus's features rippled and ebbed, as if an inner wrestling match were taking place between two parts of him at war with each another. Brusquely, he clamped an iron hand on John's wrist and marched down the drive. "Come on. Let's go for a walk."

"Why?" John asked.

"Because I have something to tell you. Something no one else must ever hear. Something that will bring you to your senses and save you and your loved ones from the same fate that befell the locksmith and the bus driver and Julia Powell, the wife of the man who owned this property before you."

"So you do know more than you're admitting!" John said, excited and confused at the same time.

Bogartus did not speak until they were over a hundred feet from the dwelling. "I know what's in this book. Passed on to me by the previous chief." Bogartus unbuttoned a shirt pocket and removed a small black notebook. Despite the dark, its age was self-evident. The leather cover was bent and cracked, the spine was crooked, and the pages were yellow around the edges.

"You've lost me," John admitted.

Bogartus halted and faced him. "The man who first owned this book was Larry Talbot, Spook Hollow Chief of Police from 1910 until 1918. It has been passed from chief to chief to chief ever since." Bogartus opened the book, revealing short handwritten entries. "There are forty-seven accounts in here of sightings of the Headless Horror. And worse."

John extended a hand, but the chief whisked it out of reach.

"No, you don't. I gave my word that I would be the only one to read this until the day I step down and pass it on to my successor." Closing it, Bogartus ran a hand over the cover. "Do you want to know something, Grant? I was born and raised in Spook Hollow. Spent my whole life here. And I never took the spook nonsense seriously until I had gone through this book. Now I'm a firm believer."

"You can't be saying what I think you're saying."

The chief was clearly miffed. "Do I have to spell it out for you? I'm trying to do you a favor and you throw it in my face!" He lowered his voice to a whisper. "That rider you saw the other night was no nut in a costume. It was the real McCoy. And it's been killing people since shortly after the Civil War."

"But—"

"Let me finish. I can appreciate your skepticism. I was once the same way. But you have to face facts. You saw Kimble's body. That poor son of a bitch had his head ripped clean off. No human could do that. No animal either, unless we have a gorilla running loose I don't know about."

All this was too much for John to take. "I can't believe any sane person would fall for such superstitious drivel. Surely there must be a better explanation."

Bogartus had the air of a bulldog about to pounce. "What does it take to convince you?" He flipped the notebook open, scanned a page, then read. "October 29, 1911. The body of forty-two-year-old Anthony DeKalb was found today on the bank of his favorite fishing hole along Blackgap Creek. His head had been torn from his shoulders, and was located on a flat boulder on the other side of the creek. It had been placed so that it faced South Mountain. Someone had overturned his wagon and one wheel was busted. The harness had been ripped to shreds. His horse was discovered late in the afternoon unhurt. Plenty of hoofprints and the tracks of a very large man were found around the body. There were no witnesses."

The lawman quickly flicked the pages. "October 30, 1937. The Headless Horror has struck again. This time it was Doctor Willis. He was called out to the old farmhouse on the hill to deliver a baby. By all accounts it was four in the morning when he headed back. His car was found parked on the edge of the dirt road on south side of the Monongahela Bridge. The windshield had been shattered and the door ripped from its frame. His body was down a bank, near the creek. I regret to note that his head had been sheared off, as if by a long blade or an axe. We searched and searched, but could never find it."

Unbridled horror crept up John Grant's spine like a venomous spider. He shuddered as the enormity of the entries hit home.

"Or how about these?" Bogartus said. "October 26, 1955. Thirty-five-year-old Becky Edwards and her twelve-year-old daughter Sally arrived at the station tonight in hysterics. They reported that while heading into town from their home at the end of Blackgap Road, they were chased by 'a headless giant on a gray horse that breathed fire.' The figure swung at their car with a 'sword that must have been seven feet long.' Mrs. Edwards sped up and eluded it. I suspect they exaggerated. We calmed them down and I inspected their vehicle. The roof bore six slash marks over a quarter-inch deep in the metal. Darnedest thing I've ever seen."

Bogartus wasn't done. "Here's another, dated the 25th of October, 1983. Twenty-two-year-old Fletcher Kiley reported that while hiking home from Monogahela Creek this evening, he spotted what appeared to be a headless rider in the distance. The rider made no attempt to come closer." The chief paused. "In parentheses, it says that Kiley's family recently moved here from Georgia. They were known to be heavy drinkers, but Kiley was sober when he told his story."

Slapping the book shut, Chief Bogartus shook

it in John Grant's face. "What more proof do you need?"

John had to force his vocal chords to work. "But if it's true, why don't you let everyone know?"

"Who the hell would believe it? And what would happen to me? I'd be booted off the force, that's what. So would any lawman who came forward with a cock-and-bull story like this." Bogartus shook his head. "No, the way we're handling it is best. Each new chief is given all the information ever collected. Then it's up to him to put a stop to the spook, once and for all." His next statement bordered on abject despair. "So far no one has succeeded."

John cleared his throat. "Why have you told me?"

"Because of what happened to Julia Powell. Because if I had warned them, she might still be alive." Bogartus gripped John's arm so hard the biceps hurt. "Take my advice before it's too late. Get the hell out of Spook Hollow." He gazed at the surrounding countryside. "If you don't, whatever happens to your family will be on your shoulders, mister, not mine."

As the chief walked off, John Grant turned toward the house he had prayed would be the salvation of his family and wished to high heaven he had never set eyes on it. "What do I do?" he said bleakly.

The only answer was a stiff gust of chill wind.

Chapter Sixteen

Laurie Grant couldn't sleep.

It had been an awful day, what with having to put up with her sister's constant nagging from the moment Tina arrived until they turned in. By the middle of the afternoon Laurie had resorted to her old trick of tuning Tina out, of letting her drone on without paying any attention to what was being said.

Laurie had wanted to find time to talk with her husband, alone, sometime during the evening. He hadn't shown up for supper, so afterward she had gone looking for him. John had been on the front porch, seated in the shadows. She had known by his knit brow and his hooded eyes that he was deeply troubled. He wouldn't say why. When she'd asked about a vehicle she had heard drive off earlier, he'd revealed that Chief Bogartus had paid them a visit. She'd pressed him, but he'd been evasive as to the reason.

As if that were not enough for Laurie to cope with, her kids were suddenly acting strange. They had been unusually quiet at supper, giving one-word answers when Tina tried to get them to open up. Then Laurie had noticed that they were being exceptionally nice to one another. That in itself had been a major shock, so out of character for them that she'd suspected they were up to something.

During supper Laurie had observed a cut on her son's cheek and a bandage on her daughter's forearm. On inquiring, Kip had told her that he'd been in a game of touch football at school, while Shery had said she'd hurt herself while fooling around in a tree in the front yard.

There was only one problem with that. Kip had no interest in sports, and Shery had stopped climbing trees when she was eight.

With all these factors swirling in her mind, Laurie Grant tossed and turned for hours after sliding under the covers. Beside her, John snored lightly. His sleep was uneven. Many times he sucked in his breath and held it for unbearably long spells. At other times he groaned softly. Or gnashed his teeth. She suspected he was having nightmares, but there was nothing she could do short of waking him up, and he needed rest badly.

It was close to two in the morning when Laurie happened to roll onto her back and gaze toward the foot of the bed. Beyond it sat her dresser, topped by a mirror. She was about to close her eyes and try for the umpteenth time to doze off when she detected a peculiar . . . something that seemed to be floating in the air between the bed and the dresser. She looked closer, perplexed.

It resembled a ball of writhing smoke, an oval shape about the size of a human head. As she watched, it solidified, acquiring the sheen of satin, the side facing her forming into definite features. First a long, beaked nose protruded from the center. A pair of ears sprouted. The chin molded itself into a jutting square wedge. High cheekbones took shape, as did a thin, cruel slash of a mouth. Next to appear were overhanging brows. Lastly, a pair of eyelids.

The whole head was slate-gray, from top to bottom.

Laurie held her breath, too scared to move. She told herself that she couldn't be seeing what she was seeing, that she must be asleep after all, and dreaming. Then the gray eyelids snapped open and a pair of blazing red eyes focused on her. They were smoldering flames, those eyes, flames that radiated cold, not heat.

The demonic head floated nearer. Laurie gasped. She could not bear to look into those horrid eyes, but neither could she bring herself to tear her gaze away. The features rippled, the mouth curling back, the flames becoming slits. It was as if she gazed on an intricately sculpted mask embodying raw elemental hatred, hatred so potent that she could feel it in the depths of her being, hatred so vicious that she quaked and nearly screamed.

Just as the head reached the foot of the bed, Laurie closed her eyes, unable to endure any more. For tense seconds she held herself rigid, dreading the feel of its alien presence on her body. But nothing touched her. She fanned her courage and cracked an eye.

The impossible monstrosity was gone.

Laurie looked right and left. Cautiously, she sat up and peeked over the side of the bed. Nothing was there. Afraid of what she might find, she inched to the bottom. The room was empty, save for her and her snoring husband.

Trembling, Laurie rested her brow on the blankets. She had to get a grip, she chided herself. Now she was so overwrought, she was seeing things.

Deciding that enough was enough, Laurie slid out of bed and padded to the closet. Donning a robe over her short nightie, she went out, closing the door so John would not be disturbed. She passed the guest bedroom on her way downstairs and beheld her sister sound asleep, snoring loud enough to be heard in Spook Hollow.

A cup of coffee was in order, Laurie thought. Since she couldn't sleep, she might as well make use of the time and clean up the supper dishes. The wooden stairs felt cool on her soles. Descending silently, she was almost to the bottom when she heard a swish of movement.

The living room was as dark as pitch. Laurie could make out the outlines of the sofa, the chairs, and the entertainment center. The front door was closed, the bolt thrown. Figuring her nerves were to blame, she walked on.

The hall was blacker than the living room. Laurie yawned as she padded toward the kitchen. On reaching it, she glanced back, and for a fraction of a second thought she saw an object about the size of a basketball close to the floor. She rubbed her eyes and looked again. It was gone.

"The tricks the mind can play," Laurie groused. She reached for the light switch. As she did, behind her rose the swishing sound, rising in volume as if whatever made it were rushing down the hallway toward her at great speed. At the instant she turned, she flicked on the light.

As usual, nothing was there.

"This is getting ridiculous," Laurie chided herself. "Next, I'll be seeing werewolves or vampires." She stepped to the coffee maker, tossed the old grounds in the trash, and set a new brew to perking. Meanwhile, she tidied up the plates, glasses, and silverware she had been too depressed to bother with earlier. Once they were arranged in the dishwasher, she closed the door but did not switch it on. The dishwasher was an old clunker which made more noise than a diesel truck and was bound to wake up her family.

Presently, the tantalizing aroma of brewed coffee filled the room. Laurie poured herself a cup, then sat at the table. She added two spoonfuls of sugar, sighed, and leaned back to take a sip. As she raised the cup, there came a scratch at the back door.

A shiver coursed through her. Laurie hesitated to investigate for fear it might be the madman her husband and son had seen. A whine put her at ease. Setting the cup down, she went to the door, worked the bolt and the latch, and opened it.

Buck was there. He did not wait to be petted or greeted. Darting past her, the mongrel swung around and stared into the night. He growled low in his chest, the hackles on his neck rising, his tail held stiffly erect.

Laurie looked out. The sky was overcast, the yard as dark as the bottom of a well. She couldn't be sure, but she thought something moved off toward the orchard. Whatever it was, it was big. Gulping, she closed the door, locked it again, and threw the sturdy bolt.

Stepping back, Laurie bumped into Buck. The dog looked up at her and whined. She squatted to stroke his neck. "What's the matter, fella?" she asked. "What's out there that's got you so upset?"

It had been days since Buck last set foot in the house. Laurie had tried on several occasions to lure him in with a bowl of food, but he had stubbornly balked. Since he had never been much of an indoor dog anyway, she hadn't attached much significance to his behavior.

Now the big mongrel faced the hallway and growled again. Laurie released him to see what he would do. He slunk forward on his belly, his teeth bared. It alarmed her. She rose and edged around the table to see what had him so agitated. En route she snatched a butcher knife from a rack on the wall.

The hallway was empty. Buck halted near it, but would not go in. He sniffed, then cocked his head as if confused. After a few more loud sniffs, he relaxed and came over to rub against her leg.

"So this place is getting to you too, is it?" Laurie said, placing the butcher knife on the counter. Sinking down, she hugged Buck, who laid with his head on her thigh. Idly stroking his thick coat, she commented, "Frankly, I don't know how much more of this I can take. John must be out of his mind to want to stay here. The kids too. What's so special about this old house that it's worth risking our lives over?"

Buck licked her hand.

"I hate to say it, but Tina is right. We're acting like a bunch of idiots. I should put my foot down and demand the kids go with me. If John wants to wind up like sweet Mr. Eldridge and that bus driver, it's his business."

Laurie sagged against the counter. She felt slightly silly talking to the dog, yet at the same time it was nice to have an outlet for her pent up emotions. At least the dog wouldn't criticize her to death, as her darling sister was prone to do.

After a while, Laurie went on. "Who am I trying to kid? I could no more desert John than I could stop breathing. After all we've been through, despite all the hard times, I still love him, Buck. He's a fine man with a good heart and he's trying his best to do what's right for all of us. Tina can take a flying leap, as far as I'm concerned."

"I second that sentiment."

Startled, Laurie shot to her feet.

John Grant filled the doorway. He had been awakened by the sound of the bedroom door opening, but when he opened his eyes, no one had been there. He'd stretched, then rolled over to go back to sleep. His hand had brushed the spot where his wife should have been. Consulting the clock on the nightstand, he'd sat up. Faintly, he'd heard someone moving about on the lower floor.

Worried, John had hastened downstairs. The sound of his wife's voice had reassured him that she was all right. As her words had registered, an ache had formed in his chest, a longing for the days when they had been close, for the days when they had rarely bickered, when every spare moment had been spent in the other's company though they had never grown tired of being together.

The old gleam in her husband's eyes, the longing on his face, filled Laurie with an ache of her own. She took a step toward him, saying simply, "Dearest." And suddenly he was there, in her arms, holding her and whispering words in her ear she had never thought to hear him say ever again.

Tears gushed. Laurie tried to stop them, but could not. The release she so fervently needed would no longer be denied. She cried and cried, sobbing into her husband's shoulder, and she didn't care.

For his part, John held her close and let tears of joy trickle down his cheeks. The tender moment was all the more special because it was the first they had shared in their new home.

For the longest while they stood locked in a warm embrace. Laurie, sniffling, was the first to draw back. Swiping a sleeve across her nose, she gave a lopsided grin and said, "Look at us. Acting like a couple of high school kids."

"All of a sudden I feel twenty years younger," John said, taking a napkin from the holder on the table and passing it her. Removing one for himself, he saw the front of her robe part as she raised her arms, and a hunger he had not experienced in more months than he cared to remember came over him.

Laurie saw, and opened her arms again to receive him. Just then, off in the living room, sounded a soft thump.

Buck sprang erect, growling like before, his nostrils flaring.

"What was that?" John wondered.

The mongrel started toward the hallway, but stopped after taking a few steps. Ears erect, he darted under the table. From behind a chair, Buck snarled at the dark passageway, then pawed at the tiled floor.

"I'd better check," John said.

Laurie almost told him about the floating head. It had been a dream, she was certain. Regardless, she felt compelled to let him know. As she decided to, he strode into the hallway, so she held her tongue and trailed along, unsettling unease afflicting her like a virus.

John Grant remembered the police chief's warning, and regretted leaving the shotgun upstairs beside the bed. Not that he would recklessly resort to the weapon indoors. Buckshot could blow a hole in a wall the size of a melon. He wouldn't risk accidentally harming his wife or one of the kids. Tina was another matter.

A second thump gave John pause. It definitely came from the living room, where no one was supposed to be. His wife's hand brushed his back, inspiring him to go on. He didn't want her thinking he was a coward. At the corner, John halted to scour the living room from end to end. It was as peaceful as a nursery. Why, then, was he racked by an almost overpowering impulse to bolt?

John took a short step, half in dread of having the Headless Horror of Spook Hollow pop out of nowhere and seize him by the throat. No such thing happened. He chuckled at his groundless fears, then observed two of the throw pillows on the floor in front of the sofa. They had not been there when he'd walked by minutes ago.

Right before John's eyes another throw pillow shot off the sofa and thudded next to the others, as if tossed by someone in the shadows. "Back up," he whispered urgently, disturbed for his wife more than himself.

From out of the upper right corner swooped an object about the size of the pillows. John attempted to see what it was, but the thing rammed into his stomach so astoundingly quick that he was on his backside, wheezing for air, before he quite knew what had transpired. Grunting, he sat up.

And was face to face with a demented mind's idea of sculpted perfection. It was a head with smooth skin the color of a rhino's hide and eyes that belonged on a denizen of the Inferno. In addition, waving wildly next to both temples were long strands of black hair. The image reminded him of the ancient Greek legend of Medusa and her snakelike locks.

"Oh, no!" Laurie moaned. She could no longer deny the truth. It had not been a dream or a figment of her mind. It had been real. And it was right in front of them, about to do—what?

In response the head hissed and dipped. Its hair wrapped around John's right wrist. At the contact, an electric charge flowed up his arm into his brain, freezing him where he sat. Its mouth gaped wide, revealing tapered gray teeth that would have done justice to an alligator. They chomped down, slicing into John's arm above the wrist, ripping through skin and flesh as if they were paper.

Seldom had John Grant ever known such exquisite agony. Blood spurted. Instinct bid him tear loose and get the hell out of there, but his limbs wouldn't move. His brain lacked the power to command them. Those razor fangs yawned wide again, drawing near to his shoulder, to his neck.

Laurie had been rooted speechless. A spreading inky stain on her husband's arm was the impetus needed to spark her into grabbing his other arm and hauling him backward. A sharp tingle shot into her body when her palms made contact, but the tingling subsided quickly. Straining, she heaved.

The moment Laurie touched him, John regained some control of his arms and legs. He pumped with the latter and snapped his wounded arm back. His intent was to tear loose, but the loops of hair around his wrist clamped tighter. The head, which was larger than his own and appeared equally as solid, proved to be as light as a balloon. When he snapped his arm, it whipped into the wall. Bounding off as if made of rubber, it streaked at his face. He ducked in the nick of time.

Laurie was pulling him as fast as she could. She wanted to get into the kitchen, into the light, where they could see the thing clearly and would have room to move. The goblin's crimson eyes flashed at her; then it dived at her arms. Its own hair jerked it up short. Hovering, it hissed and extended a gray, forked tongue over a foot long. Light as a feather, the barbed tips stroked her skin.

Searing heat exploded up Laurie's arms to her shoulders. For a second she thought that she was on fire. She almost let go of her husband. Sheer grit made her hold on. Legs driving, she drew him closer to her goal.

The head rotated as a flying saucer might, and dove at John's neck again. Balling his fist, he swung, but it easily evaded him, rotated again, and speared at his jugular. John raised his hand to ward off the attack. The head slammed into him. While it was unnaturally light, it felt solid to the touch. Its ice-cold skin writhed and rippled. John swore he could feel scales.

Then the head zipped back as far as its long hair would allow. Its high cheeks were sucked in. John understood why when they puffed out again and a noxious cloud of foul breath enveloped him. It was like being maced, only worse.

John gagged, his lungs seared by the gaseous discharge. He tried to breathe, but couldn't. Wheezing and sputtering, he gulped like a fish out of water. The hallway spun in front of his eyes. He feared he would pass out.

A glance showed Laurie she was within six feet of the kitchen. She braced booth feet and pulled. The ghastly head zipped toward her. It exhaled a grayish vapor, as it had at John. She was ready, though, and took a breath a heartbeat before. Averting her face, she saved herself from the misery her husband was undergoing, although the rank odor did make her cough.

The head uttered its trademark hiss of baffled fury. It swept at her wrist, those teeth poised to rip and rend.

One last titanic exertion brought Laurie into the light. She tripped over her own foot and fell, pulling John along with her. They spilled onto the tile.

A viperish cry burst from the head. Its hair unwound from John's wrist and it retreated rapidly. Eyes dancing with feral fury, it was almost to the hallway when the incredible occurred.

John and Laurie both saw it.

The head lurched to a stop short of the dark corridor. Its tongue extended, flapping wildly. Its hair wriggled like so many snakes. It began to spin, going faster and faster with each passing second, spinning around and around until, in a cascading shower of tiny sparks and scarlet embers, the head appeared to implode in upon itself. One second it was there; the next it was gone, the sparks raining down. They never hit the floor, but rather dissolved into nothingness as they fell.

"Sweet Jesus!" Laurie breathed, scrambling to sit up.

John rose more slowly. He looked at his arm,

at the teeth marks and the blood, then at the spot where the head had vanished. His dizziness had left him.

"Is it gone for good, do you think?" Laurie asked.

"I don't know," John said. He did not know what to make of any of it. The incident bordered on the unreal. Part of him accepted that it had happened, while another, more rational part, denied the evidence of his own senses and the wound he had suffered. It couldn't happen, therefore it hadn't happened. Yet it had, and something told him that he would never be the same man again.

Laurie gently took his forearm in her hands. "This needs to be dressed right away. It might get infected. I'll go upstairs for the first aid kit."

"We'll go together."

Neither of them moved. They weren't eager to confront the flying nightmare a second time. Under the table, Buck lay with his head between his paws, quaking and whimpering.

John draped his good arm around his wife. She pressed against him as if trying to climb into his skin. Stroking her hair, he gathered his wits. "We'll go up in a minute," he said, "and turn on every single light along the way. From now until Halloween, we keep them on all night, every night."

Laurie locked her eyes on his, the question they mirrored self-evident.

"This is our home," John said. "We can't let

this thing drive us off, as it has so many others since who knows when. There has to be a way to beat the spook, and by God, we'll find out what it is."

John could tell she wasn't convinced, so he went on. "We let the rat race in Philadelphia get the better of us. When our careers were in conflict with our commitment to each other, we let our careers get the better of us." He paused. "Well, I'm tired of being beaten. I'm tired of forces over which I have no control making a shambles of my life. Here's where I draw the line. We have to fight this thing, honey. Sink or swim, win or lose, at least we'll have stood our ground. Together."

Laurie bowed her head. By all rights, she should demand that they leave, that they forget about the Headless Horror of Spook Hollow and try to rebuild their lives somewhere else. But deep down, she agreed with every word her husband had said. If they ran, they risked making a habit of running every time life became too hard to bear.

There was more at stake than their lives. Their marriage, their family, everything they had worked toward, everything they had ever cherished, hung in the balance.

"All right," Laurie declared, astonished she was saying it even as she did. "We fight the bastard. Come what may."

Chapter Seventeen

They took the offensive the very next day.

After turning on a light in every room, including night-lights in each bedroom, John and Laurie stayed up late plotting strategy. It was close to five in the morning when they lay on the sofa, embraced snugly, and fell asleep. They were awakened by Tina, who clumped down the stairs at 6:30 and let out a squawk of surprise at seeing them in each other's arms.

Breakfast consisted of a pot of black coffee and muffins. Once the kids left for school, husband and wife showered together for the first time in many years, dressed, and drove into town.

The Spook Hollow Memorial Library was a two-story brownstone on Main Street. Weekday mornings few patrons were present, so John and

Laurie pretty much had the place to themselves. The white-haired librarian, Mrs. Agatha Harkness, conducted them to a small room on the ground floor where microfiche records of the town newspaper were kept.

Mrs. Harkness gave detailed instructions on how to retrieve material, how to use the microfiche machines, and how to properly store the files when they were done. At one point, when John's attention strayed to a landscape painting on the wall, she said crisply, "Pay attention, sir. I'll not have valuable library equipment damaged through your negligence. The ability to concentrate means the difference between success and failure in life. At your age, you should know that."

John didn't debate the point.

The *Spook Hollow Gazette* had been in continuous publication since 1849. It had the distinction of being one of the longest-running papers in the state.

They started with the previous year's editions first, then worked their way back. Laurie had brought a thick tablet and pen, and for the next three hours they made a record of every reported sighting of the Headless Horror of Spook Hollow, as well as suspicious incidents the paper tended to gloss over.

John was hoping to stumble on a set pattern of goblin appearances that might provide a clue as to how to combat the specter. But there was none.

What they did find was a startling wealth of reports, stretching back over a century.

Other than Mrs. Powell's death the year before under mysterious circumstances, there had been no confirmed reports of the Horror as far back as 1990. That had been the last big year for spook sightings. Five people claimed to have seen the apparition, either at dusk or near dawn, and in each instance the spook had seemed more ghostly than solid. Several witnesses claimed the thing had faded in and out, like the image on a TV with bad reception. No one had been attacked.

The next year a rash of reports were filed was 1983. Once again, there were none involving violence. Most were accounts of the Horror being spotted at a safe distance. In many, the rider was seen to be zigzagging every which way, almost as if he were confused, or else searching for something.

A 28-year gap took them back to 1955. That was the year the Edwards woman and her daughter had been chased while in their car. Seven sightings were mentioned, but the Edwards case was the only one in which the Headless Horror tried to kill anyone.

John sat back and thoughtfully regarded Laurie. "No wonder there hasn't been a public clamor for the authorities to do more. The reports are spaced far apart over the years, and most don't amount to much. So the majority of townspeople must think it's basically harmless."

Laurie responded, "Maybe that's to be expected. From what we've seen, the thing is mainly active at night, when fewer people are abroad. Since, for some reason, it shies away from bright lights, it's doubtful it would get too close to a well-lit house."

"If that's true," John mused, "then the frequency of reports should increase the farther back we go. People would have seen it more often in the days before electricity was in common use."

His hunch proved correct.

The next big year was 1937, the year Dr. Willis met his grisly fate. So did a hunter by the name of Isaac Johnston, found dead in the deep woods three weeks after hunting season had ended. Scavengers had feasted on the corpse. The police claimed that a bear had apparently made off with the man's head. Four other sightings were also on file.

In 1928 there had been nine reports, in 1921 five, in 1916 only two. No one had been killed. But Laurie found a short story on a rash of animal mutilations and the disappearances of pets, and brought this to John's attention.

He frowned. "Damn. I forgot about Powell's horse and dog. We should have been looking for those all along. If we have the time, we'll go back and see if we can uncover more."

They hit the jackpot in 1911. That was the year the fisherman named DeKalb was decapitated and his head placed on a boulder facing South

Mountain. Another possible victim, a lumber-man cutting trees west of the mountain, van-ished without a trace. Six sightings were also on public record.

Then came 1899. Laurie's interest perked on hearing her husband read the name of a man found dead under the grisliest circumstances so far. Lyle Helstrom, who had recently inherited the "haunted farmhouse on the hill north of town," had been literally hacked to bits. His head had been ripped off, then impaled on a short stake. Both eyes had been gouged out, his ears had been loped off, and his tongue re-moved.

"Helstrom," Laurie repeated. "That's the name Doc Syms mentioned. He told me that a man named Arkady Helstrom bought the farm before the Civil War and passed it onto his son about the turn of the century."

"Lyle must have been the son," John guessed.

From there on back, every five or six years the Headless Horror was encountered by the locals, often with fatal results. John tabulated twice as many sightings as there had been for the period between 1910 and the present. Seven more deaths were chalked up to the supernatural killer. Two others were possibles.

Four of those murders occurred on the Hel-strom farm. Three involved farmhands.

The account of one of them, in the year 1871, sent a thrill through John. "Maybe we're finally on to something here," he said. "Listen to this."

Clearing his throat, he read "Farm worker Barnabus French was slain two days ago at Arkady Helstrom's farm. According to the only witness, another worker named Jeremiah Collins, the two men were returning from a day in the fields. It was late, so they decided to cut through the orchard. Collins maintains that they stopped on hearing a loud hiss in the nearby darkness. He claims that as French moved toward the noise, a 'fiendish face with blazing eyes swooped out of nowhere and tore French's throat open with teeth the size of a wolf's' "

"Its what we saw!" Laurie exclaimed.

"There's more," John said, and quoted, "The sheriff believes French was killed by a wild beast. The teeth marks on the doomed man's neck prove that beyond a doubt. He further believes that Mr. Collins was so terrified by the ordeal, his mind became unhinged, and Collins only thought he saw a demonic head. Collins has been taken to the sanitarium in Harrisburg for treatment."

"That poor man," Laurie said. She tried telling herself that the same fate wouldn't befall them if they came forward and told what they had seen. But she had to be honest. The more enlightened a society believed itself to be, the less tolerant its members were of someone who challenged society's concept of the way things were. Anyone in their day and age who came forward with tales of spooks and goblins would be laughed to scorn, or worse.

John drummed his fingers on the machine in disappointment. They had uncovered a lot of information, but none of it provided the crucial answers they needed to pertinent questions: What *was* that monstrosity on the horse? What *was* that thing with the red eyes and the serpentine hair? How were they tied together? More importantly, what could be done to put a permanent stop to the century-old reign of terror?

They continued to scan issues of the *Gazette* clear back to 1850, but they found no more mention of the Headless Horror. Evidently, 1871 was the first year the thing had been seen, the first year it had killed.

John could well understand how the legend had become so entrenched in local folklore without acquiring the national notoriety of, say, the Jersey Devil or the California Bigfoot or Florida's notorious Skunk Ape.

Spook Hollow lay in a remote nook in the mountains, isolated from bigger towns and cities by distance and terrain. Since the locals were loath to share the legend with outsiders, and since the police played down all ghastlier aspects, the Headless Horror had been branded as a quaint folktale and nothing more. Hardly newsworthy by any standard.

"Bogartus should have told us the truth when we first moved in," John mentioned. "It isn't right, him being the only person in town who knows the whole story, yet he won't confide in a soul."

From the doorway came the lawman's voice. "Yet another reason why I went out on a limb and warned you."

Bogartus entered, his thumbs hooked in his belt. "You should be careful what you say in public. Sometimes the walls have ears." Sliding into an empty chair, he pushed his hat back and nodded at Laurie. "Hello, Mrs. Grant. I saw your car parked out front. Made me curious. I figured your family would be halfway to Philadelphia by now."

"We've talked it out," John said, "and we're not leaving."

The chief did not hide his displeasure. "Did I waste my breath last night, or what? You impressed me as an intelligent man, Mr. Grant. I thought you saw the light. Where did I go wrong? What made you decide to stick?"

"About seven hours ago the damn thing tried to kill us." John held out his arm and rolled up his sleeve, exposing the bandage his wife had applied. They had thought it best not to go to a hospital. It would only draw unwanted attention.

The chief was very still for a moment. "I still don't follow you. How can you want to stay? You know as well as I do the danger you're all in."

Laurie spoke up. "We're not letting it run us off like it did Mr. Powell and the rest. We're going to fight for what's ours."

Bogartus scrutinized them. "I can tell you're both bound and determined, but you're making a mistake. How do you fight something that shouldn't even exist?"

"You tell us," John said. "You and every other police chief since the turn of the century have been trying to put a stop to this thing. You must have some idea how to go about it."

"I wish," Bogartus said, and sighed. "To tell you the truth, I don't know any more about what we're up against than you do." Rising, he walked to a window and forlornly looked out. "If it were up to me, I'd dump this whole mess in the county sheriff's lap and let the county boys take the heat. Legally, though, I can't. Blackgap Road is the official town limit, so anyone who lives along it falls under my jurisdiction."

"Do your officers know the whole story?" John asked.

The chief chuckled. "I can see it now! I sit them down and fill them in, and what happens? Simmons wets his pants, Deever buys an elephant gun and spends every spare minute hunting the spook, and Malcolm suggests that I have a psychiatric evaluation." His chuckle became hearty mirth. "Be serious, friend. The burden is on my shoulders and mine alone."

"Not any more," Laurie said, feeling sorry for him. It was enough of a nightmare having her husband and kids to watch out for. She couldn't imagine being the guardian of an entire town, and being so helpless.

John had been mulling over their next move. "Is there anyone else who might have the answers? Someone whose family has lived here since it all began?"

"Do you have any idea how many old-timers there are in Spook Hollow? Most of the people grew up here. About half have roots stretching back to when this valley was settled." Bogartus turned. "If there is anyone who has all the answers, I'd like to know who it is. No one has ever come forward to fill me in."

"All this work, and we're back to square one," Laurie said bitterly.

John placed his hand on hers. "We're not done yet. Our research is just beginning."

"It is?"

Chief Bogartus adjusted his hat while crossing the room. "Take care, you two. I've stepped up patrols of Blackgap Road, but I doubt it will help much." Pausing with a hand on the door jamb, he said, "The spook has a knack for eluding anyone who goes after it. Last year, after we found Mrs. Powell, my men and I spent entire nights parked out your way, hoping it would show itself. It never did."

John perked up. "What about the other chiefs? They must have tried too. Did any of them have better luck?"

"Nope. Several tried tracking it down. Others posted men all along the creek and in the woods. Not one man caught so much as a glimpse of the thing."

"There has to be a way to deal with it," John insisted.

Spook Night

"If you find the key, call me. There's nothing I'd like better than to personally blow the son of a bitch to kingdom come."

Bogartus left, and they were alone again. John gave Laurie a peck on the cheek. She surprised him by molding her body to his and kissing him as if there would be no tomorrow. When they broke for air, they replaced the files and turned off the machines.

John's next stop was one of the computer terminals located at the front of the library. His fingers flew over the keys. In no time he had a list of nine books that might prove helpful in their quest. None were currently on loan. Laurie gathered four of them. He collected the rest.

Mrs. Harkness happened to be manning the front desk. She read off several titles as she stacked the volumes. *"Ghouls and Goblins through the Ages. Were-Things: A Jungian Perspective. Creatures of Myth and Legend. Things That Go Bump in the Night. Witches, Warlocks, and Imps."* Sniffing, then scrunching up her patrician nose, she muttered, "Pity. You seemed like such a nice couple too."

Laurie began paging through the books on the ride home. She learned that ghouls were creatures that robbed graves and fed on corpses, while goblins were reputed to be grotesque sprites, sometimes evil, sometimes not.

One of the books included a chapter entitled, "Spooks in the Night." She scanned it eagerly, only to discover that the word "spook" was synonymous with ghost and encompassed a wide variety of spectral entities. Nowhere did she find any reference to headless ghosts, though.

"This might be harder than we figured," she said.

John took his eyes from the road. "We're not giving up. If I have to, I'll fire up my computer and cruise the Internet to see what I can come up with. Maybe the Library of Congress will have something. The information we need has to be somewhere."

Laurie had forgotten how resolute he became once he put his mind to something. She tenderly caressed his arm, and was about to tell him how very much she cared when a disturbing oversight rocked her. "My sister!"

"What about her?"

"We forgot to tell her about the attack last night."

"So? She'd only laugh in our faces," John replied. "If you want to let her know, fine. But count me out. Her opinion of me is low enough as it is. Any lower, and I'd have to look up to see earthworms."

Laurie stared down Blackgap Road toward the distant hill. Darkly silhouetted against the bright sky was their farmhouse. Their *haunted* farmhouse. "What if we're wrong? What if the spook comes out during the day as well? Tina is there all alone."

On the tip of John's tongue was the statement that his sister-in-law would probably talk the thing to death, but he wisely held his peace. He did accelerate. Presently the Monongahela Bridge materialized. Past it, lumbering down the middle of the road, his back to them, was Bobby Harper, a fishing rod propped on one shoulder.

Harper heard them when their tires rolled onto the old bridge. Stepping to the side of the road, he smiled, waved, and waited.

"I'll make this short," John promised, rolling down his window as he braked. He was genuinely delighted to see his friend. Despite the differences in their backgrounds and interests, he liked the carefree Virginian immensely. "Morning, neighbor. Are they biting today?"

"Howdy, you-all," the big bear of a man said in his Southern twang. "I wouldn't rightly know about the fish. I plumb forgot my bait. On my way to fetch it now."

"Are you taking the day off?" John asked, recalling that Harper had recently been hired to work part-time at the market.

The Southerner grinned and inhaled loudly. "Smell that sweet air? Hear them birds twittering yonder? Why, I took one step out the door this morning and figured it was too beautiful a day to waste lugging boxes and such. So I called in sick." His jowls worked. "You should have heard that boss of mine. Raised a fuss, he did. Claimed it's not right a man should call in sick four times in two weeks."

John could sense his wife's growing urgency.

But he had to say, "Did you ever stop to think, Bob, that the reason you get laid off so often is because you don't give yourself one hundred percent to your work?"

Harper never batted an eye. "Why the dickens should I? I give a hundred percent of me to the Good Lord, sixty percent to my family, and keep the last forty percent for myself. Heck, a man's got to sit back and smell the roses when he gets the urge or life up and passes him by. Know what I mean?"

Correcting the man's math would be futile. John smiled and was about to drive on, then hesitated. "Say, Bob. I've been meaning to ask. Have you or your family seen anything unusual around here lately?"

"What sort of things? UFOs? Bogeymen? Black mountain lions? What?"

The angle of the sun was such that John had to squint to see Harper. Consequently, he couldn't determine if his friend was being serious or "poking fun," as Harper liked to say.

The man wasn't done. "Or maybe you mean the spook that has my boy Tommy Lee so fired up? That boy thinks he's going to go out and catch it and bring it home in a net like he does critters all the time." Harper chortled. "Between his shenanigans and my wife's carrying on lately about some guy on a gray horse, there hasn't been a dull moment."

Laurie was raising her arm to poke John in the ribs. She urgently yearned to get home and verify her sister was safe. But the mention of the rider made her freeze. "What did you just say?" she asked.

Harper bent lower. "Susie has been having a fit over some guy who keeps riding by our place every other night or so. It's been going on for about a week. He hangs back in the trees and stares at the house. Don't ask me why."

John's mouth had gone dry. He had to swallow twice before he could ask, "Have you gotten a good look at him?"

"I haven't set eyes on the gent. Susie has seen him three times, though. The last time she marched on out there with her rolling pin in hand to find out what he was up to."

John did not doubt it for a minute. Susan Harper was nearly as big as her husband, and he had once seen her help Bob lift an engine block. She'd hardly been breathing heavily afterward.

"Funny thing," Harper continued. "She got close enough to see the guy and his horse standing there in the shadows, but when she called out, he wouldn't answer. And when she tried to get closer, he backed off. She said that she must have tried four times to get close enough to see his face, but he wouldn't let her."

"Maybe it was good she didn't get too close," John suggested.

"Oh, don't start," Harper said. "My son claimed it must be that Headless Horror spook we've been hearing so much about, but it couldn't have been."

"Why not?" Laurie asked.

"Because, little darling, I went out for a look the next morning and found a slew of tracks leading off into the trees. When was the last time you heard of a ghost leaving tracks?"

"Maybe it's something else," John said. "A zombie of some sort."

Bob Harper roared. "You've been watching too many monster movies, bud. Zombies are dead folks who scrabble up out of their graves every night to munch on live folks. They never ride horses. And they don't go around headless. They couldn't eat thataway."

Laurie could delay no longer. She poked her husband's elbow. John bid the Southerner good day, and they drove on to their driveway.

"The nerve of that man," she complained. "I've told him a hundred times that I don't like to be called his 'little darling,' yet he does it anyway."

"He doesn't mean anything by it," John said. "It's just the way he is."

Their car growled around the curves. The house came into view. John saw a figure burst around the rear corner, flying as if for dear life. It was Buck. He braked, fearing that his wife had been right, that the spook was active during the day. Then Buck's pursuer appeared.

Tina Brewster waved a broom on high as she panted after the mongrel, screeching, "Come back here, you damn mutt! That's mine!"

Half of a Danish pastry dangled from the dog's mouth.

Spook Night

John and Laurie exchanged glances. For the first time in many days, they laughed long and hard. He pulled up at the end of the walk. As he placed his hand on the door handle, he glanced toward the barn. One of the doors was wide open, and for a brief instant, deep in the murky shadows inside, he thought that he saw a pair of scarlet orbs glaring malignantly at him. They faded the moment he saw them.

So did his laughter.

Chapter Eighteen

Saturday dawned cold and windy. The trees had begun to change color, and streaks of orange and brown lent contrast to the verdant foliage.

Kip Grant buttoned his coat as he paced on the front porch. He had been pacing for 15 minutes. His cheeks were chilled from the blustery gusts. His hair was touseled. He kept running his hand through it, but the very next gust would mess it up again.

It was past one o'clock. Everyone was late.

Kip half hoped that no one would show up so they could forget about Tommy Lee's harebrained scheme. There was no guarantee they would find anything. And since they planned to be out past sunset, they stood a very real risk of running into the Headless Horror.

Why, then, was he going? The answer was as

plain as the longing in his heart every time he thought of Amy Westbrook. If she intended to go, he would too.

From inside the house came upraised voices. Kip shut them out. It was only his mom and Aunt Tina, arguing again. His aunt had become more insistent than ever that they pack up and get out of there. His mother, to his surprise, had grown just as insistent that they stay. Usually Aunt Tina was able to wrap his mother around her little pinkie and convince her to do whatever Tina wanted. Not this time.

Equally surprising to Kip was how well his mother and father were getting along. Not once in two days had he heard them snap at each other. At meals they sat holding hands. They were practically inseparable, spending every spare moment together. It reminded him of the old days. He didn't know what to make of it.

Maybe he had his holidays mixed up, Kip mused. Maybe it was Christmas instead of Halloween.

The thought made Kip think of the dance the night before. His original intention had been to dress up as a bizarre alien from a popular space movie, but he had changed his mind when Amy agreed to be his date. With a white shirt and a black vest and an imitation blaster at his side, he had gone as the rakish hero instead. His dad had driven him.

Kip had felt stiff and awkward and not a little bit silly as he walked up the front walk to the

Westbrook home and rang the bell. His palms had been so sweaty that he wiped them on his pants three times while he waited. Then the front door opened, and he forgot all about how nervous he was.

Kip had never beheld anyone so beautiful. Amy had refused to tell him about her costume in advance. So he was unprepared for the stunning vision of loveliness she presented, dressed as she was in a flowing white dress and a sequined tiara.

"I'm a princess," she said beaming when he stood there gaping.

"You sure are," Kip agreed.

From then on, the evening qualified as the most fantastic of his entire life. They sat in the back seat, nearly touching, Amy chatting about this and that. It was just as well she did most of the talking because he was tongue-tied until they reached the junior high.

There, Kip finally quelled his nerves. They danced and talked and danced some more. He brought her punch and held her smooth hand, and it seemed like the most natural thing in the world for him to do.

At one point Tommy Lee and several boys showed up. They asked him to join them out back of the school. Tommy Lee, it turned out, had swiped a silver flask from his dad's liquor cabinet and filled it with whiskey.

Kip did not want to go. They refused to take no for an answer and badgered him. He was torn between his friends and his date, until Amy squeezed his hand and ran a warm finger along his wrist. "I'm staying here, where I belong," he declared, and received another squeeze in gratitude.

Muttering something about "another good bud going down the drain," Tommy Lee departed.

"Thank you," Amy said, gazing at him with stars in her eyes.

"No big deal," Kip answered. Then he was startled out of his mind when she kissed him, lightly, smack on the mouth.

The rest of the night a blur. They danced and danced, hugging each other so close during the slow tunes that Kip worried they might be expelled for indecent behavior.

The Halloween dance was one of four "mixers" throughout the school year, where the junior and senior high kids were allowed to mingle socially. Spook Hollow being so small, it was one way of insuring a solid turnout.

Kip had expected to run into his sister and her date, and he was not disappointed. He flinched inwardly on seeing Shery sashay toward him, certain she would tease him in front of Amy.

Shery Grant was in her element. She'd dressed as Cleopatra, wearing her long hair Egyptian-style and darkening her eyebrows. But it was her costume, or lack of one, which caused the eyes of every boy she passed to widen. She loved every minute.

Spotting her brother, Shery led Bryce Harcourt across the floor. She imagined herself the envy of every girl there, which lent added zest to the evening. Head held high, her shapely hips swaying, she was every inch the queen she pretended to be.

Shery saw Kip tense as she approached. His features betrayed a glimmer of anxiety. It was in her mind to say something like; "How's it going, dork? Have you stepped on her toes yet?" But she hesitated. She surveyed him from head to toe, and then said, "Not bad, stud-muffin. Keep this up and every girl in your class will be after you."

Kip blushed. Amy fidgeted. And Shery sailed on, her hunk in tow, savoring the looks and the attention.

Kip Grant stared after her, speechless. She had complimented him, not insulted him! First his parents, now this! Next, the world would come to an end.

Those thoughts came back to Kip now, as he paced the front porch, and he grinned. It had been an unbelievable night from start to finish. He touched his lips, where Amy had kissed him a second time when he dropped her off.

A pair of figures came around the first bend. Tommy Lee and Amy. Kip smiled and waved at her. Both of them waved back. He hurried to the drive, searching her face for some sign that she might feel differently from the night before, that maybe he had taken too much for granted. But no, her expression left no doubt how she felt. She confirmed it by taking his hands in hers and kissing him on the cheek.

"I missed you," Amy said.

"And I missed you."

Tommy Lee stuck a finger in his mouth and pretended to retch. "Gag me with a spoon! Am I going to have to put up with this soap opera all day?"

"What if you are?" Kip demanded. "She's my girlfriend now, so you'd better get used to it."

"I knew this was coming." Tommy Lee grinned smugly. "It never fails. Every time a girl starts hanging around, one of my buds is sure to lose his marbles."

The roar of a car engine punctuated his statement. Up the drive cruised a shiny red Corvette. Behind it trailed a green sedan. Kip recognized the muscle car. Everyone in Spook Hollow knew who it belonged to. He gave his sister the thumb's-up sign.

Shery Grant returned the favor, then placed her other hand on Bryce Harcourt's shoulder and delicately traced a line on his neck with her fingernail. "Now remember, lover. Bear with us. And don't be giving my brother and his yo-yo friend a hard time. This is important to us."

The star quarterback playfully nipped at her finger. "After last night, babe, whatever you want, you get. Just don't blame me if Jerry and Debs do any griping. Debs isn't exactly thrilled about this."

Shery made no comment. The real reason Debra Coker was on the rag had nothing to do with their trek to South Mountain, and had everything to do with the fact Shery and Bryce were an item. Coker wasn't a good loser.

Sliding out of the car, Shery greeted her brother and Amy. They were holding hands, and if ever there had been a case of puppy love, this was it. She merely nodded at Tommy Lee, then caught him ogling her chest. Smiling seductively, she stepped up to him and stroked his earlobe. "How's it hanging, big guy?" she asked sweetly.

Kip was tickled when his friend imitated a radish and sputtered like a drunk whose tongue wouldn't work right. As Shery turned, she winked at him.

A new feeling came over Kip. For the first time ever, his sister was treating him as he had always wished she would, instead of dumping on him all the time. They were a brother and sister again, not adversaries. It was almost too good to be true.

Shery introduced Jerry Dern and Debra Coker, who got out of the other car. The hulking linebacker slipped a backpack on while studying the farmhouse. "So this is the Helstrom place, huh? It doesn't scare me none."

"It would if you . . ." Kip caught himself before he gave away too much. Shery had made him promise not to tell a soul about their experience in the barn, not even their parents. His conscience had pricked him, but he had to admit that if he did, it might give Aunt Tina the leverage she needed to overcome their mother's objections. The last thing he wanted was to leave Spook Hollow, and Amy.

"Would what, runt?" the bigger boy asked rudely.

"Nothing," To change the subject, Kip quickly asked, "What's in your backpack?"

"Nothing," Dern said, mimicking him.

Tommy Lee turned his back to the newcomers, crossed his eyes, and contorted his features to portray the perfect imbecile. Amy giggled. Kip struggled to control himself to avoid antagonizing the mountain of muscle, who still stared at their house.

Debra Coker walked around the front of the Corvette. She had on a sweater which clung to her every asset as if it were a second skin, and if her jeans had been any tighter, her circulation would have been cut off. She stifled a sham yawn, then cracked, "So let's get this show on the road. I don't intend to waste an entire Saturday making like a Brownie Scout."

Bryce Harcourt draped an arm on Shery's shoulders. "Which way, gorgeous?"

Shery looked at Kip. All she knew was that the crazy lady who lived down the road had pointed out a strange greenish light to him somewhere at the base of South Mountain. Since Kip was the only one there who had seen it, he had to lead.

Kip suddenly found all eyes on him. He didn't have the heart to confide that the best he could do was make a rough guess, so he wheeled and led off, Amy at his side.

It didn't occur to Kip until they were a hundred yards into the woods that they might need a flashlight since they were going to stay out so late. But he wasn't about to make himself a target of ridicule by confessing his mistake and running to fetch one. Nor did he want to leave Amy alone with the gorilla his sister had invited along. So he said nothing.

That the woods were alive with small game and birds helped to put Kip at ease. With brilliant sunlight everywhere, sparrows and finches chirping, and squirrels scampering about high in the branches, it was easy to forget about the gravity of the situation. He strolled along, deep in conversation with Amy.

Shery listened to Bryce go on and on about the deplorable state of the Spook Hollow football program, and how he couldn't wait to graduate and go to Temple or Penn State where they had *real* football programs. As if she cared. She let him drone on and lost herself in her own thoughts, just as she did when her parents were on her case or when a teacher went into a long-winded spiel.

South Mountain loomed steadily larger. Forest blanketed its lower slopes, while the upper elevation was starkly bare of plant growth, unlike neighboring mountains.

As the crow flies, it was about three quarters of a mile from the farm to their destination. They had covered half that distance when Jerry Dern bellowed, "Far enough, people. Let's take a break while I break out some refreshment."

Shery, who had observed suspicious bulges in his backpack, suspected the truth. "What did you bring along? As if I can't guess."

Dern placed the pack on the ground, unzipped it, and with a flourish produced a six-pack of beer. "The line forms here," he said, smacking his left elbow.

Deb immediately stepped next to him. "Count me in, big guy. If I'm going to be bored to tears, I might as well be half-blitzed."

"Right on, sweetcakes," Dern declared. "A little buzz never hurt anybody." With a snap, he popped a can. The first one went to her. The second he offered to Bryce. "Here you go, dude. Join the party."

Harcourt glanced at Shery, then shrugged. "What harm can one do?" He took it and gulped.

Shery was royally ticked off. Without being specific, she had made it clear to Bryce that there was more to the hike than their usual fun and games. She'd asked him not to drink, as was his habit on weekends, until after they'd made it back safe and sound.

Dern shook a can at her. "How about you? Or your kid brother? I brought enough for everybody."

"No, thanks," Shery said sullenly.

Kip shook his head when the linebacker offered him one, as did Amy.

Tommy Lee, however, was not one to let a golden opportunity pass. He eagerly took the beer and held it as if he had just been given the crown jewels of England.

Amy leaned close to Kip, whispering, "I don't like this. What happens if these guys get drunk on us?"

"We split." Kip had heard his sister boast one too many times about the wild escapades of her friends. He wasn't about to be a party to their high jinks. Especially with Dern involved. The kid had a reputation for being a brawler, a troublemaker who went around picking fights when there was nothing better to do.

"We should keep going," Shery said. Her brother's annoyance was readily apparent to her even though he tried to hide it. She didn't blame him. Her only consolation was that it wouldn't get dark for another two and a half hours. By then the effects of the beer were bound to have worn off.

"Whatever you say," Dern said. Replacing the unused cans in the backpack, he draped it over his left arm. "Just don't stand downwind when I head for a handy tree."

Bryce laughed. Deb snorted, spilling beer on her chin.

Shery smiled, but her eyes were razor-sharp daggers. "Don't worry on that score. I wouldn't want to distract you when you're focusing your microscope."

The quarterback laughed louder.

Jerry Dern's brow creased. "My what? What the hell are you talking about, girl? I hate science class. It's almost as boring as algebra, which ranks right up there with history class. I don't even know how to use a microscope."

To prevent an argument, Kip went on before the linebacker figured the insult out. He had to admire how his sister stood up to Dern, how she could hold her own anywhere, anytime. She was a lot tougher than he had ever given her credit for being.

They made slow progress. Dern and Coker dragged their heels, drinking. Often they whispered to one another as if sharing great secrets. At other times they laughed loudly, scaring the sparrows into taking wing and silencing the squirrels.

The forest grew thicker, the shadows longer. The group constantly had to go around thickets and skirt other obstacles. It slowed them down even more.

Kip stopped once to climb a tree and get his bearings. From a lofty perch he could see the roof of the Jackson house to the southwest. Accordingly, he fixed on a specific spot on the mountain as the area where the green glow had likely come from. A jagged slab of rock higher on the slope served as a convenient landmark.

Kip then started to descend. He had always

liked climbing, and spent many an idle hour in his favorite park in Philadelphia pretending to be the Lord of the Jungle. As he neared the bottom of the tree, he heard voices directly below.

Jerry Dern had backed Amy against the trunk, and was leering at her as if she were a centerfold pinup. His hairy, strapping arms were propped on either side of her to keep her from slipping away. "What's the matter, girlie?" he was saying. "Cat got your tongue?"

"Please," Amy said.

Dern kept on leering. "Please what?" he taunted her, and puckered his lips. "Are you begging me for a little smooch, girlie?"

Shery started toward them. She realized it had been wishful thinking on her part to expect the linebacker to behave himself for one whole afternoon. "Let her alone," she snapped. "She's done nothing to you."

"Butt out," Dern said. "I'm just having me a little fun."

Kip saw Bryce Harcourt move to intervene. He didn't wait for the quarterback. Swinging onto the next lower branch, Kip coiled, then leaped feet-first onto Jerry Dern's back, yelling as he did, "Get away from her, damn you!"

Yelping in surprise, the linebacker was sent tumbling. Like any skilled athlete would, he rolled with the blow and swept up into a crouch, anger clouding his face, his fists cocked to swing.

The impact threw Kip off balance. He landed

on one foot, tried to regain his balance, and sprawled onto his hands and knees.

Taking quick strides, Dern reached for Kip. "Jump me, will you? I'm going to pound you to a pulp, boy, and enjoy every minute of it."

No one had been more startled by Kip's attack than Shery. She'd never thought he had it in him. Now she darted between them, her fingers clawed to scratch Dern's eyes out if need be. "Back off, idiot! You started it."

Dern drew back a hand. He might have struck her had Harcourt not seized his wrist and held on.

"That's enough, Jerry! Jesus! What's gotten into you?" Harcourt shouted. "First you hit on the jailbait, now you're ready to slug Shery? How many beers have you had?"

Dern ripped free and stepped back, glowering at all three of them. "The beers had nothing to do with it, man. And where do you get off taking her side against *me*? We've been best friends for ages. Now along comes Miss-Hot-to-Trot, and I'm second string."

Shery couldn't help herself. Her slap left a red mark the size of an apple on Dern's cheek. She braced for his response, but there was none. Sneering, he backed off.

"See what I mean? The bitch hits me and you stand there and let her," Dern raged at Harcourt. "Deb was right about her."

As if on cue, Coker sidled up to the linebacker and put her arm around his muscular waist. "I told you, didn't I? I knew she'd show her true colors sooner or later. And poor Bryce is so far gone, he'd rather be her trained seal than hang out with us anymore."

Harcourt was furious. "What the hell are you up to, Deb? What bull have you been feeding him?"

Shery butted in. "Don't you see, handsome? She's pissed because you picked me over her. So she's taking petty revenge by turning the two of you against each other. Divide and conquer, as our history teach would say."

Coker flipped Shery the finger. "Come on, Jer," she urged, pulling on Dern. "Let's go. We know when we're not wanted. Let's polish off that beer on the way back, then head into town and have us some fun."

Dutifully, the linebacker obeyed. Harcourt called out to him, but Dern made no reply. Soon the vegetation swallowed them both up.

"That bitch!" Bryce said. "I should go after them and teach her a lesson."

Snatching his wrist, Shery said, "If you do, you'll play right into her hands. My guess is that she's been putting out to him and has the big dope on a tight leash." She touched his hot cheek. "Wait a while, lover. Let Jerry simmer down. Look him up when she's not around and I'll bet you can set things right."

The quarterback stared in the direction the couple had gone. "I suppose you're right," he conceded.

Afraid he would change his mind and go after them, Shery motioned for Kip to resume their trek. As Kip and Amy moved out, she steered Bryce northward.

Kip walked next to Amy, his blood speeding at the velocity of light through his veins. Dazzled by his own audacity, he marveled that he hadn't gotten his fool head kicked in. He'd stood up to one of the toughest guys in Spook Hollow and lived!

Chugging beer, Tommy Lee overtook them. "Don't be so proud of yourself," he commented. "Hercules might have come in handy if we run into the spook later on."

The reminder was like a splash of cold water on Kip's face. He remembered the monster on the bus, and had half a mind to grab Amy and run like hell for home while they still could.

South Mountain now towered above them. They were paralleling the broad base, moving through some of the most rugged terrain he had ever seen. To glimpse the summit, he had to tilt his head back.

Meanwhile, the sun dipped steadily lower. In due course it would sink below the horizon, plunging the forest into darkness. And with the coming of night would come something else.

The Headless Horror of Spook Hollow would be on the prowl.

Chapter Nineteen

Half an hour before sunset John Grant went looking for his kids. Laurie and Tina were in the kitchen, setting out pizza Tina had picked up in town. Her comment about a "cool Corvette parked out front" prompted him to venture onto the porch. He knew it was Bryce Harcourt's car since Harcourt had dropped Shery off every night that week. The owner of the other vehicle was unknown to him.

John surveyed the farm from one end to the other, but did not see any sign of them. It bothered him. He had specifically told Kip and Shery not to stray off unless they let him or Laurie know where they were going. They had better be back before dark, he reflected, or they would both be grounded for a month.

Hanging from the top of the porch, to his left,

was one of three large spotlights he had installed out front the day after the phantom head had tried to kill him. Two more were on each side of the house, and an additional three out back. He'd gone overboard, perhaps, but since learning that bright light had an adverse effect on the spook, he had kept the house lit up like a Christmas tree from dusk to dawn. The spook had not shown its horrible face since.

John was hopeful they could get through their ordeal without further tragedy. According to local legend, as confirmed by his research, sightings of the Headless Horror were cyclical. They began about a week or so before Halloween, and lasted through Spook Night itself. So if his family could get through this one last night, they would have an entire year in which to come up with the answers needed to put an end to the nightmare for all time.

Stepping onto the lawn, John cupped his hands to his mouth and hollered, "Shery! Kip! Time for supper!"

No one answered.

John opened his mouth to try again. Already he was rehearsing the lecture he would give them. The older they got, the less they listened. As so many parents claimed, the teen years really were the hardest.

"They can't hear you, Mr. Grant."

The unexpected strange voice, so close behind him, caused John to jump and whirl. A tall, elderly patrician woman in an ankle-length brown dress stood on his porch, a purse primly clasped at her waist, her penetrating eyes fixed on him with hawkish intensity. "Who the hell are you?" he blurted out, forgetting himself.

"Alva Jackson," the woman said. "I live down the road a piece. Figured it was time we had us a talk."

"About what?" John asked, irritated that she hadn't thought to call first rather than drop by unannounced. Especially so close to sunset. "Now isn't the best of times, Ms. Jackson. We're about to sit down to the table. I hope you won't think me rude if we take a rain check."

"You do, and everyone you love will die. I came here to warn you."

"What?"

The woman turned haunted eyes toward South Mountain. "Some years the power of the Pit is weaker than others, and he never shows. Other years, the power is strong. That's when he's seen the most, when he kills the most." Those eyes shifted to him. "This year, the door to Hell is wide open. The evil is stronger than ever. Can't you feel it? There will be no stopping him this time." She sadly shook her head. "You're all doomed. Unless . . ." Stopping, she shivered.

John wasn't quite sure what to make of her. "I appreciate the warning," he said, not knowing what else to say. He suspected she might be a crackpot. Which was the last thing he needed right then.

Her head snapped up. "I'm in my right mind,

Mr. Grant. Don't fret on that score."

Startled, John said, "How did you—?"

Alva Jackson cut him off. "Where are your manners, Yankee? Aren't you going to invite me in? Or is your family of so little importance to you that you would spoil the only chance you'll ever have of learning the whole truth about the goings-on around here?"

She had an air about her. John had to concede that much. Crackpot or not, her words crackled with authority. "Fair enough," he responded. "Why don't you come in for some coffee or tea, and you can tell us what's on your mind."

Stepping to the door, Alva Jackson waited for him to open it, then squared her wide shoulders and entered. She glanced sharply to either side and up the stairs. "You better put the lights on early tonight, Mr. Grant. The more powerful Evil is, the earlier its minions are abroad."

John hesitated. The sun was still above the horizon. There was no rush, in his estimation, and he would much rather be out looking for his children. But he did as the woman wanted anyway, going upstairs to flick on a light in every room. It gave him time to organize his thoughts, so when he returned to the living room he bluntly demanded, "What's your connection to the spook, Mrs. Jackson? How is that you claim to know so much?"

"Claim?" Jackson said, and tittered. "If you don't mind, sir, and even if you do, I'll wait until the lady of the house is present also. She deserves to hear the whole story as much as you do."

They were halfway down the hall when the woman stopped so abruptly that John nearly collided with her. "Is something wrong?" he asked.

"Who else is here?"

John wondered how she knew. No voices issued from the kitchen and no one had appeared at the other end. "My sister-in-law. She's staying with us a while."

"If you care for her, you'll get her out of here right this minute."

It was John's turn to laugh. "Tina and I don't exactly see eye to eye on very much. To be honest, she wouldn't listen to me if her life depended on it."

"It does."

Laurie and Tina had stepped out back so Tina could indulge in a smoke. Laurie hated cigarettes and would not abide them in her home, a legacy of her childhood. Their mother had been a heavy smoker, up to three packs a day, even smoking during meals. Eventually Laurie had reached the point where the smell of a cigarette made her feel ill.

Now, standing upwind of her sister, Laurie folded her arms and solemnly regarded the sweeping vista of the lush valley below. Spook Hollow. No one would ever guess that under its quaint surface lurked living terror.

"Hicksville," Tina grumbled, gesturing at the

rooftops with her cigarette. "What was that lame-brain husband of yours thinking of when he dragged you out out to the boonies? I mean, what does this place have that the city doesn't, besides a few more trees and lots of bugs and horse turds in the middle of the road?"

Suddenly the spotlights came on. The screen door opened. Out walked a stately woman Laurie had never seen before. She caught her husband's eye. He put an arm around her shoulder and made introductions. Tina gave the woman the once-over, then nodded curtly.

"You're our neighbor?" Laurie said. "I'm surprised we haven't passed each other on the road once or twice, or run into each other in town."

Alva Jackson fiddled with the strap of her purse. "I tend to keep pretty much to myself, Mrs. Grant. Most folks hereabouts think I'm a mite touched in the head."

"Do tell?" Tina said dryly.

"I wouldn't be so sassy, dearie, were I you," Alva said sternly. "We never know when our allotted time is up. And given the life you've lived, you shouldn't be so eager to visit the nether realms."

Tina chortled. "What *are* you talking about, old woman?"

Laurie resented her sister's attitude. "That's enough out of you, Tina," she warned. Facing their visitor, she smiled and said, "Please pay her no mind. She has never had any manners and I doubt she ever will. Now, what can we do for you. Ms. Jackson?"

"It's what I can do for you," the woman said soberly. "I shouldn't, but I like that sprout of yours. His soul is pure, ma'am. He doesn't deserve it, like some I could mention."

The implication made Tina frown.

Laurie hadn't quite followed the woman's drift. "I'm not sure I understand."

"She's here about the Headless Horror," John clarified. His opinion of the woman had improved; anyone who disliked Tina at first sight was a kindred spirit. "She claims to know the whole story behind it."

To Laurie it was apparent the woman was nervous. "Would you care to step inside? You might be more comfortable sitting down."

"No, thanks, Mrs. Grant," Alva said. "It's safer for you if we stay out here." The sun drew her interest. "I'd better hurry, hadn't I? We're about out of time." Taking a breath, she remarked, "It's just that this is so hard for me. I'm breaking my word to my mother, who made me swear on the Good Book. Just as her mother did with her. I reckon they'll both toss in their graves when they learn what I've done." Her voice cracked. A low sob passed her lips.

John was puzzled by the woman's transparent torment. "Are you sure that you're all right?"

"Hear me out," Alva said. "Let me finish, or I might change my mind. This is the hardest thing I've ever had to do." Leaning against the wall for support, she asked the last question John would have anticipated. "What do you folks know about Gettysburg?"

"The town?" Laurie said.

"No, the battle." Alva did not wait for them to reply. "It was the turning point of the war, you know. If Lee had won, we'd all be saluting the Stars and Bars." She smiled wistfully, but the smile quickly faded. "So many precious Southern lives were lost there. The flower of the Confederacy hurled themselves at the Yankee lines and were cut to ribbons."

Tina impatiently fluttered her lips. "Just what we need. A history lesson."

Alva Jackson did not seem to hear. "Cemetery Ridge was the worst. Lee knew that if he broke the Union line at that point, he'd send the rest packing back to Washington. So he ordered General Pickett to charge the ridge. Fifteen thousand men stormed the Yankee positions. Hardly a third survived."

"Break out the violins," Tina quipped.

Once more the elderly woman ignored the barb. "One of the men under Pickett was Captain James T. Beauregard. He was badly wounded during the charge. So was his horse. Apparently, Beauregard tried to make it back to the Southern lines, but missed them in all the smoke and confusion." She looked up. "Somehow, he wound up here."

"You mean, in Spook Hollow?" John asked.

Alva tapped the ground with a foot. "No, I

mean right *here*. At this very farm."

An awful feeling came over Laurie. The lower third of the sun had disappeared. Soon the rest would be gone, as well.

"A man named Arkady Helstrom owned this place at the time. He was a mean-spirited so-and-so, a braggart who took up the Union cause but who didn't have the grit to volunteer and go fight. Helstrom and his workers hauled Captain Beauregard to the barn. Then Helstrom sent a man to town to get others." Alva swallowed. When she resumed, she did so in a rush. "The Yankees held a meeting, and it was decided to turn Beauregard over to the Union Army. But Helstrom wouldn't hear of it. He said it was their sworn duty to dispose of the rebel as they saw fit. So he had his men drag the captain into the barn. They threw a rope around Beauregard's neck." Tears formed. Jackson sniffled. "Beauregard was too weak to resist. He asked them to do the decent thing and get him to a hospital. He told them that he had a fiancée waiting for him back home. But Helstrom laughed him to scorn. Then they hung him."

John felt Laurie's hand slip into his.

Acting as if she were under the greatest of strains, Alva Jackson grew ashen, her breathing erratic. "They botched it, the scum! The rope decapitated Beauregard. Helstrom impaled the head on a pole and boasted he would parade it down Main Street." Closing her eyes, the woman raised a forearm to her forehead. "Along about then a man hurried out from Spook Hollow. He informed them that a cavalry patrol was in town, that a notice had been posted for everyone to be on the lookout for deserters and stray Confederates. Anyone who found either was ordered to turn them over to the military. Under no circumstances were the Johnny Rebs to be harmed unless they attacked someone."

Tina shook her head. "I've heard enough," she said, opening the screen door. "I'll pop the pizza in the microwave."

John was glad to see her go. Her snide comments had been uncalled for. "What happened next?" he goaded.

"Arkady Helstrom lost his bluster. He decided it would be best to hide the body and never tell a soul what they had done. So Beauregard was thrown onto a wagon and carted off to South Mountain. They took his horse and saddle too." Alva grinned. "They weren't as smart as they thought they were, though. In their haste, they forgot the captain's head."

"Wait a minute," Laurie said. The story so far seemed plausible enough, but there was something she just had to find out. "How do you know all this, Mrs. Jackson? Where did you hear it from?"

Sorrow welled up. "From my ma, ma'am. Who heard it from her mother. Who in turn heard it from *her* ma. Who just happened to be Captain James T. Beauregard's fiancée."

John was so shocked that he hardly noticed

the sun was almost gone. "She came to Spook Hollow?"

Alva straightened, dabbing at her eyes. "That she did, Mr. Grant. You see, Helstrom was worried someone would report what had happened to the Army. To cover himself, he took Beauregard's effects and a couple of workers to back his story, and went to Gettysburg. He reported that he had found a wounded Southern officer on his property and tried to help the man, but that the officer had been too far gone. So they buried the body."

"The Army believed him?" Laurie asked.

"Why wouldn't they? Helstrom had witnesses. Eventually, Beauregard's things were returned to the South, along with a brief note on his death." A gust shook a nearby tree. Alva moved away from the house, facing into the brisk wind. "We don't have much time, I'm afraid. I had better finish this fast."

John was glad the spotlights were on. They lit up the yard as if it were the middle of the day.

Alva stared at the springhouse before going on. "My great-grandmother loved the captain dearly. She wanted to see the spot where he had died, so she traveled to Spook Hollow and spoke to Helstrom. His account didn't quite match the one he had given the Army. It made her suspicious. She nosed around and eventually learned the truth."

"What did she do?" Laurie inquired.

"What could she do? It was her word against

his. She wanted to be near Beauregard's final resting place, so she bought property on Blackgap Road. Years later, out of loneliness, she married another man. Our family has lived there ever since."

"How does all this tie in with the Headless Horror?" John asked. The question proved unnecessary. In a dazzling burst of insight, he made the connection which should have been so obvious. It all added up. A decapitated Confederate officer. A headless apparition who wore a gray uniform and rode a slate-gray steed. "Dear Lord!" he breathed, staggered. "It can't be!"

"It is," Alva said. "The Headless Horror of Spook Hollow is Captain James T. Beauregard. Or rather, part of his ghostly self, destined to roam the earth every year about this time. All Hallow Even, when Evil Incarnate flourishes and the restless dead come to life."

Laurie was doing her best to digest the information. But it was one thing to accept the facts of the captain's hideous death, and quite another to make the leap of faith needed to believe that once a year he came back from beyond the grave. Then it hit her. The key word Alva had used. "The Headless Horror is *part* of his ghostly self?"

"No body is complete without its head." The recluse glanced at the corner of the house as if she had heard something. "You see, Mrs. Grant, down below the Mason-Dixon, folks believe that a corpse has to be buried intact. That if it's not, it will rise again to find the missing parts. I know this for a fact because my mother sent me to a private school in the South." She gestured at the inky woods bordering the yard. "Captain Beauregard has been searching for his head for over a century."

"And what about the head? Is it looking for the body?"

Alva shook hers. "No, ma'am. The head can't go roaming all over the place. It haunts the last place where the two were intact." Reaching out, she smacked the house. "This here farm. And that's the way it will go on being until the two are reunited."

John moved closer. A dozen questions were on the tip of his tongue, but he never got to utter a single one. For at that moment, from within the house, a piercing scream rent the air. He lunged for the door. His wife beat him by a hair and flew inside, heedless of his shout. "Be careful! You don't know what you're rushing into!"

Laurie didn't care. Tina was in danger. Their disagreements, their fights, none of that counted in the final analysis. They were sisters. As corny as the old saying might be, blood *was* thicker than water.

Tina wasn't in the kitchen, nor the hall. As Laurie dashed down it, she noticed the living room lights weren't on. Yet John had insisted that no one turn them out. Slowing, she stopped short of the doorway. No red eyes glared at her out of the darkness. "Sis? Are you in there?"

John was right behind her. The rustle of clothing, or something else, made him think of the shotgun. It was upstairs in their bedroom. He should have kept it handy. Tina, though, had nagged him to tears to quit carrying it around after dark. So he'd relented.

"Laurie?"

It was Tina's voice, yet it wasn't. Tiny, timid, quavering, it sounded more like the voice of a petrified five-year-old than an adult woman.

Laurie started to advance, but her husband clasped her wrist. She would have broken his grip had something not slid along the floor toward her. Its outline was vague. Then a pale face appeared, and she cried gratefully, "Sis! You're safe!"

Tina Brewster was chalk-white. Her thin lips trembled. She held her left hand clamped over her right wrist, using her elbows to propel herself along. Her hair was in disarray, as was her blouse. Most unsettling of all were her eyes, wide with terror, tinged with momentary insanity. "I just wanted some rest," she whimpered, more to herself than to them. "I had a headache and wanted to lie down, so I turned out the light. How was I to know?"

"Know what?" Laurie asked.

The answer came from elsewhere. It came in a sibilant hissing. It showed itself in the shape of a gray demonic head which swept down from high up near the ceiling and floated in defiance of gravity a few inches above Tina. The ogre snaked its forked tongue at them, its Medusa hair writhing like a nest of demented serpents.

Tina tilted her head, and froze. "Please, no! Leave me alone!" she pleaded pathetically.

John knew his wife as well as he knew himself. He guessed what she would do next, so he was ready when she lunged, and caught her around the waist. "Don't get close!" he warned. "Can't you see that's just what it wants? It's using her as bait."

"Maybe I can help, Mr. Grant."

Alva Jackson moved past them, her countenance set in stone. A tiny cross, which she wore around her neck, was in her right hand. "Back, hell-spawn! This has gone far enough! Too many have died already!"

The head gaped its sharklike maw wide, its tapered fangs resembling circular saws. But suddenly it retreated a foot or so, its eyes flaring brighter.

"I don't fear you!" Alva declared. "You only kill Yankees, and you know I'm a true daughter of the Southland. Just as I know your ways, spook. Just as I know how to end your rampage."

John struggled to hold onto Laurie. It would have helped if Tina kept coming, but she was transfixed to the floor.

Venting a feral screech, the head streaked in an airborne frenzy, zipping back and forth, up and down, around and around, over and over. Several times it dived at Alva, although not near enough to harm her. She continued to press forward, the cross extended.

The head ceased its mad whirling. Hissing louder than ever, it backed up to the foot of the stairs.

"Get your kin out of here, Mrs. Grant," Alva said without glancing around. "I'll try to keep it from attacking you." Like Joan of Arc wielding a sacred sword, she crossed the living room, the cross on high. Again the head gave way, flying up to the landing, where it hung stationary above the rail.

Alva didn't stop. "Where is it?" she demanded imperiously, climbing. "Where is the skull? Give me a sign. Show me. The bloodshed must end!" She scaled six steps. Eight. Then 13. When, without warning, the monstrosity screamed like a hawk and dove toward her face. Alva instinctively threw a hand up to protect herself. She missed the next step. Losing her balance, she toppled.

John and Laurie both dimly saw her flail her arms for support which wasn't there. They both saw the back of her thin neck strike the hard edge of a step near the bottom. And they both heard the crisp crack of her spine. Her body twitched once, then was still.

Just like that, the only person who could combat the spook on its own terms was dead.

And the thing that shouldn't exist and yet did, the abomination of reality as they knew it, the unholy creature that had ripped the wife of the previous owner to pieces with its teeth, spun toward them and attacked.

Chapter Twenty

Tommy Lee Harper was so excited that he dropped the empty beer can he had been crumpling into as small a ball as he could make. "Look, you-all!" he cried in awe. "There it is!"

Kip Grant and Amy Westbrook were seated on a log, facing South Mountain. Moments ago the last vestige of sun had dipped below the western horizon, plunging the wilderness into instant darkness. Enough light remained for them to make out objects close by, but at a distance the woodland was a murky blur.

Kip regretted not bringing the flashlight. It was uppermost in his thoughts when his friend called out, and he looked up. Amy gasped.

They had stopped in a clearing at the very base of the mountain. Undergrowth choked the lower third of the slope. And from somewhere deep in that undergrowth gleamed a pale greenish light which flickered and dimmed and died. The luminosity lasted no more than five seconds.

Shery Grant saw it, and was glad. She had been leaning against a tree trunk, snuggled close to Bryce to keep him content. For the last half hour he had been grumbling about the monumental waste of time the day had turned out to be, and how maybe Coker and Jerry had had the right idea about going back.

Now the quarterback uncoiled to his full height. "Well, I'll be damned," he said. "I didn't really believe this garbage. But there is something there."

"Let's find out what," Shery said, pulling on his arm as she made for the spot where the glow had appeared.

Kip rose and followed, Amy brushing his shoulder. Part of him was confident they were doing the right thing, that the only way to rid themselves of the nightmare which had invaded their lives was to learn all they could about the Headless Horror of Spook Hollow, then use that knowledge to eliminate it.

Yet another part of Kip was not so sure. A tiny pinprick of doubt formed as they moved as quietly as possible into the brush. They had no idea of what they were up against. The light might, or might not, be linked to the spook. All they had to go on was the raving of an old lady who half the time did not appear to be in her right mind.

What if the spook knew they were coming?

That thought jolted Kip to a stop. It could well be that they were blindly waltzing into a trap. Hadn't Tommy Lee told him that some people were known to have gone off into the forest and never been seen again?

Speaking of his friend, Kip saw Tommy Lee barreling along ahead of them. He was like a bloodhound on the scent of something. But what? None of them knew the full extent of the spook's power. Their quest might get them all killed.

"Is anything wrong?" Amy whispered.

Kip shook his head, held her hand more firmly, and hurried on before he lost sight of the others. They were committed now. There was no turning back, even if he wanted to.

The undergrowth thickened to the point where they were forced to twist sideways between gaps in branches and to crawl on occasion to make any headway. A briar patch necessitated a detour to the right.

Kip could still see Shery and the quarterback, but not his friend. Tommy Lee had the agility of a monkey. No one could navigate dense woods as quickly as the country boy. Kip glimpsed a pale pair of sneakers up ahead, but lost them moments later.

A yelp spurred them all on.

Shery had not been paying much attention to her brother's friend. Of more concern was the Headless Horror. She had brought Bryce and Dern along in the belief that the two bruisers could handle whatever came along. Dern was gone, though. And her main man, while as tough as any guy in school, might not be able to handle the Horror by his lonesome.

Unexpectedly, the brush ended at a barren plot of earth. In front of her rose a 15-foot-high wall of rock, a miniature cliff, as it were, in no respect remarkable except for the black cavity at its center.

"A cave!" Bryce exclaimed.

A pencil-thin beam of light suddenly stabbed out of the opening and struck Shery in the eyes. She recoiled. Squinting, she tensed, anticipating an attack.

"Come in here, you guys!" Tommy Lee said. "You just have to see for yourselves!"

Kip arrived and hurried past his sister. In the pale glow, his best buddy's face was lit by the pulsing thrill of sheer adventure. "You've had a flashlight all along?" he asked, incredulous.

Tommy Lee seemed surprised by the question. "Sure. We knew that we were going to be out after dark, so I snuck my ma's from her nightstand."

"Why didn't you tell me? Why didn't you use it before now?"

"What's the big deal?" Tommy Lee rejoined. "I figured you had your own." He shook his. "The batteries in this one are weak. I didn't want to waste them." Grabbing Kip's arm, he moved into the cave. "Forget about the stupid light. You won't believe what we've found."

It wasn't what Kip expected.

A narrow tunnel no more than four feet long brought them to a circular chamber ten feet in diameter. The walls were pitted with small holes. From the ceiling jutted jagged fingers of solid stone. Covering most of the floor was a massive slab of rock, as smooth as polished glass, a perfect rectangle in shape. It did not appear to be a natural outcropping. How it had gotten there was anyone's guess.

"Ain't it awesome?" Tommy Lee said, running a palm over the surface.

"Awesome," Kip repeated.

Even more so because on that slab lay a large human skeleton still intact from the neck down, the old bones mingled with the tatters of gray clothing and the shredded leather remains of a belt and a pair of boots. A rusty buckle was covered with dust.

"Where's the skull?" Tommy Lee wondered.

Shery had been asking herself the same thing. She stepped closer, moving around the slab, and bumped something with her foot. It rattled. "Shine the light down here," she directed.

More bones were strewn between the slab and the wall. Huge bones these were, the limbs and rib cage of a big animal. Its identity was no mystery.

Tommy Lee hunkered by the skull and tapped it with a finger. "Don't this beat all! It's the skeleton of a horse." Reaching for a leg bone, he started to pick it up. "These are awful brittle," he announced.

Abruptly, the chamber lit with an eerie green light. Tommy Lee sprang erect, dropping the bone, which cracked below the knee. He backpedaled to Kip's side, muttering, "Sweet Jesus, Joseph, and Mary!"

The enormous polished slab was *glowing*. The green light radiated outward from within it, lending the skeletons of the headless man and the horse a vivid emerald cast which grew brighter with each passing moment. The bones soon glowed so brilliantly, it hurt to gaze directly at them. They glittered. They throbbed. They *moved*.

"Son of a bitch!" Bryce Harcourt blurted out, backing toward the tunnel. "What the hell is going on?"

Shery didn't respond. She inched away from the slab, where the bones jerked and twitched as if coming to life. They slid toward one another, fusing where they should, crackling and snapping, molding themselves into a whole frame again.

"I don't like this!" Tommy Lee said.

Amy pulled at Kip, but he was riveted to the spot. It was insane, but he had to see. It was suicide, but he had to know.

The skeletons were nearly complete. On the slab, a foot connected to an ankle. The toes uncurled. On the floor, four hooves reattached themselves to four legs. The eye sockets on the skull shone with green light.

Then, for a bit, all was still.

Kip could hear Amy breathing, hear his heart pounding in his chest. The bones were rigid, as if awaiting the breath of life. It came, but first the green light intensified more than ever and the air around the skeletons glittered and sparkled and took on form and substance. Literal substance, shaping into human flesh, or a macabre imitation of flesh, adding bulk second by second, growing more solid moment by moment.

Presently a green horse lay on the floor, a headless green corpse on the slab. Yet the transformation wasn't complete. Clothes and gauntlets and boots materialized on the man, a saddle and bridle on the animal.

Bryce Harcourt reached the tunnel. "Let's get out of here while we still can!"

Nodding, Shery complied. She nearly bumped into Tommy Lee, who was not watching where he was going. Her brother and Amy dallied, Kip acting mesmerized by the pulsating light. "Come on!" Shery goaded them.

The green light blinked out, plunging the cave into blackness. Shery couldn't see a thing, not even her own hand in front of her face. Her eyes needed time to adjust. Close to her there was a click, and Tommy Lee's flashlight pierced the gloom. He fumbled with it. The beam danced from side to side, then settled on the slab, on the Headless Horror, just as the abomination sat bolt upright. Beside the slab, the horse spasmed to life, kicking its legs three or four times before it rolled up off the floor.

Tommy Lee screamed and ran, his scream serving as the catalyst that galvanized all of them into motion.

Shery caught up with Bryce, who seized her wrist and bolted. Tommy Lee was hard on their heels. A glance showed no sign of Kip or Amy, however. "Hold it!" she cried. "Where's my brother?"

The quarterback was not about to slow down. Hauling her after him, he dashed into the forest. She dug in her heels, but Bryce was too strong.

In the cave, Kip Grant became aware of Amy yanking on him and pleading softly for him to hurry. Dimly, he saw the Headless Horror shift, saw it swivel in their direction. The gray steed rose and shook itself.

"Please!" Amy pleaded. "For the love of God!"

The word triggered a jarring concussion within Kip's mind. It was as if a bomb had detonated, or a spell had been broken. His head cleared. As the Headless Horror slid off the slab and reared to its full height, he whirled and fled, Amy's arm brushing his. They sped down the tunnel and out into the cool night. Hooves clattered in their wake as they crossed the narrow strip of barren earth to the undergrowth. With no regard for tearing limbs or slashing thorns, they dived on in.

Kip and Laurie covered ten yards. Then 15 yards. Kip glanced at the mountain. An enormous figure was emerging from the cave, leading the horse by the reins. The Horror hiked a boot to a stirrup, gripped the saddlehorn, then forked leather. Its cape swirling in the wind, it applied its spurs and gave chase.

As the bloodthirsty apparition swooped toward John and Laurie Grant, he dropped to his knees, pulling his wife down beside him. The head whisked over them, so close that air fanned his cheek. It hissed madly. He swung and missed.

It was going so fast that John was sure it would overshoot the living room and fly out into the hallway, where hopefully the bright light would cause it to implode. Yet it stopped at the edge of the living room, almost within reach, and hung stationary a few feet from the floor, its tongue and hair waving wildly.

Laurie dashed to her sister's side and helped Tina to rise. A moist liquid spattered on her arm. Drops of blood were dripping from Tina's wrist, which her sister had covered with one hand. "You're hurt!" Laurie said. "How badly?"

Tina did not seem to care. She stood and retreated toward the stairs, her lips moving but no words coming out. A budding maniacal gleam hinted at her mental state.

"Snap out of it!" Laurie cried, shaking her.

John stayed between them and the demon. He cast about for a weapon, and had to make do with an ashtray he snatched off the coffee table. The head made no attempt to come after them. Instead, it glared at the hallway light. Its eyes flared wider and wider. Wisps of smoke which weren't smoke rose from it, as if it were about to combust, only it didn't burst into flame. It shook and quaked, harder and harder, until just when John thought the monstrosity might explode, the light fixture and the light bulb in the hallway shattered in a crashing shower of glass slivers.

Now the living room and the hallway were both dark.

Too late, John remembered his sister-in-law saying that she had switched off the living room light. It would still work! Darting to the switch, he flicked it. The light came on, but by then the spook was safely in the hall.

"Damn!" John said. Laurie and Tina were at the bottom of the stairs, the latter slipping steadily deeper into shock. He ran to them, grabbing Tina's free arm. "Upstairs!" he directed. "I left the shotgun up there."

The head appeared close to the living room but still in shadow. It focused on the overhead light, just as it had on the one in the hall. Again its eyes grew in size, its body shook and shuddered.

"Go! Go!" John cried, realizing that if the light burst before they gained the upstairs corridor, the monstrosity would be on them in a flash. Tina's legs gave out when they were halfway to the top, compelling him to bear most of her weight. She happened to set eyes on the head, and wailed pitiably.

The light fixture commenced to rattle in its socket. They were only a few steps below the landing when it blew up. The retort was like the crack of a pistol. John shielded Tina with his body. His back and legs were pelted with stinging glass fragments, but none were imbedded in his skin.

The instant darkness claimed the room, the head streaked toward them.

John saw it coming. Whipping his right arm, he heaved the ashtray with all his might. Yet it was as if he had done so in slow motion, for the head evaded the ashtray with ease, zipped to the right in a tight loop, and hurtled toward them.

"Keep going!" John yelled, giving Tina and Laurie a shove. Spinning, he cocked his fist. Before he could punch, the head rammed into his chest. The impact lifted him off his feet and flung him onto the landing like so much discarded dirty linen. Landing in a crumpled heap, he struggled to stand, to breathe, to regain his chaotic senses. A semi could not have hit him harder.

Laurie shouted her husband's name as he went down. She levered her sister onto the landing, then let go of Tina to run to John. From out of the shadows swept the spook. Its forehead caught her low in the legs and bowled her over as if it were a bowling ball and she a bowling pin. She landed on her back on the steps and started to slide lower. Frantically, she clutched for purchase. Clamping her fingers on a riser, she arrested her descent.

As Laurie twisted onto her hands and knees, Tina screamed. Below lay Alva Jackson, blank features fixed on the ceiling. Laurie shut the older woman from her mind and scrambled to the aid of her sister. She reached the first step, pushed up high enough to see the landing. And almost retched.

Tina was flat on her back, her arms and legs thrashing, her body bucking. Poised above her neck was the spook, its hair clasped on either side of her head, one strand encircling an ear. The lower half of its face was flush with her throat. Its cheeks rippled. Its eyes were closed.

Tina had hold of the thing and was pushing against it.

"Hang on!" Laurie shouted, leaping onto the landing. Sinking to one knee next to the fiend, she swatted its forehead. She boxed its ears. She gouged at its eyes. For all the good it did. The demonic entity paid no attention to her. It was as if she didn't exist.

"Sissssssssss!" Tina cried, sputtering at the end, blubbering as a scarlet froth rimmed her lips and blood gushed from the corner of her mouth.

Laurie grasped the thing's hair and jerked as hard as she could. All she did was jerk the head a fraction to the right. Drawing back a step, she bent her knee to kick it.

Those infernal eyes snapped open. In a slow aerial pirouette, the head rose up off of Tina and into the gloom above. Blood caked its mouth, dripped from its teeth, coated its chin.

Spook Night

A ragged hole was all that remained of Tina's throat. The skin had been gnawed through, the flesh chewed up. Her veins had been severed. Her larynx box was gone.

Bile gushed into Laurie's mouth. Automatically, she covered it and staggered back, fearing she would be sick. Nauseous, she doubled over. She tottered. Then strong arms were clamped on her shoulders and she was being steered along the corridor. "Tina!" she said weakly, attempting to cope. She mustn't let the shock overwhelm her or her turn to be eaten alive might be next.

"I know," John replied. As much as he had disliked his sister-in-law, he took no perverse pleasure in her passing. That had been no way for someone to die.

The bedroom door was partway open. John smashed into it with his shoulder. Moving swiftly, he guided his wife to the bed and gently eased her onto her side. As he dashed to the doorway, one of the two hall lights exploded. The spook hurtled through the air, striving to reach him before he could close the door. At the last possible instant, he did. Fortunately his back was to the panel, because it rocked to a blow which would have torn it from its hinges otherwise. Another blow resounded through the house. And a third.

The shotgun was just out of John's reach, propped in the corner. To grab it, he would have to take a step, which he didn't dare do so long as the vile abomination was trying to batter the door down.

The blows ceased. John listened, but heard only his wife's smothered sobs. "Laurie!" he whispered. "I need your help!"

Laurie had her face pressed to the quilt. Grief had disoriented her. She couldn't think straight, couldn't seem to get her body to move as it should. Feeling sluggish, she gazed at him, saw him point at the shotgun. It took every ounce of willpower she possessed for her to get up and totter toward it.

From down the hall came the crash of the second light. John put his ear to the wood. Presently a muffled pop confirmed that the spook was going from room to room, shattering every last bulb. Soon the entire upper floor would be dark except for the master bedroom.

The contact of cool metal on Laurie's palms snapped her out of her funk. She stared at the weapon, thinking how gratifying it would be to blow the flying nightmare to bits. She wasn't a bloodthirsty person, by any stretch. As a rule, she shunned violence. That included movies, books, and magazines that glorified it as a means to an end. But now she realized there were times when violence was the only solution, when a person either fought or perished. It wasn't fair. It wasn't right. It was just the way things were.

"Here."

Laurie gave the shotgun to John, who worked

the slide handle, feeding a shell into the chamber. He was tempted to fling open the door and step into the open to lure the spook out so he could give it a taste of buckshot. Prudence dictated that he work up a plan to get his wife out of there first. He would sacrifice himself, if need be, to insure her safety.

"We have to make a run for the car," John announced. That way, if something happened to him, she could speed into town for help.

"Why?" Laurie responded. "We can't go anywhere until the kids show up."

John wanted to kick himself. Kip and Shery and their friends might come walking in at any moment, and he was in no position to warn them. "We should be safer out there. So far as we know, this thing only haunts buildings."

"You hope."

"I'm open to suggestions," John said. None were forthcoming, so he tweaked the knob and cracked the door. Revealed in the sliver of light which spilled out was the dark corridor—and the floating head. It wore a devilish grin. He pushed and dug in his heels, but it wasn't enough. The door buckled inward, catapulting him against the footboard of the bed. He cracked his head, hard. The light above him exploded.

Laurie was clipped by the flying door. Knocked into the wall, she stayed on her feet only to find the ghoulish wraith hovering at arm's length. Its eyes blazed with degenerate

David Robbins

delight as its forked tongue licked the rim of its drooling mouth.

Feinting to the left, toward the door, Laurie dove right, toward her husband. The thing was on her before she reached him. Its writhing hair snatched at her wrist, but she shook free. Its tongue lanced at her face, nicking her cheek when she dodged. Her foot caught on the door. Her ankle seared with pain. Stumbling, she smacked onto her knees.

The leering spook rose higher, regarding her with satanic scorn. Then it exposed its fearsome fangs, hissed, and descended for the kill. Or would have, had the room not thundered to the roar of the 12-gauge. The buckshot blasted the spook out into the hall, where its shattered form plopped to the floor and lay still, its skin twitching in spots. Holes riddled its face. Where its nose had been was a gaping hole, and half of its mouth had been blown away.

John Grant rose. Working the slide, he stepped closer. "I nailed the bastard!" he declared. "It's history."

Or was it? For as John looked on, the holes closed, the skin began to mend, the mouth to reform. Terror seized him. *The creature was indestructible.* Spinning, he grabbed Laurie's wrist and yanked her off the floor.

They were too late.

The head was rising.

Chapter Twenty-one

Kip Grant sped through the wilderness with the clomp of heavy hooves in his ears and his heart in his throat. He was so scared that he was afraid to look back again for fear the Headless Horror would be almost upon him and Amy with its sword upraised. Furiously pumping his legs, he ran without taking any stock of where he was running. He had no sense of direction, no sense of purpose other than the preservation of his life, and Amy's. She kept pace, her own stark panic conveyed in the iron grip of her hand.

Up ahead, Kip spied Tommy Lee Harper. He had lost track of his sister and Harcourt, and figured they had taken another direction.

"Come on, come on!" Tommy Lee beckoned. "It's gaining on us!"

And it was, although not as rapidly as Kip had

dreaded. Mustering the courage to glance around, he saw the spectral rider pursuing them at a brisk walk, not a gallop. The horse, it seemed, was limping. Something was wrong with one of its front legs. Suddenly Kip remembered the cave, remembered Tommy Lee dropping a leg bone and the bone cracking. Could it be, he marveled, that whatever happened to the bones during the day affected the demonic pair when they rose from the grave at night? If that were the case, all he had to do was return after the sun rose and smash every last one to bits!

Provided, of course, he survived until dawn.

"Look out!" Amy yelled, hauling on his arm.

Kip had not been paying attention. A tree had reared before them, and if not for Amy he would have run right into it. They veered into the brush, then had to veer again or be torn to ribbons in a patch of briars. He could no longer see Tommy Lee, but he could hear someone crashing through the undergrowth off to the right and assumed it must be his friend. The vegetation cut off their view of the Headless Horror. He had no idea where it was.

Without warning the undergrowth ended at the rim of a six-foot-high bank. They looked at one another. Kip nodded, and they leaped, landing on spongy ground which cushioned their fall. Kip was about to rise and run on when the crashing off to the right grew louder. He flattened against the bank. Amy did likewise.

Not a second later Tommy Lee burst into the

open. He was gaping in horror behind him, and consequently he tripped over a downed tree limb, sprawling onto his hands and knees.

Kip started to shout, to let his friend know they were there. Then something else burst into the open and the shout died in his throat.

It was the Headless Horror. The rider reined up and swung from the saddle.

Tommy Lee had whirled to face the demonic creature. He was scuttling backward like a crab, blubbering, "Oh, God! Oh, God! Oh, God! Oh, God!" over and over and over. In his blind flight, he collided with a log. Quickly, he turned, or started to, to climb up and over the obstacle, but the Headless Horror reached him before he could.

A wail of mortal horror was torn from Tommy Lee as the Horror closed a gloved hand on the front of his shirt and effortlessly lifted him bodily into the air. Tommy Lee went limp, paralyzed with fright. The rider reached up and gripped the top of Tommy's head, and Tommy did what most others would have done under the same circumstances; he fainted.

Kip Grant almost screamed. He was sure his friend's head was going to be ripped off, just as Mr. Kimble's had been. He couldn't let that happen, yet he was powerless to prevent it. The next moment, to his astonishment, the Horror hesitated, then released its grip on Tommy's head and gently set the boy down, leaning him against the log.

"What in the world?" Kip blurted out.

Which proved costly. Immediately, the rider stiffened, shifting toward the bank. It knew where they were.

Kip tugged at Amy and they renewed their frantic flight, plowing through waist-high weeds into dense woodland, then weaving through a maze of trunks.

A strident, ghostly whinny rent the night. Hooves drummed once again.

The chase had resumed.

John Grant didn't stop. He pointed the 12-gauge at the rising head and fired at near-point-blank range. The buckshot slammed it back against the wall, ripping the lower half of the spook to shreds. John knew the thing would heal itself, that he had bought them half a minute at the most. Grasping his wife, he ran.

Laurie watched the monstrosity flop like a be-headed chicken as she ran past. Those infernal eyes alighted on her and blazed like red-hot coals. The hatred they radiated was so intense, so potent, she felt twin jabs in her shoulder and a brief, searing heat.

They had to jump over Tina on their way down. Laurie averted her gaze. She couldn't stand to see the butchery a second time. Weakness assailed her again, but she shook it off. When they came to Alva Jackson, she stepped over the corpse without flinching. At the bottom of the stairs she started to turn right, to make for the kitchen where a light still shone. Her husband had other ideas. Darting to the front door, he pushed her through ahead of him, then slammed it shut behind them.

The cool night air chilled John's perspiring skin. He backed to a post and leaned against it to catch his breath. Thankfully, the outside spotlights were all still on. The spook couldn't get at them so long as they stayed in the radius of bright light.

Laurie stepped next to him. "What now?" she wondered, scanning the windows. "Are we safe, do you think? Will it blow up the bulbs out here like it did those inside?"

That was the crucial question. John doubted it would try. The combined glare of the three big spotlights might be too much for the wraith to endure. And the way they were arranged, it couldn't get close to one without being caught in the glare of another. So long as he and Laurie stayed right where they were, they were be safe.

"Look!" Laurie whispered, pointing.

A nebulous shape had appeared on the other side of the nearest pane, far enough back that the light could not reach it. While the shape was blurred, its pair of diabolical eyes were not. They glared balefully, latent with menace. The thing hovered in the darkness, making no attempt to crash through the window to get at them.

"We beat it!" Laurie said.

John felt no elation. It was a temporary reprieve at best. Unless they destroyed the fiend, it would reappear next year or the year after that or maybe five years down the road, and the whole awful ordeal would resume all over again. They had to put an end to it then and there, as Alva Jackson had wanted to do.

But *how?* John asked himself. Alva had claimed the Headless Horror and the ghastly head would go on roaming the earth until the two were reunited. Reunited in what way? Did they have to touch one another? Just be in close proximity? Or was there more? Was there something he was missing?

Unbidden into John's mind came the image of the stern-faced Southerner advancing up the stairs with her cross in hand. She had been addressing the demon. Her words rang like the peal of a bell: "Where is it? Where is the skull?"

Was that the key to the whole affair? It tied in with something else the woman had said, when describing Beauregard's death: "In their haste, they forgot the captain's head."

Did that mean Arkady Helstrom had hidden the grisly trophy somewhere on the farm to keep the authorities from finding it? Had he buried the evidence, perhaps? Maybe in the orchard, which would explain why those two farmhands had been attacked there. Or maybe in the basement of the farmhouse, which would explain why the house was haunted but not the other buildings.

John Grant tensed and turned, appalled by his stupidity. He was wrong. At least one other building had to be haunted. The one where Laurie had heard pounding. The one where George Eldridge had been brutally slain. And the only one on the property fitted with an immense iron door which had been locked for generations. Why? To keep nosy people out? To keep something in? Or both.

"I know," John said softly, wishing he didn't.

Laurie was searching for the head. The eyes had vanished, and she had no inkling where it had gone. "What was that?" she asked absently.

"I know where the skull is. I know what must be done." John moved to the west edge of the porch. Shrouded in the mantle of night, the springhouse had a malevolent air. He told himself that his imagination was getting the better of him, that it was just a building, like any other. But he didn't believe that for a minute.

"What are you talking about?" Laurie asked, upset by his expression. "What are you planning to do?"

"End this nightmare permanently." John glanced at their vehicles. Under the front seat of hers was a flashlight. It hadn't been used in ages and the batteries might be dead. "Stay put," he cautioned. "I shouldn't be gone long."

Laurie was not going to let him run off without explaining. Stepping in front of him, she said, "Answer me, damn it! What do you know that I don't?"

John told her his theory. "If I'm right, if I can find the skull, we have a fighting chance."

"It's a long shot," Laurie said skeptically. The idea of being left there alone frightened her, although not nearly as much as the thought of him entering the springhouse alone. "But if you're going, so am I."

"No." John grasped her by the shoulders and moved her to the right. "One of us has to stay here in case Shery and Kip show up. We can't let them go in the house."

It was true. It was logical. Yet Laurie balked anyway. "You can't go alone. You'll need help."

"We have no choice," John reminded her. That was it in a nutshell. He offered the 12-gauge, but she shook her head, so he shoved the shotgun at her. Reluctantly, she took it. John stared into her eyes, kissed her on the cheek, and bolted for the driveway before he changed his mind. She called his name, but he didn't answer.

John had to focus on the task at hand to the exclusion of all else. Thinking of her or the kids would weaken his resolve, and if he faltered, he was dead. He had to remember that he was doing this for them, for their future together as a family.

In the past few days their lives had been turned upside down, had been transformed into a living hell. Yet against all odds, the hardships had brought them closer together, not driven them farther apart. That proved there was hope for them, that in her soul Laurie cared for him as much as he for her. And he was not going to let that hope be destroyed by anyone—or anything.

The car was unlocked. John crouched and rummaged under the seat until his fingers closed on the cool metal handle. A flick of the switch produced an adequate beam. Not as bright as he would have liked, but it would have to do.

John could feel Laurie watching him as he sprinted down the hill. The iron door was still propped open. A fresh layer of dust covered the floor, obscuring the tracks made in previous days. He played the flashlight beam over the walls and ceiling. Nothing stirred, not even a spider.

He could not help glancing up at the farmhouse one last time. Laurie was rigid with fear for his safety. He almost waved. Then he spotted a pair of scarlet eyes framed by an upstairs window.

The monstrosity knew what he was up to.

John ducked into the springhouse and hurried to the far corner. The surface of the spring was smooth and shiny, like patent leather. He played the beam over it, then dropped to his left knee and bent to probe the depths. The light did not penetrate very far, two or three feet at the most. He couldn't see the bottom, and he certainly didn't see any sign of a skull.

Maybe he was wrong, John speculated. Maybe Helstrom hadn't tossed the incriminating proof of his crime into the last place anyone would think to look. Helstrom might have simply burned it, or concealed it in the forest. There was no guarantee the skull lay at the bottom of the spring.

Yet he knew it did.

John lowered the flashlight until the lens nearly brushed the surface. Diffused by the water, the light roved over the uneven stone sides. The depths, as before, were murky. He moved the flashlight in a wide circle. Something glimmered briefly, a pale flash of white against the bleak background.

Switching off the flashlight, John stared at the spot, waiting for his pupils to adjust. A black veil claimed the interior, blacker than the house had been with the lights out, blacker, even, than a moonless night, so black that John felt as if he had been cast into the remote reaches of outer space and was the only sentient being in existence.

Gradually, the blackness brightened. Not much, but enough for John to confirm there was a pale object way down at the bottom. It could be anything. A rock. An old bucket. A farm implement. Or a human skull.

Switching the flashlight back on, John set it beside him, angling the beam so that it illuminated the surface. Swiftly, he stripped off his shirt, shoes, and pants, leaving on his underwear and his socks. The air had grown colder since he entered, and was growing even more so by the minute. Clasping his arms, he shivered.

The last thing in the world John Grant wanted

to do was what he had to. Extending a foot, he tested the water with his toe. He knew it would be cold, but it was much worse than that. It was liquid *ice*.

John inched to the edge, curled his feet over the lip, inhaled to fill his lungs, and then, before he could change his mind, dived. The onslaught on his senses jolted him. A frigid, clammy sheath encased him from head to toe. Water seeped into his ears, into his nose. His vision blurred. Mechanically, he stroked lower, finding that he could not move his arms as freely as he would have liked thanks to the cramped confines.

It seemed like another world or dimension, that gloomy twilight realm. John Grant sought some sign of the pale object, but saw none in the swirling water. Deeper, ever deeper he went, careful not to scrape himself on the stones.

Suddenly John flung out his right arm and brushed the bottom. His hand buried itself to the wrist. Treading in place, he jerked his hand loose and shook it to remove the gunk.

The reason for his being there was nowhere to be found. John worried that he had imagined the pale object, that he was wasting his time. He twisted to the right and the left. At length his lungs screamed for air, so he surfaced and wedged his forearms onto the stone rim to keep from slipping back in.

John did not rest too long. already the chill was seeping into his bones. Pushing off, he doubled in half, kicked, and knifed downward. At the bottom he groped the wall for a handhold and found one. His other hand probed the mud, poking and digging, clouding the water worse than it already was. Just when he was about to give up, his fingers brushed a hard surface. Clawing at it, he pried it loose, pushed off the side, and rose.

Only when John surged clear of the water could he see what he held. Mud coated most of the lower portion, and part of the crown had been caved in by a heavy blow, but there was no mistaking the outline. It had to be the one. He had found the skull of Captain James T. Beauregard of the Confederate Army. Grinning, he placed it on the floor, propped both hands on the edge, and began to climb out of the spring.

A sibilant hiss froze him in the act.

Between the corner and the entrance, amid a showery sparkle of green fireflies, its red eyes alive with demonic rage, the vengeful Gorgonian head was materializing.

Shery Grant had never run so hard or for so long in her life. Her right side throbbed with pain, her lungs strained for her next breath. She wanted to stop, not only to rest but to locate Kip and Amy, but Harcourt was not about to let her. Several times she had tried to slow him down, and in each instance he had clamped harder onto her wrist and virtually dragged her along.

"Damn it, Bryce!" Shery snapped. "We can't

leave the others!" As usual, he jogged on. At her wit's end, she kicked him in the leg with all her strength.

The quarterback finally halted. "What the hell is the matter with you?" he demanded. "I'm trying to save your hide and you're busting my chops."

"We have to go back," Shery said. "We have to—"

The crackle of brush to their rear made them both whirl. Harcourt pressed a hand to her mouth and pulled her behind the nearest tree. Shery, furious that he was treating her as if she couldn't hold her own, shoved his hand off her face.

About 40 feet away, tall brush parted to reveal Kip and Amy, fleeing for their lives. They were exhausted; scratched and torn and stumbling every few steps, Kip supporting Amy, who could barely lift her feet.

Shery's first impulse was to call out to them, to go help. Then, beyond them, an enormous figure flitted through the trees, now visible for seconds at a time, now hidden by the vegetation. It was the Headless Horror, closing in on her brother and his girlfriend.

Kip knew the living horror was still after them. Repeatedly he had tried to lose it, sometimes by stopping and not making any noise, sometimes by throwing stones to make it think they were heading in a different direction.

None of his tricks worked. Inexorably, the gray rider dogged their steps, never riding faster than a brisk walk.

Then Kip remembered the cracked leg bone again, and realized the horse was slowing the Horror down.

Now the spook was almost on them. Kip darted to a pine tree and flattened at its base, curling an arm around Amy. She trembled, her face the color of snow.

Shery blanched when the Headless Horror plowed through the last of the brush and reined up at the exact spot Kip had turned aside to hide. The monster started to swing toward the pine tree, and lowered a gauntlet to the hilt of its saber.

Almost of their own accord, Shery's legs moved. She sprang into the open, waving both arms, and hollered, "Over here, you suck-egg son of a bitch! Forget about them and come after us!"

Bryce backed away from her, shaking his head. "Are you crazy? You'll get us killed!"

Shery continued to wave. "Try *us*, bastard!" she taunted.

The Headless Horror had shifted toward them. It made no move either way, but sat fingering its saber until, in a blur, it erupted into motion, cracking the reins to bring its steed to a trot as it whipped the sword from its scabbard.

"I told you!" Bryce screeched, flying eastward.

The pain in Shery's side had suddenly become unimportant. If she wanted to live, she had to run, so run she did, doing her utmost to keep up with the boyfriend she was having second thoughts about, getting smacked in the face when he swept past a tree and a limb he had swatted aside flew back at her. They came to a low knoll sparse with growth. Bryce sprinted up and over, so she did the same. As he raced over the crest, he drew up short, but only for an instant. She learned why when she reached the top.

Jerry Dern and Deb Coker were lying at the bottom in a small clearing. Dern had his pants down around his ankles, while Coker was naked. Discarded clothes and empty beer cans ringed them.

"Jer!" Bryce shouted, bounding to the linebacker and shaking him violently. "Get up, dude! Get the hell out of here! Hurry!"

Both Dern and Coker shot to their feet. Dull from sex and sleep and too much beer, they blinked in confusion. "What the hell is going on?" Coker growled.

"It's the thing!" Bryce said. "It's after us! For God's sake, run before it's too late!"

Shery ran past the three of them, and slowed at the edge of the clearing to see if they were following. Bryce had taken a few more steps, but the other two, incredibly enough, were laughing.

"Nice try, buddy," Dern was saying. "But you're not going to fool us with that old gag.

David Robbins

How old do you think we are? Ten?"

Pounding hooves chopped their laughter short. The Headless Horror drew rein on the knoll, its cape flapping in the wind, its saber dully reflecting the starlight.

Deb Coker screamed.

Jerry Dern backpedaled, fumbling with his pants, hiking them so his legs could move unrestricted.

Shery resumed her flight, one eye on the ground ahead, one on the unfolding tableau in the clearing. Bryce Harcourt bolted to the north. Jerry turned to join him. Deb Coker, too petrified to move, screamed and screamed.

A jab of spurs brought the Headless Horror down the slope in a blinding rush. The saber cleaved the air, catching Coker at the nape of her neck and shearing clean through as if she were made of putty rather than solid sinew and bone. Her head sailed from her shoulders in a bloody arc, struck the earth a dozen feet away, and rolled to a stop, her face in the dirt.

Jerry Dern wailed as the flying steed rammed into him. Propelled off his feet, he was smashed to the ground near the trees, but not close enough for him to reach them even if he were able. Which he wasn't. His left shoulder was bent at an unnatural angle, and through the flesh covering his right knee poked splintered bone. Stunned, groaning loudly, he eased onto his back.

Exhibiting no haste, the Headless Horror dismounted. It sheathed the saber, then walked to the linebacker. Slowly, almost nonchalantly, it raised him off the ground with one hand. The other gauntlet seized the top of Dern's head.

Jerry came to life. Blubbering hysterically, he struggled to break the thing's grip. For all his bulk and muscle, he was a babe in the grasp of a giant.

Involuntarily, Shery slowed again. She could not bring herself to miss what happened next.

The rider wrenched Dern's head from side to side. Jerry screeched one last time, his cry strangled off when the fiend in gray ripped his head from his body. Giving the now-worthless husk a push, the rider turned. The Horror carefully cradled Jerry's head in both hands as if it were a valued prize, then raised the head and *placed it on its own shoulders*.

Flabbergasted, Shery halted.

The scourge of Spook Hollow stood quietly, although not for long. It savagely seized the head, dropped it at its feet, and proceeded to stomp the skull to a shattered, gory pulp.

"I'm out of here," Shery whispered to herself, and sprinted with renewed vigor. Bryce Harcourt had deserted her, so she was alone now.

Or almost alone.

The Headless Horror was back in the saddle and on her trail.

Its fangs glistening in the pale glow of the flashlight, its long hair writhing like a roiling nest of snakes, and uttering another viperish hiss, the monstrosity with the hellish eyes dived.

John Grant knew the thing would be on him before he could scramble out of the spring, so he ducked instead, pumping himself under the water with a fraction of an instant to spare. The head whisked overhead, then looped to the left, gaining altitude.

John had not let go of the edge. Bunching his arms, he executed a reverse jackknife, hurling himself up and over the rim and rolling when his shoulder made contact with the stone floor. He surged into a crouch next to the flashlight and the skull, and grabbed both.

Whirling, John sought his demonic nemesis. The beam revealed a few cobwebs and plenty of dust, but that was all. Every nerve tingling, he roved it over the ceiling, starting at the rear corners and working forward. Once he thought he heard a rustling noise, but when he shifted the light nothing was there.

At the same time, John crept toward the entrance. He had to reach the house, had to gain the sanctuary of the front porch. Suddenly he sensed rather than saw something to his left. Swiveling, he caught the head full in the glare of the beam. It vented its trademark hiss while zipping into the darkness.

John smiled grimly. He had a fighting chance. No sooner did the thought occur to him than the flashlight weakened, the beam fading to a feeble sparkle. He gave it a shake. The beam brightened, but not much. Realizing it would not last long enough for him to reach the doorway, he threw caution aside and broke into a desperate sprint. The beam dwindled rapidly with every stride he took.

John was ten feet from his goal when he detected a whisper of movement behind him. He glanced back—and the head was on him, striking him high in the shoulder. The impact slammed him off his feet and he crashed to the floor, scraping his chin, elbows, and knees. Razor teeth sheared through his flesh, clear down to the bone.

John couldn't help himself. He screamed. Twisting, he struck at the head with the flashlight, pounding it twice but having no effect. The thing's teeth were clamped fast; it was gnawing on him as if eating him alive. He smashed it a third time, and its wriggling hair wrapped around the front of the flashlight and held on fast. Jerking his arm to free it proved ineffective. The impossibly strong monstrosity maintained its grip.

Releasing the handle, John rose and staggered toward the entrance. Blood poured down his back. The pressure on his shoulder eased, and suddenly the fiend was in front of him, barring his escape, floating in the air at chest height, dark drops dripping from its lower jaw.

John stopped. He couldn't fight the thing on its own terms. Without the light, he didn't stand a prayer. In boiling frustration, he elevated the skull to hurl it.

To John's amazement, the thing's features rippled and a new look came over it, one he had never seen before, a look that could only be described as sheer panic. It darted to the left, hissing and growling.

John was on to something, although he didn't know what. Holding the skull in front of him as Alva Jackson had held her cross, he warily inched forward. The monstrosity darted toward him, but immediately backed off when he swung the skull toward it.

Up on the hill, there were yells. Someone— Laurie perhaps—screamed.

In a flash John was out the door and running up the slope. Its eyes dancing with elemental hatred, the grotesque head came after him. It swooped toward his shins, as if to bowl him over. Twisting, he bent down low, the skull extended, causing the thing to sheer off.

John continued running. The shotgun boomed once. Twice. Another scream rent the heavens. And around the first curve on the driveway roared a vehicle, a four-wheel-drive truck bearing the emblem of the Spook Hollow Police Department, its overhead lights flashing. Doing well over 80, it bumped over the small ditch and charged across the lawn toward the porch.

John reached the porch heartbeats behind the vehicle. He took in the scene at a glance; Shery sprawled breathless on the edge of the porch,

Laurie straddling her with the shotgun tucked to one shoulder, Chief Bogartus leaping from the truck with his service revolver out and cocked, and the Headless Horror astride its phantom steed, reining up just outside the circle of light, near his wife and daughter.

Laurie and Bogartus fired at the same time. The tall gray figure rocked to the blasts, but stayed in the saddle. Chief Bogartus adopted a two-handed stance and fired four more times in swift succession, his rounds punching holes in the rider's chest and abdomen.

The Headless Horror was hardly fazed. Swinging to the ground, it drew its saber.

John fairly flew across the lawn. In his worry over the headless figure he forgot about the head, and was brutally reminded by its teeth ripping into the back of his right thigh. He nearly went down. Swiveling, he swung the skull, and his adversary retreated. Two more bounds brought him to the porch, where the light would keep the head at bay long enough for him to do what had to be done.

Chief Bogartus had reloaded using a speed loader. Rushing between the Horror and the porch, he emptied the cylinder in the thing's sternum, blowing a cavity the size of a melon.

The rider's left gauntlet snaked out, closing on the lawman's neck. Turning away from the light, the figure lifted Bogartus off the ground and began to squeeze. Bogartus struggled mightily.

John Grant was almost to the west end of the

porch. He remembered Alva Jackson saying that the only way to end the nightmare was to reunite the head and the body. So, not knowing what would happen, he hurtled past Laurie and Shery, coiled, and leaped. The Headless Horror had its broad back to him. He landed on its shoulders, hooking one leg over them even as he swept the skull on high. Feeling himself start to fall, John jammed it onto the stump of neck.

The Headless Horror of Spook Hollow stiffened, then staggered backward. John fell at its feet as it dropped the chief, who clasped his throat and gasped for air.

A brilliant green glow enveloped the immense figure. It pivoted. With painstaking slowness the rider climbed onto the horse. The glow spread, engulfing the animal. Wispy tendrils rose from the skull, becoming streamers of green smoke, which thickened into a cloud that hid the head from view. Tiny pinpoints of green light swirled in and out of the smoke, growing brighter and brighter until, in a dazzling flash, both the lights and the smoke disappeared. In their place was the perfectly formed green head of a handsome man in his early twenties. The man looked down.

John thought he saw a hint of a smile. Then both the rider and the horse started to glow steadily brighter. Just when he could barely stand to gaze at them, they blinked out of existence.

For half a minute no one moved. Laurie broke

the spell first and ran to John, helping him sit up. "Is it over?" she asked in an awed whisper. "Is it honest-to-God over at last?"

Shery was standing. From out of the woods jogged Kip and Amy. Around the corner of the house, whining and wagging his tail, came Buck. John Grant, smiling, took it all in. "Yes," he said simply, and embracing his wife, molded his lips to hers.

PRANK NIGHT

DAVID ROBBINS

Bestselling Author Of *Hell-O-Ween*

Beneath sky pitch-black and moon full bright
Lurks terror twice as dark as night.
Newly arisen from the grave,
Hot, fresh red blood it does crave.
Grisly death it brings the brave;
the cowardly will rant and rave.
Halloween is a time for fright,
But madness stalks the gloom of prank night.

_3676-2 $4.50 US/$5.50 CAN

Don't Miss These Novels of Bone-chilling Horror from Leisure Books!

The Lake by R. Karl Largent. From out of the murky depths rises a horror born of a technological disaster—a terrifying force that defies the laws of nature and threatens mankind. To save the environment, it has to be controlled. To save the town, it has to be destroyed.

_3455-7 $4.50 US/$5.50 CAN

Borderland by S. K. Epperson. Not much has changed in remote Denke, Kansas, since the pioneer days. For over one hundred years, the citizens of Denke have worked far outside the laws of man and nature, hunting down strangers, stealing their money and their lives. But the time has come at last when every one of them will pay for their unspeakable crimes....

_3435-2 $4.50 US/$5.50 CAN

Madeleine by Bernard Taylor. To all appearances, Madeleine and Tess are identical in every way. But beneath Madeleine's beauty, her soul is possessed by a dark nature. Slowly, relentlessly, she turns her sister's happy life into a horrifying nightmare, pushing Tess to the very edge of sanity, waiting for the day she can claim Tess's life for her own.

_3404-2 $4.50 US/$5.50 CAN

RED TIDE
R. KARL LARGENT

"A writer to watch!" —*Publishers Weekly*

COUNTDOWN: 72 HOURS

Aboard a yacht on the peaceful Caribbean, a secret meeting between the leaders of the U.S. and the former Soviet Union is set to take place. Protected by the most sophisticated technology known to man, they will have nothing to fear— if one of their own isn't a traitor.

OBJECTIVE: DESTROY THE NEW WORLD ORDER

In a tangled battle of nerves and wits, Commander T.C. Bogner has to use his high-tech equipment to defeat a ruthless and cunning foe. If he fails, the ultimate machines of war will plunge the world into nuclear holocaust.

_3366-6 $4.99 US/$5.99 CAN